Tote Bags
and
Toe Tags

Books by Dorothy Howell

HANDBAGS AND HOMICIDE

PURSES AND POISON

SHOULDER BAGS AND SHOOTINGS

CLUTCHES AND CURSES

TOTE BAGS AND TOE TAGS

Published by Kensington Publishing Corporation

Tote Bags and Toe Tags

DOROTHY HOWELL

KENSINGTON BOOKS
http://www.kensingtonbooks.com

Mys
Howell

KENSINGTON BOOKS are published by

Kensington Publishing Corp.
119 West 40th Street
New York, NY 10018

All Kensington titles, imprints, and distributed lines are available at special quantity discounts for bulk purchases for sales promotion, premiums, fund-raising, educational, or institutional use.

Special book excerpts or customized printings can also be created to fit specific needs. For details, write or phone the office of the Kensington Special Sales Manager: Attn. Special Sales Department. Kensington Publishing Corp., 119 West 40th Street, New York, NY 10018. Phone: 1-800-221-2647.

Kensington and the K logo Reg. U.S. Pat. & TM Off.

Library of Congress Card Catalogue Number: 2012932551

ISBN-13: 978-0-7582-5332-3
ISBN-10: 0-7582-5332-X

First Hardcover Printing: June 2012

10 9 8 7 6 5 4 3 2 1

Printed in the United States of America

To David, Stacy, Seth, Judy and Brian

ACKNOWLEDGMENTS

The author is eternally grateful to the many people who generously gave their time, effort, and support to the writing of this book. Some of them are David Howell, Stacy Howell, Judith Branstetter, Seth Branstetter, Brian Branstetter, Martha Cooper, Hannah Dennison, and William F. Wu, Ph.D. Many thanks to Evan Marshall of the Evan Marshall Agency, and to John Scognamiglio and the talented team at Kensington Publishing for all their hard work.

ACKNOWLEDGMENTS

CHAPTER 1

A whole new me. That's what I wanted.
Not that there was anything wrong with the old me, really. But there had been some comments. A few whispers. An occasional eyebrow bob in my direction. A couple of—

Well, anyway, a whole new me seemed in order.

After a run of not-so-great luck—long story—I knew I had to turn things around. So I did—big time.

I'd finally figured out—for now, anyway—what to do about the fact that, at age twenty-four, my life was almost gone and I hadn't accomplished much. Jeez, *thirty* wasn't that far away—and everybody knew it was all downhill after thirty.

So I, Haley Randolph, with my red-carpet-worthy dark hair, my enviable five-foot-nine-inch height, and my even-though-they're-mostly-recessive beauty-queen genes, had taken a giant leap forward in improving my life.

Even without that flash of brilliance, my personal things-were-going-great category looked pretty good, despite that patch of bad luck. I'd scored a huge chunk of change—long story—that kept me from roaming the parking lots at malls, asking total strangers for handouts—not that I would have actually done that, but still.

My best friend Marcie Hanover and I were giving killer

purse parties and raking in the bucks. I had a fantastic apartment in Santa Clarita about thirty minutes, give or take, from Los Angeles that I'd fixed up just the way I wanted and absolutely loved.

Of course, my personal things-were-*not*-going-so-great category was stacked kind of high, too.

I still had my crappy part-time job at the crappy Holt's Department Store, bringing down a crappy seven bucks an hour, and the crappiest part was that the store management actually wanted me to wait on customers. I mean, really, come on. How much could they expect for minimum wage?

I was still slogging my way through college. The fall semester would begin in a few weeks and I'd have to register soon. I saw no need to overwhelm myself with a full load of classes. Or even a couple of classes. The one I'd picked out of the college catalog was plenty.

And, then, of course, there was my official boyfriend, Ty Cameron.

I wasn't sure which category he belonged in.

A few weeks ago, Ty practically put the smack down on me to move in with him. He'd made all sorts of fabulous—and I mean *totally* fabulous—promises. But, well, let's just say we're still living apart and neither of us has mentioned it since—not even on our flight home from Las Vegas.

I whipped my Honda into a parking lot a block off Figueroa Street in downtown Los Angeles, paid the attendant, and slid into a space near the entrance. The lot was packed, which wasn't unusual, and I was running late, which wasn't unusual either. I was meeting Marcie for lunch. She had a job at one of the banks on Fig, as everybody called it, in the financial district. She wouldn't mind that I was late. *That's* what good friends we were.

By the time I hoofed it a block to Fig, the office buildings had already let out for lunch. The thing about downtown L.A. is that anything goes, fashion-wise. Some women were decked out in full-on business suits and pumps. Others went for a trendier look. Still others dressed comfortably. Men had it easier, of course. It's hard to go wrong with a suit and tie, sport jacket and crew-neck sweater, or even a tie and shirt with the sleeves rolled back.

Up the block, I spotted Marcie coming out of the bank building where she worked. She looked great in a Donna Karan suit. I had on sandals, a yellow top, and check-out-my-butt white capris.

"I'm starving," Marcie said, as I walked up. "Let's go to—oh my God, what happened?"

After only one quick look at my face, Marcie knew I had major news. See what great friends we were?

Not that I'm a drama queen, or think that I'm *all that*, but moments such as this required a certain amount of hesitation to allow the suspense to build. But right now, I couldn't hold back.

"I passed!" I screamed.

Marcie grabbed my arm. "You passed? Already?"

"Yes!" I told her, and broke into my own personal X-rated Snoopy dance. A guy in a convertible stopped at the traffic signal honked. I threw one last booty pop his way and he drove off.

"Wow, Haley, you said you were turning your life around, and you really have," Marcie said.

In her official capacity as my best friend, Marcie had been the only person privy to my life-changing declaration of a few weeks ago—plus, I didn't want a lot of people to know if I couldn't pull it off and ended up falling on my face.

"How are you doing on your other changes?" Marcie asked.

Best friends can really be a mood spoiler sometimes.

Okay, the whole-new-me idea wasn't exactly *my* idea. A

few weeks ago, I met a girl who was kind of weird and, honestly, not all that bright. I didn't really like her. She got on my nerves big time.

But she'd yammered on about how easy it was to change your life. She called it the "reverse world." If you didn't like how things were going, just do the opposite. So that's what I'd done.

"Things are going good," I told Marcie. "Really good."

She gave me her I'm-your-best-friend-so-don't-lie-to-me look.

I hate that look.

"I'm working on them," I told her.

In retrospect, maybe I'd overreached on some of the changes in my life. Like not eating chocolate and laying off the mocha frappuccinos—the best drink in the entire world—from Starbucks.

"When was the last time you had a Snickers bar?" Marcie asked.

Jeez, having a best friend this good was kind of getting on my nerves all of a sudden. I hadn't expected her to really hold me accountable for my actions, or anything. So what could I do but change the subject?

"I got a certificate," I said. "Want to see it?"

"Sure."

I dug into my totally fabulous Chanel tote and pulled out the certificate I'd earned after passing my final test. As of this morning, I was a graduate of UM, the University of Mixology—bartending school.

"Look," I said, pointing. "It has a gold seal on it and everything."

Marcie nodded appreciatively. "Cool, Haley. Really cool."

Yeah, okay, I knew bartending school wasn't something I'd ever considered before. But my life wasn't going the way I wanted, so I'd taken this drastic step to change things.

UM seemed like a natural for me. After all, who would make a better bartender than someone like me, who loved to party? I went to all the best clubs. I knew lots of people there, and everyone knew me, of course.

"UM has a job placement service," I said, slipping my certificate back into my tote. "I'll be working in no time."

"Cool!" Marcie threw both arms around me.

"Way cool!" I said, and hugged her back.

"What's so cool?"

A man's voice spoke from beside us. I whirled and saw Ty Cameron, my official boyfriend, standing on the sidewalk. His office was nearby so I figured he was heading out for lunch.

My stomach did its usual flip-flop, just like always when I saw Ty. He was so handsome. Tall, light brown hair, gorgeous blue eyes, athletic build. He looked great in his suit.

Ty was the fifth generation of his family to be completely devoted to, out of his mind dedicated to, and unreasonably consumed with running the Holt's Department Stores. Yes, the same chain of stores that paid me a whopping seven bucks an hour—long story. Anyway, Ty wasn't content with the dozens of stores the family owned. He'd recently opened a boutique he'd named Wallace, after some ancient Cameron ancestor, and he'd just concluded negotiations for Holt's International—at least I think it's concluded; I usually drifted off when Ty talked about business.

Ty and I had dated since last fall. We'd had a few rough patches—okay, more than a few. But we were doing great now. Well, good. Kind of good.

Ty thought I should be more understanding about his duties and responsibilities to the Holt's Corporation. I thought he should actually remember our dates, show up on time, and not spend the entire evening texting or phoning somebody because of some problem at Holt's.

Call me crazy.

Anyway, we were trying to work it out, although I didn't think it would kill Ty to put a little more effort into it.

"What is it?" Ty asked, smiling and waiting for an answer. "What's so cool?"

"Haley graduated from UM," Marcie exclaimed.

I'd never gotten around to telling Ty I was going to bartending school—not that he'd have listened anyway.

Ty's expression morphed into disbelief, then to surprise, and, finally, into a smile again.

"You graduated from college? Already?" Ty asked.

Oh, crap. Ty knew I'd been taking classes to earn my bachelor's degree. Now he thought I'd done it.

"Why didn't you tell me?" Ty asked.

He threw his arms around me and pulled me into a big hug. He's so strong and he always smells great. Ty's way hot.

After a few seconds, I eased back a little. "Well, really, it's not—"

"Get a room, you two," someone said.

I glanced around and saw Sarah Covington walking up to join us.

I hate Sarah Covington.

Sarah was the vice president of marketing for Holt's. She wasn't much older than me and already had her BA and made a ton of money so she could buy fabulous clothes and terrific handbags—which was reason enough to hate her—but she was all over Ty all the time. She was forever calling him about every tiny decision, every problem, every situation that came up. And the worst part was that Ty didn't get it. He thought the world rotated around Sarah Covington.

I snuggled closer to Ty and threw Sarah an I'm-being-a-bitch-by-pretending-to-like-you smile, and said, "Maybe we'll do that."

Ty, of course, missed the whole exchange.

"Great news," he said. "Haley just graduated from UM."

Sarah's eyes widened in surprise. "The University of Michigan?"

The University of . . . *what?*

"They have a fabulous online program," she said.

What the heck was she talking about?

"A friend of mine graduated from UM. It's very demanding. Quite an accomplishment," Sarah said. "Congratulations, Haley."

She said it like she really meant it—which just made me hate her even more.

"Was your degree in business?" Sarah asked.

Oh my God. She actually thought I'd graduated from the University of Michigan.

"Of course," Ty said, smiling down at me. "Right, Haley?"

Oh my God. Ty thought so, too.

Jeez, what could I say? I couldn't announce that I'd really graduated from the University of Mixology and that up until a couple of minutes ago I didn't even know Michigan had a university—I'm not even sure where Michigan is. I'd look like a complete idiot—and a total loser. Ty would be embarrassed and that witch Sarah Covington would probably post it on her Facebook page quicker than Macy's took a season-end markdown.

So what could I do but smile up at Ty and say, "Yes, that's right."

Thank goodness Ty didn't mention my graduation again—but it did kind of irk me. I mean, come on, for all he knew, I really had graduated from the University of Michigan's demanding online program. But he did ask me out to dinner a few days later and told me to dress to impress—like I ever dressed any other way—and picked me up early.

"Look at this," he said as he stood in my living room dressed in a gorgeous Perry Ellis suit, crisp white shirt, and azure blue necktie that reminded me of the Caribbean, which I hoped he'd take me to one day but knew he wouldn't unless Holt's had a conference or something there.

Ty pulled out his cell phone, held it up, and made a show of switching it off.

"No calls tonight," he said.

Oh my God. I could hardly believe it. Ty had never switched off his phone before.

"You do the same," Ty said. "I want it to be just you and me tonight."

For a moment, I was too stunned to move—sort of like when you spot the latest Chloe bag in a display case and hadn't thought it would be available for another few days.

Finally, I came to my senses and slipped my cell phone out of my bag—a terrific Gucci clutch—and turned it off. It felt great knowing we were both free from every distraction tonight. Maybe our relationship was taking a giant leap forward.

Ty drove us in his way-hot Porsche to the way-hot Hollywood entertainment district. By day, thousands of tourists flocked to Hollywood and Highland to see the stars on the Walk of Fame, stick their feet into the concrete footprints outside Grauman's Chinese Theatre, snap pics, and point to famous landmarks before hitting the great stores and shops. At night, the mood changed as the crowd shifted a few blocks east to take in a play at the Pantages or squeeze into the trendy bars and restaurants.

"Let's have a drink before dinner," Ty suggested, as he left his Porsche with the valet in front of the totally hip W Hotel.

At the rooftop lounge, we ordered wine and relaxed on white overstuffed couches surrounded by lanterns and candles, potted palms and flowers. Soft music played in the background. Ty asked about my day—which was weird—and didn't tell me about his—which was even weirder. The sun went down and the lights of L.A. spread out around us like gleaming jewels on a Judith Leiber evening bag.

Wow, I didn't know how the evening could get any more perfect.

"Ready for dinner?" Ty asked, as we finished up our third glass of wine.

We held hands as we rode in the elevator. I hadn't been here before but Ty must have been, because the maître d' smiled pleasantly as we walked up.

"Everything is as you requested, Mr. Cameron, in our private dining room," he said.

Ty hooked my arm through his as we walked down the corridor to the dining room. Inside, the lights were low, candles burned, flowers were everywhere. All the tables were already filled and—oh my God, my mom and dad were there. How weird was that? Then I spotted my sister and her boyfriend sitting nearby. Wow, what a coincidence. My gaze jumped from table to table. Ty's mom and dad were here, and so were his grandparents.

I got a weird feeling in my stomach.

At another table sat Marcie and some of our other friends. Then I saw a bunch of my mom and dad's friends, and more of our relatives.

I got a really weird feeling now.

I looked up at Ty. "What the—"

Suddenly the band at the opposite end of the dining room broke into a strange song. No way could you dance to it. It sounded more like a march, maybe, or a—

Oh my God. *Oh my God.* It was that song that was always played at graduation ceremonies.

Along one wall hung a huge banner that read CONGRAT-

ULATIONS, HALEY! Then two waiters wheeled in a giant cake with sparklers burning, decorated with a diploma and graduation cap on it. Everybody seated at the tables broke into applause.

Oh, crap.

Chapter 2

"Why didn't you *call me?*" I all but screamed at Marcie.

"Shh," she hissed.

We were in the ladies' room where I'd dashed as soon as Ty finished his speech about how proud everybody was of my graduation from UM—and he didn't mean University of Mixology—and the applause had died down. Marcie had followed, as a best friend would.

I glanced around and didn't see any of my friends or family, then said, "I can't believe you didn't warn me."

"I didn't know what was going on until I got here," Marcie told me. "Ty kept it a secret."

"You should have called me as soon as you found out," I insisted.

"I tried—a million times. You didn't pick up," Marcie said.

So that was why Ty wanted us to turn off our phones. Am I an idiot or what? He didn't want the evening to be about just us—he knew Marcie would call me and ruin his surprise party.

"You can't let everyone think you got your BA from Michigan when you really didn't," Marcie said. "You have to tell them the truth."

Marcie was almost always right. But not this time.

"No way. *No way,*" I said. "Ty would look like a complete idiot—and so would everybody else who showed up here tonight. And I would look like the biggest idiot of all."

"What are you going to tell people when they discover the truth?" Marcie asked.

"Nobody is going to find out."

Jeez, I really hope nobody is going to find out.

"Haley, everybody in that room thinks you just earned a business degree," Marcie said, sounding way too sensible to suit me at the moment. "What are they going to think when you get a job bartending?"

"I'll tell them I plan to open a bar and that I'm doing research."

Marcie didn't say anything and I could see she was thinking it over.

"You can't accept the gifts," she said.

Gifts? There were gifts?

"It wouldn't be right," Marcie said.

The image of a table sitting near the buffet piled high with beautifully wrapped gifts surfaced in my mind. They hadn't even registered when I'd walked in—*that's* how upsetting this whole thing was.

Then a fantastic thought zapped my brain. Maybe one of them was the Temptress handbag. Oh, wow, that would be so cool. It was the "it" bag of the season—well, the moment, anyway. My spirits lifted as the image of that gorgeous bag floated through my mind. I'd seen it in all the fashion magazines this month. Getting that bag would be the saving grace to this whole ordeal.

"Haley." Marcie called my name in that singsong way she has, the one she uses when she thinks I need to be reeled in.

I hate being reeled in.

"I can't refuse the gifts. Everybody would know something was up if I did," I said. "Trust me, after tonight, nobody is going to remember whether I have a college degree or not. Why would they?"

We walked out of the restroom together and I spotted Ty waiting. Beyond him, down the corridor, I heard the murmur of my friends and family in the dining room.

"I have a great surprise," he said.

Jeez, I didn't think I could take another of his surprises tonight.

"Haley, now that you have your BA, I want you to come to work at the Holt's corporate office," Ty said.

I stopped, too stunned to move. Ty wanted me to come to work at the Holt's corporate office? In the same building where he worked? Where I could see him every day and we could have lunch together, and drinks after work? And everybody would know I was his girlfriend and be jealous?

I mean, it's not like I didn't have mad skills. Last year I'd worked for the Pike Warner law firm—long story—so I knew all about the corporate environment. I was great at delegating and dressing for success, not to mention disseminating office gossip.

"Oh, Ty, that would be awesome!" I threw myself against him and wrapped my arms around his neck.

"Hey, you two, get a room," I heard someone say.

I turned and saw Sarah Covington standing in the hallway watching us. What the heck was she doing here? I hate her. This was *my* party. Who invited her?

Damn. It must have been Ty.

"I was just telling Haley how I want her to come to work at the corporate office," Ty said.

"Oh?"

The word just hung there, like a loose button on a YSL skirt, annoying and sure to cause trouble at some point.

"Ty, could I speak with you for a moment?" Sarah asked.

She turned and walked down the corridor. Ty followed.

At the end of the hallway, he leaned down and listened while she talked, and talked, and talked, and talked. Jeez, did she *ever* shut up? Finally, Ty nodded and the two of them walked back.

"Sarah has a good point," Ty said. "It would look bad if you came to work at the corporate office since we're . . . involved."

What? Sarah had told Ty I shouldn't come to work with him? And he'd gone along with it?

I hate her.

"But don't worry, Haley," Sarah said. "After I learned that you'd graduated, I took the liberty of speaking with a friend of mine who works for a wonderful company. I've arranged an interview for you. It's tomorrow. Just a formality, really. I put in a good word for you."

"Isn't that great, Haley?" Ty said.

Oh my God. How could I refuse with them double-teaming me?

"Yeah, that's really great, Sarah," I said.

Bitch.

It was a Louis Vuitton day. Definitely a Louis Vuitton day.

I parked in the lot off Fig and made my way up the block to the bank building where Marcie worked. It was a gorgeous Southern California day. Lots of sunshine, warm breezes, swaying palms. I was meeting her for lunch before my interview with the company Sarah had set me up with. I was still way ticked off over the whole thing, but I hadn't been able to confront Ty about it last night after he'd thrown that graduation party for me—not that he'd have listened anyway.

It was lunch time and the sidewalks were crowded. I spotted Marcie and waved as she walked out of the bank building. She waved back.

Marcie was the best BFF ever. I wouldn't have made it through last night and this morning without her. She'd kept me from putting the smack down on Sarah Covington for sabotaging my chance to work with Ty at the Holt's corporate office. Then this morning she'd called early and made sure I updated my résumé and e-mailed it to the human resources department. She'd asked what I intended to wear, of course.

"Awesome," Marcie declared as she took in the black Michael Kors suit I had on.

It was a relic from a bygone era, way back last fall when I'd worked at Pike Warner. I styled it this morning with a power-red scarf and three-inch heels, and teamed them with my Louis Vuitton bag so the gals in H.R. would know up front who they were dealing with.

"That really was a killer party Ty threw for you last night," Marcie said as we made our way up the street.

"Yeah, I guess," I said. It was. Even though Ty had probably had his personal assistant find a venue, select the menu, arrange for the band, contact all my friends and family, and swear them to secrecy—he'd at least thought of it. Plus, he'd actually been there—not something that always happens with our dates.

"You're still ticked off about the job, aren't you?" Marcie said. "Not that I blame you, of course."

"I need a Starbucks," I said.

Marcie frowned. "What about your new lifestyle? No more frappuccinos?"

I threw her a not-even-a-best-friend-could-stop-me-now look. She interpreted it immediately and crossed at the corner with me.

"So what's the story on the company Sarah set you up with?" Marcie asked, as we went inside Starbucks and got in line.

Last night I'd been majorly ticked at Ty for letting Sarah

derail my employment at the Holt's corporate office. She'd blabbed on and on about the company. I'd drifted off, picturing her as a rag doll and me sticking pins in her.

"Some place called Dempsey Rowland," I said. "I looked them up on the Internet this morning."

Marcie thought for a minute. "Never heard of them. What do they do?"

"I have no idea," I said. "I just looked up their address."

"I can't take a whole hour for lunch today," Marcie said. "Let's just grab something here."

We got sandwiches and I ordered a venti mocha frappuccino with extra whipped cream and a double shot of chocolate—*that's* how upset I was about this whole job thing—and found a table by the window.

"Look on the bright side," Marcie said.

I didn't want to look on the bright side. I was in no mood.

"You'll make a lot of money," she said.

Hmm. Wow. I would. I'd been so upset about Ty caving to Sarah's wishes—again—I hadn't even thought about that.

My spirits lifted a little.

"Plus, you'll need all new clothes," Marcie said. "We can go shopping."

My spirits lifted a little higher.

"And," Marcie said. She leaned in a little so I knew this was going to be something great. "You can quit your job at Holt's."

I shot straight up in my chair. My eyes bugged out. My mouth flew open. I grabbed the sides of the table to keep from launching myself into the ceiling.

"You're *right*." I think I yelled that.

Oh my God. How could I have been so upset over Sarah Covington that I hadn't realized what the new job really meant?

I've seriously got to get a hold on my life.

Then, my future rolled out in front of me like models streaming down a Milan runway.

No more crappy sales clerk job. No more annoying customers. No more unreasonable store management. My own desk. A huge salary. New clothes whenever I want them. Fabulous new handbags—oh my God, I could get that awesome Temptress bag. I could get a new car—a BMW. I could move to a bigger apartment—or maybe buy a condo near the beach. I could actually tell my mom where I worked and she'd be proud of me. Oh my God. *Oh my God.*

"I've got to go," I said, jumping up from my chair.

I wanted to be early—way early—for my interview, to show them how conscientious I was, how dedicated I'd be, and what a perfect employee I'd make. And besides, I needed to brush up on my résumé and remember what I'd put on it. Yeah, okay, I'd stretched the truth a bit, but who doesn't? It's expected, really.

"Good luck," Marcie called as I slurped down the last of my frappuccino and ran out the door.

By the time I got to the office building, I'd spent my first three paychecks, in my head. No need to rehearse my take-this-job-and-shove-it speech for the manager of the Holt's store; I'd had it down since the second hour of the very first day I'd worked there.

The Dempsey Rowland Company was located in a high-rise building on Figueroa Street, just a couple of blocks from the bank building where Marcie worked and the Holt's offices where Ty worked. Great location for coordinating future lunches.

The lobby looked sleek and contemporary with lots of polished black marble on the floor and walls, and several chic-looking water features. I dashed into the restroom, checked my hair—I'd gone with a conservative updo that screamed take-me-seriously—and freshened my makeup.

I checked my phone. Ty hadn't called or texted. Jeez, you'd think he would on a big occasion like this. I was his official girlfriend, after all.

I went into the lobby again. Two guards in gray uniforms sat behind a big reception desk. I gave my name. One guy checked the computer while the other one eyed me, which was kind of weird, then finally I got a badge with VISITOR on it, which I clipped to the lapel of my suit jacket. Not a favorite fashion accessory of mine, but what could I do?

I took the elevator up to the fifth floor. The doors opened and a woman in a navy blue business suit approached as I stepped out. She was in her fifties, I guessed, neat, clean, and composed.

"Miss Randolph? I'm Adela Crosby, human resources," she said, smiling. "Please follow me."

Oh, wow, this was so cool. I had a personal escort. They must have had a really important position in mind for me.

My annual salary grew larger in my head.

Adela made small talk as we wound through a maze of offices. Dempsey Rowland looked prosperous and sort of old-school. Thick beige carpet, dark wood furniture, oil paintings of fox hunts and sailing ships on the walls. Everybody I saw seated in their offices or walking the corridor was well dressed. I couldn't wait to go shopping for new business clothes. Marcie would probably go with me tonight. I'd get the new Temptress bag. Oh, yeah, what an awesome way to start a new job.

"Please be seated," Adela said as she led the way into her office. Atop her desk was a file folder with my name on it.

We both sat down. I was mega nervous. I really wanted to work here—not that I knew what they did, or anything—so I forced myself to sit still and pay attention.

See how I'm already dedicated to this company?

"I'm looking at your job history," Adela said, flipping pages in my folder.

A knot the size of a Prada satchel jerked in my stomach. Yeah, okay, I'd changed jobs a few times—lifeguard, receptionist, file clerk, and two weeks at a pet store—but that was before I found my niche at Pike Warner last fall.

A bigger knot jerked in my stomach. Things hadn't worked out as well as I would have liked at Pike Warner— there was that whole administrative-leave-investigation-pending thing—but it had all turned out okay in the end. Sort of.

"You're currently employed at Holt's Department Store? A retail job isn't easy," Adela said. "I can see you're a very hard worker. We like that here at Dempsey Rowland."

I relaxed a little.

"And you've just graduated from the University of Michigan?" she asked.

I tensed up again.

"Quite an accomplishment," Adela said, still studying my file. "And I can see you come very highly recommended."

I guess the recommendation came from someone at the company, by way of Sarah Covington. Wow, she had really hooked me up with a great job.

I still hate her, of course.

A couple more minutes dragged by, then Adela closed my file and folded her hands.

"Mr. Thrasher heads up our human resources department," she said. "He's out of the office for a while, so I'm going to offer you a position in our contracting department."

What the heck was a contracting department?

"How does that sound?" she asked.

I had no idea what sort of position that would be and what it would entail. I'd never heard of a contracting department—let alone had a clue of what it did. So what could I say but, "Great."

"It will be a full-time position," Adela said.

My heart fluttered a little. A full-time position meant full-time pay.

"With benefits, of course," she said. "Medical, dental, retirement, everything."

Oh my God.

"We'd like to start you out at seventy thousand per year," Adela said.

Oh my God.

Adela gazed across the desk at me. I could see that she was talking but I wasn't listening. How could I? Thoughts were pinging around in my head like waistband buttons at a chili cook-off.

Then I realized Adela had finally stopped talking and was looking at me kind of funny. Jeez, had she just asked me a question or something? I didn't want her to think I wasn't paying attention—which I wasn't, of course—but still.

Instantly, I channeled my mom's I'm-better-than-you attitude. Mom's a former beauty queen. Really. On rare instances—like solar eclipses, and now—something she taught me paid off.

I downgraded Mom's I'm-better-than-you look to my own I'm-giving-your-words-careful-consideration look. I've found if I hold it long enough, the other person will eventually say something.

Jeez, I wish Adela would say something.

"If you'd like to think over our offer and review the new-hire package, that's fine," she said.

Yikes! She thought I was reluctant to accept the job here. Quickly, I morphed my expression into my I've-suddenly-made-up-my-mind look.

"Everything sounds perfect," I said, and managed to sit still when I really wanted to do a backflip off her desk.

"Excellent." Adela pulled a big folder from her desk drawer and passed it to me. "I'm so glad you could come in today because we've got several other new hires going through orientation. We'll put you in with them and you can start working tomorrow."

My heart hammered in my chest as I walked the corridor with Adela. She was gesturing and explaining which department was which, where things were, who worked where. At least, I guess that's what she was saying. I drifted off.

All I could think was that I could stop by the Holt's store on my way home and *quit my job.*

I'd call Marcie right away and give her the news. We'd have to go shopping immediately. Maybe she could leave work early today.

I'd go by Ty's office and tell him. He'd be so happy for me—as long as I wasn't interrupting a meeting, of course.

Adela led the way into a large conference room. Two men and a woman, all dressed in please-hire-me suits, were seated at the table clutching the same big folder as me. I took the chair farthest from the front of the room— old habit.

A woman stood at the head of the conference table pulling a screen down from the ceiling. My spirits dipped a little. Apparently we were in for the Dempsey Rowland version of Death by PowerPoint.

Adela introduced me to the other new hires, then gestured to the woman at the front of the room.

"This is Violet Hamilton. Violet heads up our security department," Adela said, then left the room.

Violet looked kind of old to head up much of anything. She was a tiny woman, barely five foot three, and I doubted she weighed much more than the last pair of thigh-high boots I'd bought. Her snow white hair was styled in an I-never-got-over-the-fifties helmet, and she had on a bright pink suit.

She looked like Retirement Home Barbie.

But maybe she had a little New Millennium Barbie in her. A laptop sat on the conference table near her. And perhaps she also had some I'm-Better-Than-You Barbie in her because a Burberry laptop case sat close by. Granted, it was an older style—a special line of pink and black accessories they'd trotted out a few years ago—but it was a designer label and she was working it big time.

"I'd like to stress to each of you the importance of completing your paperwork," Violet said, gesturing to the folders we'd all been given. "It's mandatory that you answer each and every question put to you. You will not receive your security clearance—and remember, you can't work for Dempsey Rowland without it—until your background investigation is done."

Wait a minute. Security clearance? Background information? What the heck was she talking about?

"How long does it take to get a clearance?" a man—whose name I'd already forgotten—seated next to me asked.

Maybe this was something Adela was talking about in her office.

"There are different levels of clearances required for different positions here at Dempsey Rowland, so the time necessary to complete the background investigation will vary from person to person. Weeks, sometimes. Months, occasionally," Violet said. "We move as quickly as possible."

I started to get a weird feeling.

"How far back does your investigation go?" the same man asked.

My weird feeling got weirder.

"Years, decades. Back to childhood," Violet said. "After all, we're handling sensitive work for the government of the United States. We can't have anyone working here whose past is questionable."

"What exactly do you mean by questionable?" I asked.

Violet smiled kindly at me. "No need to worry, Miss Randolph. I can see you're a nice young lady. It's not as if you've ever been in trouble with the law, have you?"

Did being a suspect in multiple murder investigations count?

"Or been involved in any organized criminal activity?" she asked.

Jeez, did that include the guy from the Russian Mafia who owed me a favor?

"You've never been let go from a job under a cloud of suspicion, have you?" Violet asked.

Well, there was that whole administrative-leave-investigation-pending thing from last fall. Would that be a problem?

"And everything you stated on your résumé is true, isn't it?" she asked.

Kind of. Sort of. Well, except for that part about the University of Michigan. And, well, maybe a few other things.

What could I say? Confess to everything? Now? Before I even got my first paycheck? No way. How would I explain it to Ty? And what would happen when Sarah Covington found out I got the boot because I couldn't get the security clearance? I'd never live it down.

"Haley?" Violet asked. "Is there something you'd like to tell me?"

What could I say but, "No, of course not."

"Then you have nothing to worry about," Violet declared.

Oh, crap.

Chapter 3

Was I going to get fired today? Before I'd really even gotten to work here?

The notion had plagued me all last night—I hadn't even gone shopping—and this morning, and had taken all the fun out of imagining how I'd blow my first paycheck on clothes and handbags. I hadn't even told Marcie about the whole security clearance thing—*that's* how upset I was about it.

I left my Honda in the parking garage, took the elevator down to the Dempsey Rowland lobby, and flashed the I.D. card I'd been issued yesterday at one of the guards at the reception desk while the other guard gave me serious stink-eye. I hoisted my Burberry satchel higher, then took the elevator up to five. I was early—I wanted to get my desk chair warm before they booted my butt out on the street—but so were other people. They looked happy and secure, as if they'd actually still have their jobs at the end of the day.

Jeez, I really hope I still have my job at the end of the day.

Yesterday, after several grueling hours of orientation and having us complete our background information forms, Violet Hamilton had given the three other new hires and me a tour of the office complex, then let us leave for the day. She'd left instructions for us to report to H.R. this morning so Adela could escort us to meet our new supervisor, where we'd be given *blah, blah, blah*. I don't know what she said. I'd drifted off.

I moved along the corridors with the other employees who'd reported early. Wow, a lot of people were already here. Some of them had a coffee cup in their hands, others were already seated at their desks working. Wow, what was that all about?

I couldn't help but notice that a lot of really good-looking men worked here. Not that I was interested, of course. After all, I had an official boyfriend who was fabulous—at least, he was the last time I heard from him, whenever that was.

I turned a corner, then another, and another, looking for H.R.—it was like a maze in this place—and spotted the name CONSTANCE ADDISON on a little nameplate outside an office. Constance would be my supervisor, I recalled from a lucid moment during yesterday's orientation. A long, thin window ran down the edge of the door. I peered inside and saw the usual office furniture—desk, shelves, chairs, computer, and a couple of big cabinets. The lights were off; no one was inside.

I should have been doing my X-rated Snoopy dance— I'm pretty sure upper management at Dempsey Rowland frowned on that sort of thing, but it would be a hit at the office Christmas party, if I lasted here that long—but instead I was looking at the possibility of getting canned today. All because of that security clearance thing.

With the exception of perhaps slightly misrepresenting my academic qualifications on my résumé—which shouldn't be *that* big a deal, if you ask me—I hadn't really done anything wrong, or illegal, or dishonest. Yeah, I'd been involved in a few questionable things, but none of them were my fault. Really.

So there was no reason to think I wouldn't get my security clearance and continue to work here. Right? Besides, all that other stuff was in the past. I was starting over fresh in a new job, at a new company. And as long as nothing bad happened here, I'd be fine. Right?

I glanced up and down the hallway and saw no one headed my way. Since I was lost and couldn't find the H.R. office—and I didn't want to look like a total idiot by asking—I decided I'd leave a little note for Constance, letting her know I was here—way early—and that I was reporting to H.R.

I opened her office door and walked inside. Huh. Something smelled kind of gross in here.

I got a weird feeling

I noticed that the chair was pushed back from the desk, and that the stapler, pencil cup, and paper clips were strewn across the floor.

My weird feeling got weirder.

I walked farther into the office and circled behind the desk. Violet Hamilton lay face down on the floor. I knelt beside her. She was covered in blood. Dead.

A scream pierced my left eardrum. I jumped up and saw a woman standing just inside the doorway holding a totally fabulous Prada handbag and a cup of coffee. She was a little on the chunky side and had on an I-don't-own-a-full-length-mirror burnt orange suit. I figured her age for the wrong side of fifty. Her auburn hair was cut in a short bob. Her mouth gaped open and she looked like two flying saucers had just landed in her eye sockets.

"Oh my God! My office! What did you do? What did you *do*?" she shrieked.

So this was Constance Addison, my new supervisor. Jeez, do I know how to make a first impression, or what?

She kept screaming, like a siren going off. If her voice got any more high-pitched, only dogs would be able to hear her.

"Violet! Oh my God! Violet!" Constance lurched across the desk, spilling her coffee and knocking a stack of papers onto the floor. She gasped and turned back to me. "What have you done to Violet?"

I considered bitch-slapping her—just to break her momentum, of course—but instead I pulled my cell phone from my purse.

"Gun!" Constance screamed, pointing at my phone. "Gun!"

Maybe I should go ahead and slap her.

"Don't kill me! Please!" she yelled.

I hit 9-1-1, gave my name and a brief rundown on the situation to the operator, and hung up just as a bunch of other people rushed through the door. Some of them looked familiar, but I didn't know their names.

"Oh my God!" Constance yelled, as she pointed to me. "She's killed Violet!"

Everybody looked at me funny. Then they all started screaming and jostling for position, some trying to get inside the office, others stampeding toward the door.

Constance staggered backward and collapsed into the visitor chair by the window.

There is no easy way to handle people in this sort of situation—believe me, I know. I've had experience.

Hmm, maybe I should put *that* on my résumé.

"Quiet! Everybody quiet!" I shouted, and clapped my hands together.

A hush fell over the room. All eyes turned to me.

"This is a crime scene! Everybody out," I said, motioning them toward the door. I pointed to a kind of hot-looking guy—not that I'd really noticed under the circumstances, of course—and said, "Find whoever runs this place and tell them to get over here. And call security at the desk in the lobby. Tell them what's going on and to not let anyone leave the building."

He pushed his way through the crowd, which hovered outside the door, as Adela Crosby wormed her way inside.

"What's going on?" she demanded.

"Violet is dead," I said, and gestured behind the desk.

Constance started screaming again. Adela gazed behind the desk, then turned white and grabbed the doorframe to steady herself.

"But . . . how? What . . . happened?" Adela asked.

"Somebody killed her!" Constance shrieked. She pointed to me. "It must have been her! She was the only one here when I walked in!"

Adela instantly pulled herself together and narrowed her gaze at me. She opened her mouth to say something, when a man rushed into the room. He had white hair, and wore an I'm-in-charge expression and an expensive suit.

"What's going on in here?" he demanded.

Constance started screaming again.

Adela turned a lighter shade of white. "Oh, Mr. Dempsey."

Mr. Dempsey? The Mr. Dempsey who owned the company? Wow, was I having a great first day on the job, or what?

Mr. Dempsey's gaze swept over each of us, as if to take a roll.

Adela folded her hands primly in front of her and said, "It seems that Violet is dead, Mr. Dempsey," she said quietly, like that might somehow soften the news.

Mr. Dempsey drew in a long breath and squared his shoulders, as if he'd already seen it all, many times before, and this was just another duty to dispense with.

He pointed at Constance who was still screaming. "Shut her up," he said.

Adela rushed to her side and knelt by the chair. "Shh, Constance. You have to be quiet now. Mr. Dempsey is here."

He pulled his cell phone from his jacket pocket.

"I've already called nine-one-one," I said.

His gaze drilled into me. I don't think he appreciated my taking charge.

"I've had security notified of the situation and instructed them not to let anyone leave the building," I told him.

"Who the hell are you?" he demanded, jamming his phone into his pocket.

Adela sprang to her feet. "This is Haley Randolph, a—a new employee."

He glared harder at me, then whipped around to the employees standing in the hallway.

"It's all right, everyone. The situation is under control. Let's all get to our desks, back to our routine," he said. Then he turned to me and motioned for me to walk around him, out of the office.

It miffed me a bit that I was being dismissed—I mean, jeez, I found the body—but it suited me just as well to leave. I walked to the end of the corridor, then turned back. Mr. Dempsey and Adela were outside Constance's office. I couldn't hear what he was saying, but Adela looked as if she'd heard it a couple million times before.

Since my presence obviously wasn't wanted here, what could I do but head for the employee breakroom—the one place I remembered from yesterday's tour—and sit for a while.

As breakrooms went, Dempsey Rowland's was a good one. There was a big refrigerator and a microwave, and lots of tables with chairs just hard enough to discourage employees from lingering for extended periods of time. Vending machines were stocked with an impressive array of energy drinks, snacks, and candy in an effort, no doubt, to squeeze a few more minutes of work out of the staff by plying them with excess caffeine and sugar. On the walls hung posters detailing our rights as employees, which would surely be ignored until someone filed a lawsuit.

I fed a ten into one of the vending machines and started pushing buttons.

Yeah, okay, I know I'd vowed to change my life, live in the reverse world, and lay off the sweets, but, come on, I'd had one hell of a morning.

I grabbed a stack of magazines and settled into a chair. Immediately I downgraded the Dempsey Rowland break-room from good to unacceptable when I realized the only magazines available were on business, health, and fitness. No *People*, *Glamour*, or *Marie Claire*. Working here may be harder than I realized—if I got to keep my job, of course—which I might, since the head of security had just died.

I mean that in the nicest way, of course.

It's not easy to eat a Snickers bar, M&Ms, and bite-size Almond Joys while flipping through *Women's Health*, but I persevered. After all, these were extenuating circumstances.

Thanks to the mega-watts of chocolate I'd consumed, my brain cells started firing and all rushed to the image of Violet Hamilton. I didn't know her—except from orientation yesterday and, truthfully, I hadn't paid all that much attention—but she'd seemed like a nice lady. Organized, efficient, knowledgeable, composed. Not exactly the kind of person who would incite someone to murder her.

But maybe her death hadn't been intentional. Maybe it was an accident.

When I first saw Violet lying on the office floor, I figured she'd been murdered. I'd seen murder victims before— long story—so I figured that's what happened to Violet.

But I guess she could have had a heart attack or stroke, and fallen and hit her head. It appeared as if the back of her skull had been struck, but maybe that just meant she'd fallen backwards and hit her head on something. Maybe the heart attack or stroke hadn't killed her immediately. Maybe she'd rolled over to get up, or just thrashed around and ended up lying face down before dying.

I'd gotten a look at the back of her head and it didn't look all that great. Plus blood had splattered all over the place. The stuff on top of the desk had been knocked off, so maybe there'd been a struggle. Did that mean someone had hit her? Murdered her?

I bit into another Almond Joy—just to keep my brain working at peak levels, of course—and another thought came to me.

When had she been killed or, maybe, died? Violet was sans the Barbie-pink suit I'd seen her in yesterday so I figured it must have been this morning. Lots of people were here early. I thought back and tried to remember everyone I'd seen in the parking garage, the lobby, and the Dempsey Rowland office complex. Since I only knew a few people here, all the faces were a blur.

The breakroom door swung open and a man—one of the new hires from orientation yesterday—walked in. Just about everything about him was forgettable. Average height, a little overweight, a middle-aged white guy with a comb-over. He froze when he saw me, like he didn't want to be caught in the breakroom.

"Want some?" I asked, and pushed my bag of M&Ms toward him.

"No thanks," he said, then headed for the coffeepot on the counter beside the refrigerator. He poured himself a cup and glanced back at me. "It's Haley, right?"

"Yeah, and you're . . . ?"

"Max Corwin," he said, and walked back to my table. He sipped his coffee and shuddered. "Crazy first day on the job, huh?"

I doubted he knew I'd found the body. I saw no need to mention it.

"The cops are all over the place out there," he said, nodding toward the breakroom door. He forced a laugh and said, "Somebody dying on our first day. Hope that's not an omen."

Max looked like a worrier to me. He had deep wrinkles in his forehead and his fingernails were bitten down to nothing. I figured he had a wife, kids, and a mortgage and really needed this job.

"Of course, the company has been around for over forty years. I suppose they've seen just about everything," Max said.

"Forty years? Wow."

I guess they covered that in orientation.

"Can you imagine? Arthur Dempsey founded the company with ten dollars in his pocket and built it into this." Max sipped his coffee. "Too bad his partner isn't around to see how great the business turned out."

Maybe I should start paying attention in orientations.

"Would that be the Rowland guy?" I asked.

"Freak accident, falling down the stairs like that," Max said. He nodded slowly. "You've got to hand it to Mr. Dempsey for keeping his buddy's name on the business all these years. Heck of a way to honor him."

Max drained his cup.

"This is probably going to slow down the process of us getting our security clearances," he said. "But we're here now. We're on board. We're employed. There's nothing they can do about that."

Since, apparently, Max had actually been listening during orientation, I was about to ask him what the heck the company did, but I decided I'd just look it up on the Internet tonight.

"Well, we'd better get out there," Max said. He set his cup aside. I stuffed the last handful of M&Ms in my mouth, dumped my trash, and followed him out the door.

I figured that if I just walked the halls, eventually I'd stumble over the H.R. office. Adela found me first. She looked majorly stressed.

"The detectives have been looking for you," Adela said.

I wondered how good they were at *detecting* if they didn't think to look in the breakroom.

Adela took off like a shot, leaving me to follow.

"You're going to have to talk to the homicide detectives," she said, setting a blistering pace through the corridor. I have my mother's long pageant legs—plus I'd been out-distancing Holt's customers who expected me to help them with something, for months now—so I kept up easily.

"Tell them whatever they want to know," she said. "You must be absolutely truthful when—"

"I got this," I said.

I've been interviewed by homicide detectives before—in two states, actually. I'd had a brief run-in with the FBI, too—long story—so I knew what to do.

Maybe I should add that to my résumé.

I knew I hadn't done anything wrong so I had nothing to worry about. I'd simply had the misfortune of finding Violet dead on the office floor. That's it. End of my involvement. So I had nothing to worry about.

Jeez, this whole thing seemed eerily familiar.

Adela rushed through the door into the conference room and I heard her say, "I found Haley Randolph. She's here." Then she blasted past me, back down the corridor as if she'd just stepped onto the red carpet and spotted another woman wearing her exact same dress.

I lingered in the hallway for a few seconds and reminded myself that the homicide detectives were just looking for information—no way were they going to try to pin anything on me—so I had nothing to worry about. I mean, really, this day could not possibly get any worse. Right?

I walked into the conference room. Two LAPD homicide detectives sat side by side at the head of the table. My stomach did its this-cannot-be-happening heave.

Detectives Madison and Shuman.

Oh, crap.

CHAPTER 4

Detective Madison and I had history—but not the good kind.

He'd been all set to retire last year when I'd solved a big case for him—which he didn't seem to appreciate, for some reason. So he was still on the job, on a mission, really, to find me guilty of *something*.

I hadn't seen Madison in a few months but he hadn't changed much. Thinning gray hair, heavy jowls, a gravy stain on his tie that I suspected was left over from yesterday's lunch, and a beach ball belly.

Detective Shuman and I had history, too—the better kind. Nothing romantic, of course, since I had an official boyfriend and Shuman had an official girlfriend he was absolutely crazy about. But still, there was something going on between us, only neither of us would go there and find out exactly what it was.

Shuman looked good today. Early thirties, kind of tall, nice build, brown hair, blue eyes. He had on his usual sport jacket–shirt-tie combo.

"Well, if it's not LAPD's favorite murder suspect," Detective Madison said, and sat back in his chair. "Haley Randolph. Again."

"Aren't you supposed to be working in another jurisdiction, or whatever you call it?" I asked.

Madison folded his hands across his wide belly. "You're well-known in squad rooms all over Southern California. When the call came in that you'd reported yet another murder, the word went out."

I pictured a giant "H" beaming into the heavens over city hall, just like the Bat Signal above Gotham City. Cool.

"What can you tell us about Violet Hamilton's murder?" Shuman asked, as he pulled a little notebook from his jacket pocket.

"She was murdered?" I asked, as I sat down at the table. "It wasn't an accident?"

"Like you don't know," Madison sneered. He rocked forward in his chair. "You're working here now, aren't you?"

He made it sound like it was all part of some big conspiracy.

"I just got hired yesterday," I said.

"And there's a murder already," Madison said.

Well, okay, I couldn't exactly argue with that.

"Look, all I did was walk into the office and find Violet dead on the floor behind the desk," I said. "I had nothing to do with her death."

"You had no reason to want her dead?" Madison asked.

"No, of course not," I insisted.

"No reason at all?" he repeated.

I got a weird feeling.

"No," I said. Okay, that sounded kind of guilty.

"Then let me give you a reason," Madison declared. "You've got a lot to hide."

My weird feeling turned really weird.

"Your résumé," he said.

Yikes! Had he seen it?

"You need a security clearance to work here, don't you, Miss Randolph?" Detective Madison demanded.

"Well, yeah, everybody needs—"

"But not everybody is afraid of a background check like you are," Madison said. "Because not everybody has something to hide, like you do."

Jeez, what could I say to that?

"You're afraid of a background check. You wanted to delay it in an attempt to ingratiate yourself here," Detective Madison said. "But you won't get your clearance. You know you won't. And then what will your socially prominent mother say? What will your well-to-do boyfriend and his family think of you?"

Madison pushed to his feet, planted both palms on the table, and leaned toward me. He looked like one of those bulldogs snarling through a backyard fence.

"You came to work early this morning, didn't you?" Madison demanded.

"Well, yes. I wanted to make a good first—"

"You sneaked in early—"

"I didn't sneak!"

"You were supposed to report to the human resources office, weren't you?" Madison said. "But you didn't. You went to another office. Don't lie, Miss Randolph."

"I'm not lying!"

"You found Violet Hamilton and you killed her to stop her background investigation because you have a lot to hide and you don't want to lose this job," he declared.

"No—"

"You were seen bending over her body," Madison told me. "I have a witness!"

"I was just—"

Madison straightened up. "I'm going to take apart your résumé item by item, find everything you lied about. And I don't care if doing that brings down this whole company!"

Great.

*   *   *

I didn't know why Madison would think I'd lied on my résumé, except that everyone lies on their résumé. I mean, if people didn't lie, how would anybody ever get a job?

I swung my Honda into the parking lot in front of the Holt's store in Santa Clarita, and cut off a bright yellow VW Beetle to grab a spot near the door.

This wasn't exactly how I'd planned to spend my evening. I'd envisioned myself skipping into the store, cartwheeling to the store manager's office, and claiming my little piece of the American dream by announcing my resignation at the top of my lungs. Now I didn't dare quit. Not with that whole murder investigation and security clearance thing hanging over me. Instead, I had to go inside and actually work.

I hate my life.

Of course, it was possible I had nothing to worry about—from Detective Madison, anyway. I still didn't know for sure whether Violet had been murdered or if she'd died under other circumstances. Maybe Madison was just messing with my mind.

My cell phone rang. I pulled it from my handbag—a really cool Dooney & Bourke barrel—and saw Ty's name on the caller I.D. screen. My heart did its usual—but rare—Ty's-calling flutter. I answered right away.

"I heard you had a rough day," Ty said.

His voice sounded soft and sexy. I pictured him seated at his big desk in his big office at the Holt's corporate office downtown, still dressed immaculately even after twelve hours of handling situations all more important than me. But at least he'd called. I was glad about that.

"You heard about Violet dying?" I asked.

"Sarah told me," he said.

I hate her.

I sat there in my car, looking up at the sign on top of the building that spelled out HOLT'S in blue cursive letters, thinking about Sarah Covington working at the corporate office with Ty. If it hadn't been for her big mouth, I'd be working there, too. Instead I was stuck at Dempsey Rowland, in the middle of a possible murder investigation.

Then it hit me. Oh my God. Sarah probably knew something like this would happen. She probably got me the job on purpose to make things harder on me. She could have killed Violet herself just to make me look bad.

Well, okay, maybe that was a bit of a stretch, but it *could* have happened.

"Haley?" Ty asked.

I realized he'd been talking and I wasn't listening.

"Yeah, I'm here," I said quickly. "I have to go in a minute. I can't be late for my shift."

"You're still working at the store?" he asked.

I couldn't exactly tell him that Detective Madison had declared me a suspect in Violet's death, and that there was a question about the info I'd stated on my résumé, and doubt as to whether I'd get a security clearance and remain employed at Dempsey Rowland.

I saw no reason to get into all that with him.

"I was already on the schedule and I didn't want to leave the store without coverage. It wouldn't be right," I said. "Unless, of course, you want to come over to my place. I'll call in sick."

Ty chuckled. "Sounds good, but I can't make it tonight. I have a meeting."

Damn.

"I'll see you soon," Ty said.

I was about to ask his definition of "soon"—since it often conflicted with mine—but he hung up. I sat in my car for another few minutes until there was nothing left to do but go inside.

The store was kind of quiet tonight, just a few shoppers wandering around as I made my way to the employees' breakroom at the back of the building. This area also housed the store manager's office, the training room, and a couple of other offices.

Just outside the breakroom was the customer service booth, often my assigned sector of retail hell. Grace was in the booth tonight. She's way cool. She was in college and took her classes seriously, which was kind of odd, but we're still friends. She'd recently dyed the tips of her spiky hair Martian green. It looked great.

Inside the breakroom I stowed my purse in my locker, hung my Holt's lanyard around my neck, and cued up behind the other employees in line for the time clock.

"Hey, girl." My friend Bella left her spot ahead of me in line and came back to stand next to me. "You look like your cat got run over, or something. What's up?"

Bella was my BFF at Holt's. She was tall and black, and she worked at Holt's to save money for beauty school. She envisioned herself as a hairdresser to the stars and, in the meantime, practiced on herself. Tonight she'd fashioned her hair into what looked like a sea turtle, so I figured she was in a tropical phase.

"Just one of those days," I said.

"It's always one of those days in this place," Bella grumbled, as the line moved forward.

A few weeks ago, the time clock blew up. Everybody blamed me but it wasn't my fault—not entirely, anyway— so now we had a new one. Instead of sticking our time cards into a slot, we punched in our employee number on a keypad, pressed our thumb on an I.D. screen, and that was it. Really. You'd think Holt's was preparing us to arm nuclear missiles, because Corporate had subjected us to a butt-numbing three-hour training course to tell us that. I'd avoided the entire session by hiding out in the stock room.

That's how I roll.

I glanced at the work schedule hanging above the time clock as I clocked in and saw that I was assigned to the junior's department tonight. I liked working in juniors, mainly because there was a great spot behind the clothing racks and in front of the wall of jeans, where I could sit on the floor, pretend to straighten sizes, and text my friends.

Just because I knew my department assignment, I saw no reason to rush straight there. I circled around the rear of the store, past domestics, thinking I might stop off in the shoe department and catch up on things with Sandy, my other Holt's BFF, when I spotted Detective Shuman in the housewares department.

Yikes! What was he doing here?

Immediately, I dropped into a crouch behind the display of place mats. My heart pounded. My thoughts raced. Had Shuman come to Holt's tonight to arrest me for Violet's murder?

For a minute—well, for several, really—I considered sneaking to the stock-room door and going out the back way through the loading dock. But then I realized that wouldn't accomplish anything, just prolong the inevitable. Shuman knew where I lived. If he'd really come to arrest me, he could easily find me.

And so could Detective Madison, I realized.

Hmm. I hadn't spotted him with Shuman. He sure as heck wouldn't want to miss being front and center when I was arrested.

I rose and peered over the place mat display. No sign of Madison. Then I saw Shuman looking at the stand mixers. A woman stood beside him.

I figured her for maybe thirty, kind of tall, trim, with dark brown hair pulled back in a sensible, low ponytail. She had on a black skirt, low-heeled pumps, and carried a black Coach tote. She wore a royal blue blouse and had turned up the collar and rolled the cuffs back. It made me think she'd gotten off work, ditched a suit jacket, and was going for a more informal look.

I can't say she was gorgeous. Pretty, though, in a no-

nonsense way, the kind of person who always got picked to head up a committee or something because they looked smart, competent, and capable, and would make everybody else assigned to the project look good.

Shuman sure found her fascinating. He stood close as she studied the stand mixers that were on display. He watched her expressions, moved when she moved.

Oh my God. She was Shuman's girlfriend, I realized, the lawyer who worked in the district attorney's office. They were shopping.

How come Ty never went shopping with me?

Shuman didn't take his eyes off of her, as if every word she spoke, every movement she made, was absolutely captivating.

Well, maybe we'd never gone shopping, but Ty always looked at me that way.

Seeing them together, bending their heads to talk, studying the display, discussing options, smiling at each other, laughing at some private joke, gave me a weird feeling, somehow.

I walked over. Shuman didn't look surprised to see me.

Maybe it wasn't a coincidence they'd chosen this Holt's store to shop in.

"Haley, this is Amanda Payton," he said, making introductions.

"I found my grandmother's German cookbook, so I'm redoing my entire kitchen," Amanda said, smiling broadly. Definitely a woman on a mission. She touched Shuman's arm. "He claims he's never eaten German food before, so I'm going to rock his world."

Shuman shook his head and gave her a teasing grin. "I don't know about that."

"You're going to love it," Amanda declared. "Haley, you'll have to come eat with us one night. Oh, I know. We'll have a dinner party."

"Sounds great," I said.

Ty and I had never had a dinner party, but we could. He'd love it. Kind of. Sort of. Well, maybe.

"Perfect. We'll invite the—" Amanda stopped, pulled her cell phone out of her tote and checked the caller I.D. screen. She looked at Shuman. "Sorry, I have to take this."

Amanda answered her phone as she walked away. I watched Shuman as he followed her with his gaze.

Yeah, Ty had looked at me that way before. I'm sure he had.

"She seems really nice," I said.

"She's awesome," Shuman mumbled, his eyes still on her.

Ty thought I was awesome. Probably.

After a few more seconds, Shuman turned to me, his expression decidedly different.

"Violet Hamilton was murdered," Shuman said. "Blunt force trauma to the back of her head."

"I don't suppose you caught the killer already?" I asked.

"Did you see anyone or anything unusual in the office?" he asked.

Shuman had become pretty good about sharing info with me, but he wasn't about to give up anything without getting something from me first.

"I noticed that lots of people had reported early for work, which seemed kind of odd to me. But maybe that's expected there," I said. "I guess the strangest thing is that Violet was in that particular office."

"Why's that?" Shuman asked.

"It wasn't her office. It belonged to Constance Addison," I said.

"So why were you in there?" he asked.

"Constance is my supervisor."

"Great," Shuman muttered, and shook his head.

"That doesn't mean I killed her," I pointed out.

"But it's another reason to tie you to the crime," Shuman said.

"Which is exactly what Madison is looking for. Right?"

Shuman didn't say anything. He didn't have to. I knew he agreed with me. But Detective Madison was his partner. He wasn't about to say something against him.

"Anything on the security tapes?" I asked.

"We've got all the footage from the lobby and the parking garage. It's a big building," Shuman said. "It's going to take a while to go through them, see if there's anybody who doesn't belong."

"We all have to show our I.D. card to the guards in the lobby," I said.

"Those things are stolen, duplicated, and falsified all the time," Shuman said. He shook his head. "We don't even know if the murderer was a Dempsey Rowland employee. Someone could have come from one of the other companies on another floor."

"Murder weapon?" I asked.

Shuman shrugged. "We're looking for it."

I guess a lot of murder investigations seem kind of hopeless in the beginning. I guess, too, that Shuman was used to it but still didn't like it.

"I'll let you know if I find out anything," I told him.

He didn't jump at my offer.

"There's a murderer in that office building, Haley. Watch yourself," Shuman said, and for a couple of seconds—okay, maybe just one—I thought I saw the same expression he'd used when he looked at Amanda.

Or maybe that was just wishful thinking on my part.

CHAPTER 5

Iabsolutely had to find that Temptress handbag. It was the only thing that could salvage the crappy week I was having. I'd been strong, stuck to my it's-a-whole-new-me plan, and hadn't had a mocha frappuccino in *forever,* but I didn't know how much longer I could hold out.

The realization came to me the next morning as I pulled yet another months' old business suit from my closet. So far I'd been getting by wearing my old Pike Warner clothes from last fall for my interview and the first day of work at Dempsey Rowland, but I was sick of them. Too many bad memories. Nothing less than some new clothes could lift my spirits—except the Temptress to go along with them, of course.

I'd been given a lot of gift cards from department stores for graduation presents, but after Violet had burst my I'm-going-to-make-bank-working-here bubble during orientation with that whole background investigation/security clearance thing, I hadn't been too excited about laying in a supply of black, brown, and navy blue business suits.

But who knew when all that would be sorted out. Days? Weeks? Months, maybe? I definitely had to get some new clothes.

My cell phone rang, which was weird because it was only a little after 7:30, way early for anyone to call.

My stomach did its this-can't-be-good roll. What if it was Adela from Dempsey Rowland? What if she was calling to tell me they'd completed my background check already, and not to bother coming to work today?

Since I'm not big on suspense, I looked at the caller I.D. screen. Mom was calling. Okay, this was way weird.

"Haley, you have to come over immediately," Mom said when I answered. "Something terrible has happened."

With her history of holding the crowns of Miss California and third runner-up in the Miss America contest, Mom lived in what I call the "pageant universe." The pageant universe—complete with its own time zone—existed in an alternate reality. Time, space, and the three dimensions the rest of us live in didn't apply to Mom.

Her frantic phone call at this early hour insisting something terrible had happened didn't upset me. For Mom, it could mean that her *Vanity Fair* had arrived in the mail with a crease in the cover, or that some hapless shoe salesman in Neiman Marcus had brought her open-toe, slingback pumps in the size that fit her, rather than the size she actually wore.

"I've got to get to work," I said.

"It's Juanita," Mom said.

Juanita was Mom's housekeeper. She'd worked there for as long as I could remember.

"What's up with Juanita?" I asked.

"She's dead."

I grew up in a great house in La Cañada Flintridge that was built back in the 1920s, or something, and had been left to my mom by her grandmother, along with a trust fund. Nobody in the family knew—or was willing to tell—exactly what my great-grandmother had done to acquire what amounted to a small mansion on a prestigious hillside that overlooked the L.A. basin, or to establish a trust fund for my mother, of all people.

In another yet unexplained twist of fate, Mom had been grateful enough to give me, her oldest female child, great-grandma's name. So here I was attempting to skip lightly through life with the middle name of "Thelma."

Leave it to family.

It was a great house to grow up in. I couldn't remember living anywhere else. I lived there with my older brother—now an air force pilot flying F-16s in the Middle East—along with my younger sister, who attended college and modeled. And my dad, of course, who was an aerospace engineer. In what I thought of as one of life's greatest mysteries—sort of like the origin of the pyramids—Dad had somehow managed to stay married to my mom all these years.

As far back as I could remember, we'd had a lot of household staff—believe me, Mom went through quite a few people. Gardeners, housekeepers, an herb garden advisor—organic food, anyone?—window washers, a pool service, an indoor plant service—Mom's interpretation of going green—a tropical fish tank service, nannies, chimney sweeps, decorators, landscape architects, mural artists, caterers, cooks, a Feng Shui master, a sand castle–building coach—don't ask—not to mention the parade of personal assistants Mom had, no doubt, sent running back to college determined to get a real job.

But Juanita had always been there. I couldn't remember a time when she hadn't been in the house offering a kind smile, quiet words of encouragement, and promises of better things to come.

And, believe me, I needed it, especially during those years when Mom had subjected me to a battery of lessons—singing, tap, modeling, ballet, piano—in a desperate attempt to unearth some tiny nugget of natural talent in me.

Juanita had even been there for me when I set fire to the den curtains while twirling fire batons—it was an accident, I swear. Kind of. Sort of. Well, anyway, the incident had gotten me out of taking any more lessons—that and the fact that my little sister became Mom's Mini-Me.

I didn't wait to hear what else Mom had to say about Juanita's death. I threw on the first business suit I got my hands on in my closet, then called Dempsey Rowland and left a message on Constance's voicemail that I'd be late for work, using the I-have-a-flat-tire excuse—everybody knew it was a lie, but, oh well—and hauled out to Mom's house.

I was frantic. I hadn't asked Mom for details about Juanita's death on the phone because I knew she wouldn't make any sense and I wouldn't have the patience to try and figure it out—which pretty much summed up the ongoing state of our mother-daughter relationship.

I swung into the circular driveway in front of my folks' house, dreading the thought of seeing ambulances, fire trucks, cop cars, and plain vanilla detective-mobiles parked in front, maybe even a news helicopter circling overhead. I didn't want to see one of those big ugly black body bags, knowing Juanita was inside it.

But when I pulled up, the driveway was empty. Huh. That was odd. Had emergency services come and gone already? Had Juanita died a few days ago and Mom forgot to tell me?

I left my car and hurried to the door. It opened as I approached. Mom stood in the foyer wearing a silk caftan, gold earrings, necklace, and bracelet, and two-inch heels. She had on makeup and her hair was styled in a tight updo.

Mom always dressed as if *Extra* would burst into her home at any second and film her for a "Former Beauty Queens, Where Are They Now?" segment, or something.

"Oh my gosh, Mom, what happened to Juanita?" I asked.

"That's exactly what I'd like to know," she announced as she closed the front door.

I looked around. I saw no one. The house was deadly silent. No low voices of detectives, no squawking police radios, no sign of my dad or sister.

"Where is everybody?" I asked.

"Good question," she said to me, and headed through the house toward the kitchen.

Mom bypassed the kitchen, of course, and went straight into the little dining room nearby. She stood by the glass slider and gazed outside in a pageant stance—chin high, shoulders up, back straight—as if she suspected the paparazzi were lurking in the rose bushes snapping photos.

"You told me Juanita was dead," I said, and flung my hands out. "Where is she?"

Mom turned to her right, as if offering her profile to the nonexistent photographers outside. "I have no idea," she said.

"Then how do you know she's dead?" I asked.

"She isn't here," Mom said, as if the answer were obvious. "She reports for work at seven-thirty and she's not here. She must be dead."

I'm pretty sure I was switched at birth.

"It's not even eight-thirty yet," I said. "Maybe she's just running late."

"Juanita is never late. Not once in all these years," Mom said.

Okay, that was true, but there were a lot of reasons she might have been late today.

"Maybe she's sick, or her car broke down, or she overslept, or she had a family emergency," I said. "Maybe she had a flat tire."

Mom dismissed my words with a wave of her slender hand. "She would have called."

Okay, that was true, too. Still, there had to be an explanation—other than that she was dead.

"Have you called her house?" I asked.

Mom gazed across the room for a long moment, then turned to me. "Why would I possibly have her phone number?"

"Do you have her home address?" I asked.

"Really, Haley, I insist you take this situation seriously," she said.

"You could call your accountant," I said.

"Who?" Mom looked totally lost now.

Jeez, I really hope the day doesn't come that my life depends on Mom.

"He makes out Juanita's paycheck every week," I said. "He has her contact information."

Mom pulled a handkerchief from the pocket of her caftan and touched it to the corner of her eye. "I have to know what happened to her, Haley," she said. "I absolutely have to know."

Now, I felt kind of crappy for thinking bad things about Mom. After all, Juanita had been with us for years. She was part of the family.

Mom drew a breath. "I have a dinner party scheduled for later in the week and I certainly can't get a decent caterer at this late date."

Oh, *please,* let me have been switched at birth.

"I'm going to report Juanita's death to the police," Mom told me.

I glanced at my watch. "She's only an hour late. I think it's a little too soon to call the police."

"It's never too early to notify the authorities," Mom insisted. "That's what they're for—much like household staff."

For a moment I considered giving her Detective Madison's phone number just so Mom could ruin his day, but thought better of it.

"I'll take care of it," I said. "I'll make some calls and try to locate Juanita. If nothing turns up, I'll call the police."

"Excellent," Mom said. "Meanwhile, I'll try and find a good caterer."

I left the house and got in my car, not all that worried about Juanita. Anything could have happened to delay her arrival this morning, like maybe she'd skimmed enough of Mom's jewelry and silver over the years to retire—which she totally deserved—so I saw no need to investigate her supposed death yet.

I pulled out of Mom's driveway just ahead of a yellow VW Beetle and headed to work.

"Miss Randolph?"

Camille, the receptionist at Dempsey Rowland, called my name as I stepped off the elevator. I ignored her. She scared the crap out of me, frankly. I figured her for mid-sixties, tall and rail thin. She must have had some work done because the skin around her eyes was drawn back so tight I don't think her eyelids closed anymore. Her gray hair looked like she'd styled it with a leaf blower.

"Miss Randolph!" she called again.

I stopped and turned back, pretending I'd just heard her.

Camille waved a small pink piece of paper at me. "You have a message."

I walked over and took it. It was from one of those "While You Were Out" message pads.

"Adela would like you to report to H.R. immediately," Camille said.

Just why she couldn't have told me what the message was before I walked over here, I didn't know.

Nor did I know why she was giving me the message on a slip of paper.

"Don't you e-mail the messages to the employees when you get them?" I asked.

"I think a personal touch is much better," Camille said. She made what probably would have been a frown, if her face had been able to move, then said, "I don't really like all that e-mail business. Too complicated."

I remembered that when I'd first gone into Adela's office for my interview, she'd had a paper file for me, rather than one on the computer.

"I guess Dempsey Rowland employees aren't much for technology," I said.

I'm pretty sure that came out sounding pleasant instead of a what-the-heck-is-the-matter-with-you-people kind of thing. Well, okay, *kind of* sure.

Camille smiled—I think.

"I just saw Ruth with a laptop," she said. "That's progress, I suppose. If you like that sort of thing."

I didn't know who Ruth was but I sincerely hoped she was using her laptop for something more important than a doorstop.

"Adela would like you to report to H.R. immediately," Camille said, waving her finger—which looked like an eagle talon—toward the pink note in my hand.

Great. Just what I needed this morning. I guess Constance had ratted me out to H.R. when I hadn't been in her office first thing this morning, despite the message I'd left on her voicemail.

I found my way to Adela's office after making only two wrong turns among the warren of offices, and saw that the door was open. Adela sat behind her desk studying a personnel file.

Jeez, I really hope that's not my file.

Adela looked up, waved me inside, and said, "Close the door, please."

Oh, crap. This couldn't be good.

I eased the door shut and sat down in the chair that faced Adela's desk. I eyed the personnel file. It had my name on it. Yikes!

Adela studied me for a moment. She looked tired, a little weary—or maybe she was just working up the courage to tell me I was fired.

Not a great feeling.

"I realize that yesterday—your first day with us—was difficult," Adela said. "I'm afraid I have more troubling news for you."

Did I pick a bad time to quit eating chocolate or what?

"As you know, everyone at Dempsey Rowland hired to handle sensitive work—such as you—for one of our government projects must undergo a background check and obtain a security clearance," Adela said.

Maybe I should start carrying a Snickers bar in my purse—strictly for emergencies, of course.

"Those checks can take a long time to complete," Adela said.

Maybe a couple of Snickers bars—and some M&Ms.

"Violet headed up security, as you know," Adela said, "and now she's . . . gone."

Did they sell those things by the case?

"Until a security clearance can be obtained," Adela went on, "new hires are placed in nonsensitive positions, which is why you were assigned to work under Constance."

How long would it take to eat a whole case? I was pretty sure I could buzz through one pretty quick, under the right circumstances—like now.

"Constance was our corporate event planner," Adela said. "You were assigned to assist her."

My spirits lifted a little—but I still could eat a case of most anything with chocolate on it—and I said, "I was going to help plan corporate events?"

"Business luncheons, on- and off-site meetings, retreats, dinners with clients, retirement and promotion ceremonies. The birthday club, of course. It's an extremely important position." Adela paused and drew a breath. "But something has happened."

Jeez, I hope she isn't going to tell me Constance is dead, too.

Adela shifted in her chair. "Constance isn't taking Violet's . . . death . . . well. She's not in today. But we're going to go ahead and use you in corporate events."

I was going to have to plan corporate lunches, dinners, meetings, retreats, and ceremonies? I still wasn't sure what the heck this company even did.

"Did Constance have an assistant, maybe?" I asked.

Adela nodded. "Yes, of course. That would be Patty. She's extremely competent and capable—Constance's second brain, really."

From what I remembered of Constance, she could sure as heck use a second brain.

I heaved a mental sigh of relief.

"Unfortunately," Adela said, "Patty resigned."

Oh, crap.

"With Violet's murder taking place in Constance's office—which is right next to Patty's—well, it was just too much for her," Adela said.

Adela looked at me like she expected me to say something sympathetic about what Patty had been through, but I couldn't think of anything.

"Normally, we wouldn't turn such an important position over to someone new, but these aren't normal circumstances," Adela went on. "You have a very strong résumé, Haley. Your qualifications are outstanding. So for now, you'll handle corporate events on your own."

I'd been to a lot of big events, but I'd never planned one. I didn't have the foggiest idea of how to stage a business luncheon, off-site retreat, promotion ceremony, or any of the other things Adela had mentioned. I'd be lost, completely in the dark.

So what could I say to Adela but, "Sure. Sounds great."

CHAPTER 6

Wow, my own office. I'd never had one before. It was awesome. My own desk, chair, cabinet, visitor chair, all lighted by a big window that overlooked Figueroa Street.

Jeez, I really hope I get to keep it.

Adela escorted me to the office that had belonged to Constance's assistant, Patty. The desk had been emptied of personal items and the janitors had cleaned everything. She mentioned the computer system that Patty used to track upcoming events, then left.

It creeped me out a little that on the other side of the wall was Constance's office—the door still crisscrossed with crime scene tape—where Violet had been killed, but I was determined to enjoy the place while I could. Constance would return tomorrow and, well, who knew what would happen after that?

I settled in and spent the morning texting friends, reading my e-mail, and checking out Facebook. I used my cell phone to take a picture of myself at my desk and sent it to Marcie. Then I surfed the Macy's, Neiman Marcus, and Nordstrom Web sites and looked at their business suits—and their handbags, of course—because even if I eventually got fired, I still needed to look great while I was here.

Next I checked my bank balance online, read my horoscope, and made an appointment for a manicure. I mean, that's what a private office is for, isn't it? So you can take care of your private business?

I glanced at my wristwatch and saw it was after one already. Time for lunch. So far, I was loving this job. I figured I'd ask Marcie to eat with me so we could map out a shopping plan for tonight. My cell phone rang. The caller I.D. screen read, PALMDALE REGIONAL MEDICAL CENTER.

Oh my God. Juanita.

I answered immediately and a woman's voice said, "This is the emergency room at the Palmdale Regional hospital."

My heart did a huge flip-flop. Juanita was in the emergency room? Something had happened to her? Mom was right about something?

"I was asked to contact you," the woman said. "Tyler Cameron has been involved in an automobile accident and—"

"Ty?" I shot to my feet. "*Ty?*"

"He's not seriously injured and will be released shortly," she said. "He'd like you to pick him up."

"I'm on my way!"

I grabbed my purse and ran out the door.

The Palmdale Regional hospital was in the Antelope Valley, an area up the 14 freeway about an hour north of downtown Los Angeles. It's the High Desert, hot and windy—when it's not cold and windy—with mountains that get snow in the winter and a valley floor that's covered with tumbleweeds and Joshua trees. It's a busy place with lots of family activities, a great location for people who want a place away from the hustle and bustle of a crowded city.

I'd been up there a few times because of my dad's job. Aerospace was big in the A.V. The space shuttle was built in Palmdale and recovered at Edwards Air Force Base. The air force had its flight test facility on the base, along with their test pilots' school and the NASA Dryden Flight Research Center.

I'd never made the trip up the winding freeway as quickly as I did today, darting in and out of the carpool lane, which wasn't against the law at this time of day—not that I cared. I took the Palmdale Boulevard exit, and whipped into the closest parking space to the hospital's emergency room I could find.

The woman who'd called me had said Ty wasn't seriously injured but, of course, that didn't keep me from conjuring up all kinds of horrible pictures in my mind. I raced into the emergency room mentally bracing myself to see Ty encased in a head-to-toe cast, or with one of those halos bolted into his skull, or strapped in a wheelchair drooling into a cup.

Instead, I found him sitting quietly in a chair, waiting patiently. His pale blue polo shirt had a reddish stain on the front, as did the knee of his jeans.

"Oh my God, Ty, are you all right?" I asked as I rushed over.

He looked up at me and managed a brief hint of a smile. "I'm okay,"

I pointed to his shirt. "Is that—*blood?*"

He gestured to his face and I saw a scrape on his nose and left cheek.

"Air bag," he said. "They did X-rays and an MRI. Nothing's broken. I'm just a little sore."

I dropped into the chair next to him and took his hand. "Thank God."

We sat like that for a minute, then Ty squeezed my fingers. "Get me out of here, will you?"

"Sure," I said, getting to my feet.

Ty rose slowly and handed me a little white bag. "Pain meds," he said.

I tucked them into my purse. Ty let me take his arm and we headed for the door. He moved kind of slow.

When we got to my car, Ty stopped and asked, "Will you call Mom for me?"

"Of course," I said, opening the passenger-side door.

He hesitated a few seconds. "Is it okay if I hang out at your place?"

"Absolutely," I said. I glanced around the parking lot. "Is your car here?"

"Totaled," he said.

I figured he must have already taken some of the pain meds if he looked that unconcerned about his gorgeous Porsche being wrecked beyond repair.

Ty grimaced as he lowered himself into my Honda. I drove slowly out of the parking lot. By the time we hit the freeway, I'd calmed down enough to start wondering how and why the accident had occurred—here, of all places. Holt's didn't have a store in the Antelope Valley and had no plans to build one—that I knew of, anyway. Ty usually told me everything about the company. Sometimes—well, okay, most of the time—I drifted off.

"So what were you doing in Palmdale?" I asked.

I glanced at Ty. He was asleep.

"Haley, there's been a development," Mom said as soon as I answered my cell phone.

I swung into the parking garage next to Dempsey Rowland and whipped into a spot near the elevator. I wasn't feeling all that great about leaving Ty alone at my apartment after his accident, but as soon as I'd helped him undress and get into bed, he was out cold. I figured I should put in an appearance at work this afternoon; I'd be off in a couple of hours, anyway.

I wouldn't have answered Mom's call—thank God for called I.D.—except that I hoped she wanted to tell me Juanita had finally showed up.

I could use one less thing to worry about right now.

"Good news, Mom?" I asked, as I got out of my car.

"Yes," she said, and sounded relieved. "I've found a caterer."

I'm pretty sure my real family is out there somewhere looking for me.

"What about Juanita?" I asked.

"Who?"

"Juanita," I said, and managed not to yell, "Is she there yet?"

"Of course not," Mom said. "Why else would I still be looking for a caterer?"

"I'm driving into a tunnel, Mom," I said. "I might lose you—"

I hung up and hurried into the elevator. By the time I'd crossed the building's main lobby and ridden up to five, I'd rehearsed the my-boyfriend-was-in-a-car-crash excuse for being away from the office well enough that I could say it in one smooth sentence and even work up a tear, if necessary.

Camille, Dempsey Rowland's version of the Crypt Keeper, didn't look my way when I got off the elevator. I went to my office. No yellow notes stuck to my computer monitor, no voicemail from anyone demanding to know why I wasn't at my desk.

For once I had a perfectly good excuse for being late back to work—and no one even asked. It was kind of disappointing. At least that meant I could use it at some point in the future.

I closed my office door and worked the phone. First I called Ty's mom. Her voicemail picked up, so I left a detailed message about the accident and assured her Ty was fine. I'd leave it to her to notify the rest of the family as she saw fit—no way was I getting involved in that.

There's nothing like a family tragedy to cause everyone to turn on each other.

Next I called Amber, Ty's personal assistant. I like Amber. She is about my age, short, with dark, sensible hair. Everything about Amber is sensible. I could have been jealous of Amber—she ran *everything* in Ty's life—but she made things so easy for him—which ultimately benefited me, of course—I couldn't complain. Plus, she wasn't Ty's type—or, rather, Ty wasn't her type. Once when Marcie and I were out shopping and ran into Amber, I caught Amber checking out Marcie's butt.

Amber answered on the first ring. I gave her the news and immediately she jumped into action.

"I'll inform key personnel at Corporate," she said. "I'll get the status on his car, notify the insurance company, get the accident report from the CHP, and I'll bring his clothes by your place tonight."

"Thanks, Amber," I said. "You're awesome."

"How are you holding up?" she asked.

That was nice to hear. Amber thinks of *everything*.

"Relieved he's not seriously hurt," I said. "I hope he was telling me the truth. You know how men are about medical things."

"I'll double check with the hospital," Amber said. "You said it was Palmdale Regional? What was he doing up there?"

Okay, that was weird.

"You don't know?" I asked.

"At about eleven this morning, Ty asked me to cancel all his afternoon appointments," Amber said.

Okay, that was really weird.

"I'm sure it was something to do with business," Amber said.

"I'm sure you're right," I agreed. Ty seldom did anything that didn't involve Holt's in some way, shape, or form.

"See you tonight," Amber said, and hung up.

Through the glass panel in my office door, I saw people

walking through the hallway and realized it was time to go home. Thank goodness. I'd had one heck of a day.

As I reached into my bottom desk drawer to retrieve my purse, my office door opened and Adela walked in. She didn't look happy.

"I didn't receive an e-mail announcement about tomorrow's event," Adela said.

There was an event tomorrow?

"You've made the arrangements, haven't you?" she asked, though it sounded like more of an accusation, like she thought I hadn't done it, or something—which I hadn't, of course, but still.

Adela narrowed her gaze at me. "I assured Mr. Dempsey you could handle this position, Haley. Your résumé was very strong."

Jeez, what did I put on that thing? Maybe I should have reviewed it before I sent it in.

"Was I wrong?" she asked, her eyes getting narrower.

My future at Dempsey Rowland flashed in front of me—and not in a good way. Did I now have a double chance of getting fired? Once for not passing my security clearance, and again for bungling tomorrow's event—whatever it was?

"Of course not," I said, giving her the same you-can-trust-me smile I gave Holt's customers when I sent them to the other side of the store for an item we don't even carry.

Adela didn't look relieved—obviously, she wasn't a Holt's shopper.

"The birthday club is extremely important," she said. "It's good for morale and, believe me, this office needs a morale boost after what we've been through. Kinsey Miller is relatively new with us, but I want her to feel as if her birthday is just as important as anyone else's."

"I couldn't agree more," I said, channeling my mother's I'm-better-than-you voice. "Here's the situation, Adela. All the office decorations, birthday and otherwise, are locked up in the cabinets in Constance's office, which is still sealed by LAPD's crime scene tape."

Okay, that was a guess on my part. I'd seen the big cabinets in Constance's office and I hadn't found decorations here in the office I'd taken over from Patty, so I made a logical assumption—more like a wild guess.

Sometimes my wild guesses work out.

"I couldn't possibly schedule Kinsey's birthday celebration tomorrow without decorations," I said. "It's unacceptable. I simply won't do it."

Adela's expression shifted into back-down mode. "I'll be right back."

She left my office. I logged onto the computer—luckily, Patty hadn't set a password—and clicked on the calendar. Yikes! There were all kind of events scheduled.

Jeez, if Patty did all of this, what the heck was Constance working on?

From what I could see, Patty had made detailed notes of each event. I clicked another file and saw the names and contact info for dozens of vendors.

Adela walked into my office and stood in front of my desk. She looked a little rigid and tense.

"I should have given this to you earlier," she said, in what I guessed would be the closest thing to an apology I'd ever get from upper management. She held out an envelope. "Things have been so . . . difficult."

I rose from my seat and took the envelope. I ripped it open and found a credit card and slip of paper with a PIN. The words DEMPSEY ROWLAND were embossed on the card and in the corner was the company logo.

"It's a corporate credit card," Adela explained. "A card with your name on it will be ready soon."

Light beamed down from above—I swear—reflecting off the card.

"You're to use it to purchase everything necessary for corporate events," Adela said.

Angels—really—began to sing.

"It goes without saying," Adela said, "that Dempsey Rowland events are all top rate, first-class. We have global reach. We have international clients, strong political ties, and high government connections. We have superior standards and a reputation for excellence to uphold."

I started to get light-headed.

"Use the card at your discretion, Haley," Adela said. "And remember, only the best will do for Dempsey Rowland."

Adela left my office. I collapsed into my chair.

Oh my God. *Oh my God.*

I love my job.

CHAPTER 7

I was tempted to use the my-boyfriend-was-in-a-car-crash excuse—which I intended to upgrade to a-*horrendous-car-crash*—but since I was just calling Holt's to cancel my evening shift, I didn't mention it. Besides, Jeanette, the store manager, already kind of knew I was involved with Ty, though she'd never mentioned it, and by now she would already know about his car accident.

As I hung up with Holt's, I whipped into a strip mall near my apartment and picked up Chinese take-out. It was one of Ty's favorites, but I felt kind of crappy not preparing him a home-cooked meal after his accident—not that I'd ever done that, but still.

Shuman's girlfriend, Amanda, popped into my mind as I parked outside my apartment. Maybe I should redo my entire kitchen and make German food for Ty like she was doing for Shuman. Maybe Ty and I could have a dinner party and invite our friends. Then everyone could see Ty look at me the way Shuman looked at Amanda—which Ty did. I'm certain of it. Really.

My apartment was silent when I went inside. I kicked off my shoes, set the take-out on the kitchen counter, and tiptoed to my bedroom at the end of the hall. The blinds were drawn and the lights were off. Ty was still sleeping, still lying in the same position he'd been in when I left him there hours ago.

I changed into sweats and grabbed the jeans and polo shirt Ty had worn today. The bloodstains were pretty bad but I had mad skills when it came to washing clothes.

My laundry room—which consisted of a washer, dryer, and some shelves—was situated in the hallway of my apartment, next to a coat closet and my second bedroom. I opened the bifold doors and went to work, soaking the stains with three different stain removers, concentrated detergent, dry bleach, then liquid bleach, all of which was probably against some EPA regulation, but, oh well.

I turned on the washer as I searched the pockets of Ty's jeans. I found his phone, wallet, and a couple of dollar bills and some coins wadded together with a receipt. I unfolded it and saw that it was for a soda purchased from a Chevron station in Acton, a community about fifteen minutes south of Palmdale. Ty must have stopped there for a cold drink before his accident.

My doorbell rang as I shoved his clothes into the washer. I closed the bifold doors, dropped Ty's phone, wallet, and money on the kitchen counter, then took a look through the peephole in my front door. Amber waited outside, holding a garment bag and a small duffle.

"How is he?" she asked, when I let her in.

"Sleeping," I said.

"Still?" she asked, looking troubled. "He doesn't have a head injury, does he? Did the doctors tell you to watch for signs of a concussion?"

Was Ty lying in my bedroom, dead? At this very moment? And I hadn't noticed? Jeez, what kind of girlfriend was I?

Good thing I didn't go into the medical field.

"I was just about to check on him again," I said to

Amber, which was a total lie, of course, but one I figured needed to be told.

"Where should I put these?" she asked, hefting the garment bag and duffle a little higher.

I pointed behind me as I hurried down the hallway. "In there. It's really packed. Just shove them in as best you can."

Ty—thank goodness—was breathing steadily, so I closed the door and went back to the kitchen. Amber was plugging Ty's phone into a wall charger she must have brought with her.

"I hope his phone wasn't damaged in the crash," Amber said. "His entire life is in this thing."

"Want some Chinese?" I asked.

She eyed the take-out cartons for a second, then shook her head. "Can't. Too much to do."

I followed her to my front door.

"I'll let Corporate know Ty won't be in tomorrow morning," Amber said. "There's some mix-up with his auto insurance company about the Porsche. I'll get it straightened out. Other than that, everything is handled. I'll have all the details for Ty as soon as he needs them."

"You rock," I said.

Amber gave me a grateful smile and left.

First-date sex was good—not that I've ever done that myself, of course—third-date sex was great—no comment—and so was make-up sex, but so far I liked car-crash sex the best.

Ty woke up early the next morning well rested from his twelve-plus hours of pain medication–induced sleep, which benefited me in the best way possible—twice. I told him Amber had brought his clothes over last night, but he said he wasn't going into the office today. Then he fell back to sleep while I showered, dressed, and left for work.

My afterglow was humming along nicely as traffic crawled south on the 405, so when my phone rang and I saw Mom's name on the caller I.D. screen, I didn't even cringe.

"Something terrible has happened," Mom said when I answered.

My afterglow shattered. Oh my God—Juanita. I'd forgotten all about her.

"What is it?" I asked, visions of having to dive across three lanes of traffic and head to the morgue to identify her body bouncing around in my head.

"The caterer I want is already booked elsewhere," Mom said.

The caterer? What the heck was she talking about?

She huffed irritably. "I explained to them in detail how important this dinner party was, but they absolutely refused to work with me."

"What about Juanita?" I asked.

"What about her?"

"Did she come to work today?" I asked, and managed not to scream into the phone. "Did she call? Have you heard from her at all?"

"You were supposed to handle that, Haley," Mom said. "Frankly, I'm a little disappointed in you."

Great.

"I'm working on it, Mom. I'll let you know something soon," I said, and hung up.

With one eye on the freeway traffic, I scrolled through my address book—which was against the law, I know, but this was an emergency—and punched in the phone number of Mom's accountant.

The old geezer who handled Mom's trust fund was nearly ninety and acted as if the money were *his*. He also seemed to think there was some sort of accountant–client confidentiality, like lawyers and priests, and always gave me a hard time if I called for something Mom needed.

Luckily, his secretary answered my call. She blamed my mom for causing the old guy's last two heart attacks—which was probably true—so she gave me Juanita's home address and phone numbers without question. I wanted her to text them to me, but since she was in her eighties and had tried to sign her name with a fork the last time I was in there, I copied the info down on a Pizza Hut receipt while steering with my knee.

When I stepped off the elevator into the reception area of Dempsey Rowland, I was pleased to see that at least something—besides the great car-crash sex—was going well for me this morning. Two dozen balloons, a cake, and a bag of birthday decorations sat on Camille's desk.

I'd called the bakery mentioned in Patty's notes before leaving work yesterday and ordered the cake for today's birthday girl. Then I'd figured that, hey, what was a birthday celebration without balloons to go along with the decorations? I'd Googled party supply stores and found one on Wilshire Boulevard. Just like the bakery, they'd happily agreed to deliver everything—thanks in no small part to the exorbitant up-charge I'd agreed to and charged to my Dempsey Rowland corporate credit card.

The halls were almost empty—I was super-early today—as I made my way to my office juggling the giant bouquet of balloons, cake, party supplies, and my purse, a totally fabulous Prada satchel. I passed a few people, most of whom looked at me kind of funny, and saw Mr. Dempsey talking with somebody I didn't recognize.

Jeez, that guy always came in early. If I owned the place, no way would I be the first one through the door every morning.

As I struggled to open my office door, I caught sight of two other men who were also there way early. Detectives Shuman and Madison, headed straight for me.

I doubted they'd come to tell me they'd solved Violet's murder.

My stomach did its good-grief-what-now twist, which was only marginally better than its good-grief-am-I-about-to-be-arrested-now twist.

"Stay away from there!" Detective Madison shouted. "That's a sealed crime scene!"

I guess with me partially hidden behind the bouquet of two dozen balloons, he couldn't see that I was trying to get into Patty's office next door to Constance's. Still, it didn't stop two employees who were walking by from turning to stare at me.

Not a great feeling.

I ignored Madison, went into my office, and dropped everything on my desk. The two detectives were on me before the balloons stopped bobbing.

Shuman looked pretty good for so early in the day. Neat, pressed, clean, crisp, wearing a navy blue sport coat and a nice stripped tie. I wondered if Amanda had dressed him this morning. I wondered if they'd had anything close to car-crash sex this morning—which was really bad of me, I know, but there it was.

"Oh, so you have your own office now," Madison said, and made it sound as if it were some sort of crime. "That didn't take long—especially since the background investigation for your security clearance is suspended indefinitely."

It took a second for me to realize why he'd said that, then it occurred to me that Dempsey Rowland was probably having trouble filling the head of security position—since the last person who had it was murdered.

"Maybe if you could manage to find Violet's killer, the background investigation could proceed," I told him.

Madison's sneer turned into a nasty frown. He gave me what I thought was homicide detective–stink-eye, and left my office. Shuman stayed.

"How was the German food?" I asked.

"Great," he said, and grinned, making me think there was such a thing as German-food sex, and it must be pretty darn good.

Shuman nodded toward the hallway. "Your own office, huh?"

I stepped outside and saw a little plaque with my name on it next to the door. Wow, I hadn't noticed it when I came in. I figured this must be good news. Surely Dempsey Rowland wouldn't fire me if they'd gone to the trouble to make me a nameplate.

Yeah, okay, that was a stretch, but I really, *really* wanted to keep this job.

I glanced next door and saw that Constance's name plaque was missing. Huh, that was weird. Then I figured Adela had probably taken it down to discourage looky-loos from breaking in, or maybe out of respect for Violet.

The crime scene tape was pulled away and the door to Constance's office was open, so I figured Detective Madison was inside.

"Something new going on?" I asked.

Shuman didn't answer my question, but said, "Did you know any of the three people who were hired with you?"

I rolled my eyes. "Let me guess. Madison thinks it's some kind of conspiracy. I got a bunch of my friends hired at the same time as cover so I could murder Violet. Right?"

Shuman gave me cop face. "Is that a 'yes'?"

"You know it isn't," I told him. Then I realized he wasn't asking me a question. He was trying to tell me something.

"You think one of the other new hires was involved?" I asked.

"I didn't say that."

Okay, this was kind of cool, Shuman and me talking cop-code in a murder investigation.

I wonder if he talks to Amanda that way.

"I spoke with one of them the morning of Violet's murder," I said. "Max Corwin."

Shuman's cop face held, but I saw a little light sparkle in his eyes—*that's* how well I know him—and realized I was on to something.

I wonder if Amanda knew what that little sparkle meant.

"Max seemed like he was worried," I said, remembering the conversation I'd had with him in the breakroom that morning. "He talked about how the background investigations would be on hold for a while, but it wouldn't affect us because we were already hired."

Shuman nodded slowly

"I got the impression Max worried a lot," I said.

"He should," Shuman said softly.

Madison came out of Constance's office, pulling the door shut behind him. He locked it—I figured he'd gotten the key from somebody in security or maybe H.R.—and stuck the crime scene tape back in place.

A jolt of something hit me—sort of like when you see the latest Betsey Johnson bag in a shop window and you hit the brakes and desperately look for a parking place so you don't miss a great opportunity.

"Can I check something in Constance's office?" I asked Shuman.

On the off chance that Adela might want to verify my story—like I'd made it up or something, which I had, of course, but still—that the birthday decorations were actually in the cabinets in Constance's office, I wanted to check and find out for sure. I'd meant for only Shuman to hear me, but I guess Madison had dog ears, or something.

"You want to get inside?" he asked, loud enough for the employees in the nearby offices to hear. "Why's that, Miss Randolph? So you can manipulate the crime scene? Hide evidence? Is that why you want to get inside the office where a murder took place?"

Two men walking by looked at me funny.

Not a great feeling.

So what could I do but channel Mom's I'm-better-than-you attitude and say, "The reason I need access to that office, Detective Madison, is classified information that you're not authorized to know."

Before he had a chance to call me on it, I put my nose in the air—channeling Mom big time—went back into my office, and closed the door.

Luckily, Madison and Shuman left. Whew!

I sat back in my chair suddenly desperate for a mocha frappuccino. This whole-new-me thing was really working on my nerves. How was I supposed to function without an occasional chocolate and caffeine boost?

Something—really—called my name. It drew me out of my chair and to my office window. I looked down at Figueroa Street. Lots of traffic, lots of people, but my gaze homed in on one thing—Starbucks.

For a minute I thought I was going to lick the glass.

Obviously my whole-new-me plan needed a slight modification. How could I be expected to execute the high standards of Dempsey Rowland's demanding event planning department without the necessary nutrition?

Starbucks was very nutritious. I read that somewhere. I think. Well, I'm pretty sure.

I went back to my desk, got the Dempsey Rowland corporate card, called the Starbucks, and ordered a venti

mocha frappuccino with extra whipped cream and chocolate, which they promised to deliver.

Yeah, okay, Adela hadn't said I could order myself a
frappie, but she didn't say I couldn't either. Besides, I was
only doing this to ensure that Kinsey Miller—whoever she
was—had a spirited, fun, exciting birthday celebration this
morning. I'm sure—kind of sure—Adela would approve of
my total commitment to the success of the birthday club.

That's how I roll.

A few minutes later, Camille called. I hoofed it to the reception desk and—thank goodness—found my mocha
frappuccino waiting for me. By the time I got back to my
office, I'd finished off a third of it and, already, my brain
cells were clicking like snap closures on Gucci handbags.

Shuman barreled into my thoughts—but only in the line
of duty, of course—and I recalled his not so subtle hints
that something was up with Max Corwin. Shuman wouldn't
out-and-out ask for my help, but he wouldn't have mentioned Max if he didn't want my input.

Like I'd said to Shuman, Max seemed like a worrier. A
man his age—I put him at mid-forties—probably had a lot
on his mind. Health problems; keeping his wife happy;
kids in college; a mortgage to pay. All of which required
money. Plus, he'd somehow lost his last job before taking
this new one with Dempsey Rowland, which could have
caused him more money problems. A break in income or a
loss of benefits, maybe. He could have been forced to take
a lower starting salary.

Maybe he figured killing Violet would delay the background investigation—if he had something to hide, of
course—so he'd continue to draw a paycheck until someone new was hired to fill her position.

But if he had something to hide and knew he might not
pass the background check, why would he have taken the
job in the first place? Unless, like me, he hadn't known a
security clearance was required.

I slurped the last of my frappie. There was nothing for me to do but find out what was going on with Max Corwin, and find out why Shuman was interested in him.

And I knew just how to do it.

I grabbed the cake, decorations, and bouquet of balloons and left my office.

CHAPTER 8

Wow, had this section of the office been here all along? After wandering the halls, weighted down by the balloon bouquet, cake, and decorations, I'd finally found the department Kinsey Miller—today's birthday girl—worked in. Patty had left good notes, but for a few minutes there, I thought I'd have to access Mapquest to find this place.

The SUPPORT UNIT, as the tiny sign over the main door indicated, was a giant cube farm. Around the perimeter of the room were glass-walled offices where, presumably, supervisors sat. A lucid moment from the tour I'd endured during my first day surfaced, and I recalled that this area handled all the administrative—that's code for crappy—work here at Dempsey Rowland.

Luckily, the cubes were all numbered, so I followed the signs and located Kinsey's workstation. Even though I was super early, a number of other workers were already there. They were all girls around my age.

I smiled but didn't get much in return, so I wondered if maybe nobody really liked Kinsey. But, hey, that's no reason to take it out on me. I was here to decorate her cube and start her day with a big Dempsey Rowland birthday wish.

Like anyone in upper management gave a rip one way or the other.

I tied the balloon bouquet to Kinsey's chair, took the cake from its box and centered it on her desk. I glanced around and saw that a half-dozen girls were standing in their cubes staring at me, and they definitely did not seem to appreciate all the trouble I was going to.

Jeez, who'd have thought birthday club prep would be so confrontational?

I decided to take the high road—thanks in part to the lingering effects of my mocha frappuccino—because I figured the Support Unit was a target rich environment for new friends. All the women I'd seen over in my section of the building were older than Grace Kelly's signature Birkin bag, so this would be the perfect place to find a lunch buddy or two.

I gave them Mom's pageant smile and amped it up a bit. "Hi! I'm Haley Randolph. I'm handling corporate events now."

"Yeah, we know who you are," one of the girls said.

Seemed office gossip spread fast at Dempsey Rowland.

"You're the Queen of Morale," someone else said.

I was finally queen of something. Mom would be so proud.

Everybody started eyeing my suit—but not in a good way, and I don't think it was because it was a leftover from last fall.

"So what did you do to get this job?" another girl grumbled.

I kept my smile in place and said, "Patty quit so I was asked—"

"Not the birthday club," the girl said. "The *other* job. The one they hired you for."

"Yeah," somebody else sneered. "The one you got only because that old bastard is on his way out."

Okay, something weird was definitely going on here, but that didn't mean I was willing to become the birthday club punching bag to find out what it was.

"When Kinsey gets in, tell her happy birthday and I hope she enjoys her cake," I said, keeping it light. I made quick work of finishing the decorating, then left.

Yikes! Tough crowd, I thought as I headed back to my office. I was considering ordering a whip and chair on my corporate card for the next time I had to go to the Support Unit, when I heard someone call my name. I turned and saw Max Corwin hurrying toward me.

"Are you okay?" he asked quietly. He glanced up and down the hallway, then eased a little closer. "I heard the detectives came to see you again this morning."

"They came to take another look at Constance's office," I said.

No way was I getting into the exchange I'd had with Detective Madison, though from the look on Max's face, the whole thing had already zoomed down the office rumor superhighway.

Max looked even more concerned. "Those detectives, they didn't talk to me again. Or Ray or Tina."

I remembered—barely—that Ray and Tina were the other two new hires who'd come on board with Max and me.

Max glanced around again, as if he suspected we were being spied on, or something.

"Watch yourself," he whispered. "There are lots of undercurrents in this place. I've seen it happen before at other companies. Backstabbers are everywhere. Who knows what the other employees are telling those detectives?"

He darted away as if he suddenly realized he shouldn't be seen with me.

As I headed through the maze of hallways trying to find my way back to my own office, I realized that Detectives

Madison and Shuman hadn't questioned Max again because they already had something on him and probably
didn't want to make him suspicious. Then I realized that if
they weren't questioning the other two new hires, maybe
that meant they'd uncovered something on them also.

And I knew I'd figured all of that out due to a late-firing
brain cell, which I could only attribute to the mocha frappuccino I'd had earlier.

Yeah, this whole-new-me thing definitely needed some
work.

Since finding my office again might take a while, I pulled
out my cell phone. Juanita's disappearance had been
swirling around in the back of my mind since Mom first
mentioned it. Yeah, I'd blown it off, thinking it was a typical Mom thing. Now I wondered if I should have taken
her seriously from the start.

Jeez, I really hope I don't have to start taking Mom seriously all the time.

I hit Juanita's home number, which I'd programmed in
while I was in traffic this morning. Her voicemail picked
up. I left a message. I tried her cell phone next. Same thing.
I left another message.

I'm not big on suspense so I considered calling hospitals
and morgues. But since I wasn't ready to make the huge
mental jump to my-mom-actually-knows-what-she's-talking-
about, I decided I'd take a run by Juanita's house first.

For a minute I thought about calling Ty. When I left this
morning, he claimed he intended to stay at my place all
day—which I doubted he would do since, even though it's
been in business for a hundred years or something, he thinks
Holt's can't survive a day without him. But on the off
chance that he was still sleeping, I didn't want the phone
to wake him. He'd call me when he got up. Probably.
Hopefully. Well, I'd call him later this afternoon.

The hallways were filling up now as more people

showed up to work. Lots of men dressed in great suits—not that I really noticed, since I have an official boyfriend, of course. A few of them smiled, some looked right through me, a couple looked at me weird. One of them gave me big-eyes, then glanced behind him, and quickened his pace.

I looked down the hallway. Oh my God! Madison and Shuman! I spotted them through the glass wall of one of the small conference rooms talking to Adela and Mr. Dempsey.

They were still here? Asking questions? About *me?* Okay, this was too much.

My future flashed before my eyes: Being called into Adela's office. Hearing that I was being put on administrative leave. Enduring the long walk of shame to my office. My personal belongings already boxed up and waiting. A security guard escort all the way to the parking garage.

No way—long story—was I going through *that* again.

I whipped around and headed in the other direction. If Shuman thought there was something suspicious in Max Corwin's background, I intended to find out what it was. And while I was at it, I would check out Ray and Tina, the other two new hires. Then I'd investigate every person Violet Hamilton had ever known in her entire life, if I had to, to prove to Detective Madison that I was innocent.

I hurried to H.R. and stopped outside Adela's office. I didn't know how long she'd be tied up with the detectives, but I didn't need much time.

I glanced up and down the hallway and slipped inside.

I hoped that since we'd all just come on board, the new-hire personnel files would still be on Adela's desk. No such luck. I glanced at the doorway, saw no one walk by, then eased open the bottom desk drawer. Lots of folders, but none with our names on them.

I slid around the desk to the credenza on the other side

of the room. Two huge stacks of folders sat at each end. I ran my gaze down the tabs on the closest one. No luck.

Voices sounded in the hallway. I darted back to the visitor chairs in front of Adela's desk, put on my most casual I'm-not-doing-anything-wrong expression, and pretended to study the artwork on the wall.

From the corner of my eye, I saw two men walk past. Whew!

I spun back to the credenza and eyed the other stack of folders. My heart jumped. There, near the bottom, were our personnel folders.

Darn. That meant to get to them I'd have to shuffle through about fifteen folders. Not exactly a stealth move.

I sure could use some superpowers at a time like this— or maybe just a couple of Snickers bars.

I looked back at the door again. Nobody in sight. I strained my ears for the sound of approaching footsteps. Nothing.

I turned back to the credenza and reached for the top folder.

"Haley?"

I whipped around and saw Adela and Mr. Dempsey standing in the office doorway. They both looked surprised to see me—not as surprised as I was to see them, of course—but luckily I don't think my presence uninvited and unescorted in Adela's office was the problem.

Mr. Dempsey gave me a hard look, then said to Adela, "We'll continue this another time."

"Certainly," Adela murmured. She went to her desk and kept her head down while she shuffled papers.

"I'll come back another time," I said, and headed for the door.

"No, that's fine, Haley," Adela said, finally looking up at me. Her cheeks were pink. She straightened her shoulders. "What did you need?"

Oh, crap. I had to tell her *something*.

"I wanted to ask about Constance," I said—which just proved that the lingering effects of a mocha frappuccino were indispensable when working a high-pressure job. "I noticed her nameplate wasn't outside her office this morning."

"Oh, yes." Adela sank into her chair. She drew in a deep breath and said, "Constance's condition has worsened. She's had some sort of a breakdown and won't return to work for a while."

I tried to think of something sympathetic to say. Nothing came to me.

That happens a lot.

"Which means—" Adela's phone rang. She picked it up, listened, then said, "I'll be right there."

Adela pulled open her bottom desk drawer. "That means, Haley, you'll have to take over all of the events, not just those Patty was handling."

I remembered seeing the list in her computer. Business luncheons, birthdays, meetings in the office conference rooms. Nothing major.

"No problem," I said. "It looked as if Patty was handling most of them anyway."

Adela froze, a folder halfway out of the desk drawer. "You don't *know?*"

I was supposed to *know* something?

"It's the premier event in the history of Dempsey Rowland," Adela declared, and yanked the folder out of the drawer.

Yeah, well, that sounded important, all right.

I channeled my mother yet again—which was starting to creep me out—and said, "I'm well aware of everything Patty was assigned to handle. But everything Constance was working on is inside her locked office, sealed with crime scene tape, completely out of my reach."

Adela pushed her desk drawer closed and rose from her chair.

"Mr. Dempsey is retiring," she told me. "The ceremony will be a gala affair at the prestigious Roosevelt Hotel, attended by twelve hundred guests and dignitaries from all over the globe. It will be an evening of monumental importance befitting Mr. Dempsey's outstanding and far-reaching accomplishments on the world stage."

Okay, I couldn't help it. My mouth fell open.

"Constance has devoted most of the past year in preparation," Adela said. "Now you'll take over."

"But everything is in her office." I think I whined when I said that.

"If you'll excuse me," Adela said, shooing me out of her office ahead of her.

"I don't have access to anything she's done." I'm sure I whined that time.

"You'll figure it out," Adela declared.

She locked her office door and walked away.

Oh, crap.

Around noon, my desk phone rang, startling me a bit because I'd been deep in thought.

Since my Plan A had failed this morning when Adela and Mr. Dempsey walked in on my covert op, I'd immediately jumped to Plan B. It had taken longer than expected to arrange, but finally it was done—and now I was being interrupted.

"Haley?" a girl asked when I answered my phone. "This is Shawna from the Support Unit."

Somebody in the Support Branch from Hell. Just what I needed.

"Listen, I noticed Kinsey didn't get her card from Mr. Dempsey yet," Shawna said.

There was a birthday card? From Mr. Dempsey?

I hate the birthday club.

Shawna didn't sound like a complete bitch about it, which was encouraging.

"Kinsey's at lunch. So if you want to bring it over now, it will be a nice surprise when she gets back," Shawna said.

I glanced at my watch and saw that I had a few minutes before Plan B went into effect.

"I'll bring it right over," I said, and hung up.

I couldn't imagine that Mr. Dempsey took time away from his outstanding and far-reaching accomplishments on the world stage, as Adela had put it, to sign birthday cards for specific people. I searched through the desk drawers and the file cabinet until I found a stack of pre-signed cards, which, I would have bet, his secretary had signed.

I wrote Kinsey's name on the envelope and headed to the Support Unit. I'd been there once today already, but the walk over seemed different this time.

For one thing, everyone on my side of the building dressed nicer—obviously, because we made more money—but that wasn't all of it. The carpet here was a little thicker and the furniture was nicer. Everyone here had a private office.

That still didn't explain why the girls in the Support Unit had hated me on sight.

A girl waited at the entrance to the cube farm, leaning against the door casing. I put her at about my age. She was petite, with short blond hair and a pierced lip. A tat peeked from under the sleeve of her striped sweater. Her face looked vaguely familiar from my visit earlier today.

"I'm Shawna," she said, when I walked up. "Pretty brave of you to come over here again, after this morning."

"You've got to be tough to work the birthday club," I told her.

She grinned and nodded toward the inside. "The other girls took Kinsey out to lunch for her birthday."

"You didn't go?" I asked.

"They're not exactly my peeps." Shawna said. She paused for a moment, then said, "They shouldn't have treated you that way this morning."

Already, I could tell Shawna and I might become friends.

"So what's got everybody so bent out of shape?" I asked.

She shrugged. "Some people take a job *way* too seriously."

I was liking her more every minute.

"This place," Shawna said, shaking her head. "They don't exactly have what you'd call really fair hiring practices. A lot of the girls in Support are qualified for higher positions but don't get them. H.R. is super old-school."

Maybe that explained the crappy looks I'd gotten this morning and the comments about how I'd gotten hired. It probably didn't help that I'd been brought on board so quickly by Adela.

"I'd probably hate me, too," I said.

"It's still not right," Shawna said. "None of it."

I passed Kinsey's birthday card to her. "Thanks for the heads-up."

Shawna eyed the envelope. "I don't know why anybody would want a card signed by the old bastard himself, but Kinsey's new. She'll learn."

Okay, that was a weird thing to say.

"Great job on the balloons," Shawna said, backing away. "They really livened up the place."

When I got back to my office on the other side of the complex, I saw Max, Ray, and Tina waiting outside my door. Plan B was a go.

"Thanks for coming in," I said, squeezing between them and taking the power seat behind my desk.

They filed inside looking a little confused, and sat in the three chairs I'd swiped earlier from the conference room down the hall.

Max seemed a little nervous about being here, as if SWAT might crash through my window any second and arrest me—along with the three of them, simply for sitting here. Ray seemed like one of those guys who was never upset—no matter what. He was thirty, maybe, and slender, and looked as if his mother dressed him. Tina had a few miles on her. Mid-forties, a bad dye job, and an expression that said she'd seen it all, more than once, and expected to see it all again.

"I'm heading up corporate events now," I said, "which makes me in charge of office morale, among other things."

I gave them a bright smile—a key element in Plan B— just as if I really loved the position and hadn't felt hopelessly lost since I set foot in the office.

"So first of all, I want to make sure all of you are feeling good about being here and are adjusting well," I said.

They all mumbled that things were fine. They wouldn't, of course, say anything else, since everybody wanted to keep their job.

"To be sure you're included in all the corporate events in a manner that's comfortable for you," I said, "I'd like you to fill this out."

I passed out the form I'd generated on my computer earlier. The three of them looked it over.

"You want our home address?" Ray asked. "And our spouse's name?"

I cranked up the wattage on my Queen of Morale smile.

"You never know when Dempsey Rowland is going to surprise you with something cool delivered right to your home," I said. "And if there's a special event in your honor

here at work, we want your wives, husbands, and significant others to be invited."

Tina eyed the form. "You want to know our favorite
color?"

"And what kind of ice cream we like?" Max asked, as if
it were some sort of mounting conspiracy.

Honestly, I couldn't have cared less. I'd just thrown
those questions in for cover.

"I want to personalize your birthday celebrations," I
said, smiling even wider now.

"This is too much," Tina declared. She sat back in her
chair and folded her arms. "Bad enough I need some security clearance just to do admin work."

There were several levels of security clearances, depending on what project you were assigned to and what your
specific duties were—I know this because my dad is an
aerospace engineer and has yammered on about it my entire life. It sounded as if Tina's clearance was lower than
that of the rest of us, making her more reluctant to con-
form to my totally fabricated Plan B.

Not good—for me.

So what could I do but turn up the heat—and not on my
I'm-a-really-nice-person smile.

"If you're refusing to cooperate, Tina," I said, in my
now-you're-in-trouble voice, "you'll have to sign a different form stating why you're not willing to divulge this information. I'll have to present it to H.R. where it will be
placed in your permanent record."

Max and Ray eased sideways in their chairs, distancing
themselves from Tina. She stewed for another minute,
then mumbled something under her breath, picked up her
pen, and started writing.

They all made quick work of completing their forms,
then left my office. I fell back in my chair.

Jeez, who'd have thought corporate events—coupled
with Plan B—could be so exhausting?

Really, at that moment, I'd had enough of Dempsey Rowland. How did anybody sit in an office all day? Especially in the early afternoon on a Friday?

I took care of a couple of things, then grabbed my purse and left.

CHAPTER 9

I couldn't imagine how I'd possibly live the rest of my life knowing Mom had been right about something. It would completely shatter our relationship as I'd always known it.

Not a great feeling.

So when I got in my Honda and pulled out of the parking garage, I headed straight for Juanita's house. I needed to put this Juanita-might-be-dead thing to rest quickly.

I'd never been to Juanita's place. In all the years she'd worked for my mom, Juanita had always been at our house, day in and day out, working early or late, holidays and special occasions, whenever Mom needed her. The only constant was her day off, which was Sunday. Juanita had another day off during the week but it changed, depending on Mom's schedule.

My GPS took me up the 110, then onto the 5 toward Eagle Rock, which was sandwiched between Glendale and Pasadena. It was home to Occidental College. The town had been around for decades, changing with the times, like a lot of places in Southern California. There was a wide variety of neighborhoods and houses, and everything from working-class people to young professionals and artsy types lived there.

I decided to give Ty a quick call as I transitioned to the 2. Even if he'd slept in today, he'd be up by now. I punched in his speed-dial number and was surprised when he answered on the second ring.

"How are you feeling?" I asked.

"Great," he said.

"Really?" I asked.

He hesitated a minute. "Still a little sore."

"Are you at the office?" I asked.

"No," he replied. "I'm taking care of some things."

Amber had left something undone? That was weird.

"What kind of things?" I asked.

"Seeing my mom."

I liked Ty's family, the few of them I'd met, that is. His Grandma Ada was a real hoot.

"I'll bring you something special for dinner tonight," I said.

"We can go out," Ty offered, which, I'm sure, was in no way a reflection on my nonexistent culinary skills.

"You need to rest," I told him.

Ty was quiet for a few minutes, then said, "That's really nice of you, Haley."

"See you soon," I said, then hung up.

I took the exit for Colorado Boulevard, the main street that ran through Eagle Rock. It still looked as it must have appeared back in the day when Pat Boone topped the charts, with lots of small shops, restaurants, and mom-and-pop businesses.

The GPS directed me onto Eagle Rock Boulevard for a couple of blocks, then through a few more turns, and finally onto the street where Juanita lived. I crept along, getting a look at the area. Stucco houses, fenced yards, mature landscaping. The neighborhood was older but in good shape. Kids rode bicycles and played in the yards. Not a lot of adults were out, but that wasn't unusual for a hot summer afternoon.

I pulled in at the curb and parked in front of Juanita's house. The place was neat and clean, surrounded by a chain-link fence. It had a settled look to it, as if she and her family had lived there for years. I knew Juanita had a husband. She had two grown daughters, one here in Eagle Rock and another who'd recently moved out of state; I didn't have contact info for either of them.

I got out of my Honda and went through the gate. The front windows were closed and the blinds were down. I stepped up onto the porch and I rang the bell. No answer. I rang again, then knocked. Still no response.

I glanced around, saw nobody looking, and opened the mailbox hanging by the front door. A handful of envelopes were inside, mostly bills, and the usual junk mail. I noted two different postmarks on them.

I left the porch and followed the narrow concrete strips that led from the street to the detached garage at the back of the house. I gazed through the glass panel in the big rollup door and saw Juanita's Chevy parked inside.

While I was back there, I checked out the rear yard. Neat and orderly, just like the front. I stepped up onto the porch, cupped my hand against the window in the door, and gazed into Juanita's kitchen. The light was on over the stove and several glasses sat on the counter by the sink. I knocked, but nobody appeared.

No sign of a struggle that I could see, no broken door locks, no shattered windows, no blood, no dead body. Nothing indicated Mom was right in her assertion that Juanita was dead.

Yet Juanita didn't seem like the type of person to let two days of mail accumulate; but since it was mostly bills, what was the rush in taking them inside—not that I'd ever done that myself, of course. From the look of things, Juanita had simply left the house for a while, maybe to shop or visit a friend.

Still, that didn't explain why she hadn't called Mom about not coming to work.

I rounded the house and went out the gate. The neighborhood seemed quieter. The kids weren't riding bikes now. A couple of people had come out of their houses and were gazing my way.

I probably looked like a cop or a bill collector in my suit, which wouldn't inspire anyone to talk to me, so I got in my car and left.

Okay, so my investigation into Juanita's supposed disappearance hadn't netted much, but that was no reason to go back to work.

Really, was there ever a reason to go back to work on a beautiful sunny Southern California day?

I stopped at the traffic light and accessed the e-mail on my cell phone—which I think might be illegal—and found the home address of Max Corwin I'd oh-so-cleverly acquired earlier, scanned into my computer, and sent to myself, along with Ray's and Tina's info. I punched Max's address into my GPS—which I'm pretty sure was also illegal—and hit the freeway heading west.

Detective Shuman hadn't given me any real info about why he suspected Max Corwin in Violet's murder. I guess if he had any hard evidence, he'd have arrested Max already. But that didn't mean there wasn't something I could uncover. Something that would prove Max was the killer—and I was innocent, of course.

I wasn't exactly dressed for a covert op but I didn't intend to get out of my car at Max's place anyway. I just wanted to check it out. Who knows, there might be some incriminating evidence right there in his front yard.

My GPS took me south on the 405 toward Los Angeles. Traffic moved slower now as the evening rush hour approached—not that I cared, of course, since I was in no hurry to get back to work. And, technically, finding out who killed Violet was a Dempsey Rowland matter, right? I mean, come on, what could improve morale more than finding the murderer so nobody would be afraid to walk the halls again?

That's my position on the situation and I'm sticking to it.

As I drove through the Sepulveda Pass, the high-rise buildings on Wilshire Boulevard came into view. Above them was a sandy-colored band of smog—which always said "home" to me—that gave way to a brilliant blue sky. I took the 105 west until the freeway dissolved into Imperial Highway, then turned on Main Street in the city of El Segundo.

I'd been here before when Mom was in her antique phase and we'd roamed the quaint shops and stores. I liked it here. It was sort of a back-in-the-day oasis amid major corporations and heavy industrial sites.

I turned at the library onto Mariposa Avenue, drove a few blocks, and found Max's home on a quiet residential street. The area had a mix of single family homes and apartment buildings, all neat and clean, the kind of place where you'd move if you were raising a family.

I rode past Max's house, then flipped a U at the next intersection, drove back, and parked in front of the house directly across from his. I accessed the Plan B form in my cell phone e-mail and noted that he'd indicated he had a wife and three children. The SUV in the driveway and the bikes and scooters in the yard confirmed it, along with one of those wooden signs hanging by the front door that listed the family names: Max, Mandy, Maddie, Micha, Minnie.

Huh. Well, so much for finding evidence right there in the front yard.

Now I was even more curious about what Detectives Madison and Shuman had discovered in Max's past that made them suspect him of Violet's murder. Certainly nothing at his house, as far as I could see.

I pulled out my cell phone and called Shuman. I was deciding whether or not to leave a message when he picked up.

"Have you got something for me?" he asked.

I could tell he was in big-time cop mode. His voice was low and rushed. I figured that if he took my call, he must be desperate for some info.

Since I roll with most anything, I went into big-time, talking-to-a-cop mode.

"Why do you suspect Max Corwin in Violet Hamilton's murder?" I asked.

I kind of expected him not to answer, but he said, "He lost two jobs in the past eighteen months."

"That's it?" I asked.

"So far." Shuman hung up.

I glanced at Max's house again. Three kids. A wife. A mortgage. Medical bills. Maybe private school. He had a lot on him and sure as heck couldn't afford to get the boot from Dempsey Rowland.

Still, if he'd murdered Violet to delay his background investigation, he would have had something in his past that was seriously worth hiding. Losing—translation: *getting fired from*—two jobs in less than two years might be it, depending on the reasons he'd lost those jobs, of course.

Since no clues into Violet's murder had been revealed to me in Max's front yard—which was kind of annoying—I left.

"I'm Ruth Baker, Mr. Dempsey's executive secretary," a woman said in an I'm-important voice.

I looked up from my Facebook page. Like most of the other women I'd seen at Dempsey Rowland—except for the girls in the Support Unit—she was old enough to have worn a candy stripe two piece back when it was in style. She had gray helmet hair, and dressed as if she were headed for a funeral.

I was a little annoyed to see her standing over me. I'd intended to just kill time since returning from Juanita's and

Max Corwin's houses, until the office emptied out for the weekend. She had that everybody-has-to-keep-working look on her face.

I hate that look.

I rose from my chair and introduced myself, even though I'm sure she already knew who I was.

"I want to discuss Violet's memorial service," Ruth told me.

Violet was having a memorial service?

"She deserves only the best," Ruth said.

I hadn't really known Violet, but a memorial service sounded like a great way to get out of the office for a while. I'd definitely be there.

"I expect you to see that she gets it," Ruth told me. "*Regardless.*"

Oh, crap. She expected *me* to plan the memorial.

This whole corporate-event-planner thing was starting to get on my nerves.

"You'll need to book the main conference center," Ruth said. "And you'll also—"

"I'll handle everything," I told her. I'd intended to use my you-can-trust-me voice, but it came out sounding more like my get-out-of-my-face voice.

Honestly, I didn't know that Dempsey Rowland even *had* a main conference center, but I saw no need to tell her that.

Ruth drew herself up into a more rigid stance. "Violet worked tirelessly and selflessly for decades. She was the backbone of this company."

"I understand," I said. I really didn't but this was easier.

She glared at me for another half minute like she didn't think I really understood, or something, which was true, of course, but it still kind of miffed me.

"Mr. Dempsey wants this service to be a priority, so I'll expect a full report on my desk first thing Monday morning. I'll give it to him—after I review it, of course," Ruth told me. She gave me one last hard look, then left my office.

I sank into my chair feeling a little overwhelmed. Even my Facebook page, still up on my computer screen, didn't raise my spirits.

But at least it was Friday. I didn't have to work at Holt's tonight, since I usually reserved Friday nights for partying. But I'd be staying in tonight. My official boyfriend was at my apartment—or at least I guess he was, since he hadn't called me lately—so maybe we could go out, or at least have hot car-crash sex.

I checked the event calendar Patty had made and noted that two more birthdays were scheduled for next week, along with some luncheons. I made quick work of placing orders at the bakery and party store.

I recognized the names of the restaurants on Patty's list of vendors. They were okay but not fabulous—and certainly were not worthy of the high standards expected of a Dempsey Rowland luncheon. I phoned several places that I knew were super nice, and made reservations for next week's luncheons.

Time to get on with the weekend. I got my purse and left.

So much for Friday night car-crash sex.

My apartment was empty when I walked in. No sign of Ty. Not even a note saying where he was, just a kitchen counter covered with toast crumbs and dirty dishes in the sink.

As I reached for my cell phone to call him, my doorbell rang. My heart did its usual maybe-it's-Ty flutter while my brain countered with its usual don't-get-excited-it's-almost-never-Ty buzz kill.

I looked through the peephole and saw Amber waiting outside.

"Hey, how's it going?" I asked, as I opened the door.

She was weighted down with a garment bag and two small duffles, a shopping bag, and her own purse, a department store house brand. Yikes!

I really need to talk to her about that.

"I went to the impound yard today and got Ty's things from the car," Amber said. "Want these in the usual spot?"

"Wherever you can find room," I said, pointing toward the hallway and the closet where she'd put Ty's other things. "Want a beer?"

"I'd better not," Amber called. She came back a few minutes later carrying the shopping bag, and asked, "Where's Ty?"

"Don't you know?" I asked. Amber almost always knew where Ty was. If *she* didn't know, I guess I shouldn't feel so bad—but I did, of course.

"I haven't talked to him since this morning," Amber said. She shook her head. "That car of his was completely destroyed. He's lucky to have walked away."

"I guess he'll go shopping for another Porsche soon," I said.

"He wasn't driving his Porsche. It was a Chevy Malibu. A rental." Amber placed the shopping bag on the kitchen counter. "Check this out."

She unloaded about a zillion greeting cards and a dozen boxes of candy onto the counter.

Jeez, did I pick a bad time to institute a whole-new-me policy with a say-no-to-chocolate clause, or what?

"I'm keeping a log of the phone calls and e-mails from people wishing him well," Amber said.

Really, I've been under a lot of stress lately. Maybe this wasn't the best time to strictly adhere to my new policy.

"I'll get it to him when he comes back to the office," Amber said.

I mean, really, what harm can one piece of chocolate

do? Or two, for that matter. Three, maybe. A half dozen, at most.

Amber arranged the boxes in a neat stack. "Ty will probably want me to donate this to the homeless shelter."

Ty wasn't much for sweets—which alone was reason to break up with him—but I was hanging in there, determined to overcome this vast difference between us. That's the kind of awesome girlfriend I am.

"Unless you want some of it," Amber said.

Some of it? How about *all* of it?

The vision flashed in my head: ripping the boxes open, scooping up double handfuls, shoving them into my mouth. The taste of the rich, creamy chocolate, the sugar rush, my brain cells screaming for more, more, *more!*

I've really got to get a hold of myself.

But I can be strong when I have to. Okay, I can be strong sometimes. Often. Kind of often. Occasionally.

"None for me," I said, and with monumental effort akin to the launch of a space shuttle mission, I pushed the boxes away.

Amber gave me a have-you-lost-your-mind look—not that I blamed her, of course.

I didn't want to get into the reverse world thing, so I said, "I've got this whole-new-me thing going. I'm off the chocolate."

Her have-you-lost-your-mind expression didn't change to a jeez-I-really-admire-what-you're-doing look, which kind of annoyed me. But, obviously, I was operating on a deeper level of commitment than Amber was accustomed to.

"Okay, anyway, tell Ty I'll call him later," Amber said. "I need to find out—"

The front door opened and Ty walked in. He wore the same jeans and pale blue polo shirt he had on when I'd picked him up from the hospital—stain-free, thanks to my mad laundry skills.

He didn't look so great, though. Kind of subdued. He'd

told me earlier that he was seeing his mom. Since she was nothing like my own mom—lucky for Ty—I wondered if the visit hadn't gone well, or if maybe he was still feeling the effects of the car crash.

"Oh, hi," he said, spotting us together in the kitchen.

"Gifts from well-wishers," Amber said, gesturing to the loot on the counter. "Do you want me to donate it?"

"Sure, whatever," he said. Then he paused and looked at me. "Keep it for yourself. I know you like this stuff."

"She's off chocolate," Amber said.

I got the have-you-lost-your-mind look all over again, this time from Ty. So, of course, what could I do but defend myself so I wouldn't look like a complete idiot. I mean, really, did everyone think I was too weak to stick to my new plan?

"I'm going for a whole new me," I explained, and managed to put some enthusiasm in my words. "No more chocolate."

"What about Starbucks?" Ty asked, as if he still couldn't believe it.

"I'm off the frappies, too," I declared.

Ty shrugged, then said to Amber, "Go ahead and donate all of it."

She loaded the boxes of chocolates back into the shopping bag.

"No, wait!" I screamed that in my head—I think.

I followed her to the front door, drawn by the vapor trail of chocolate that wafted from the bag. She said something and left. I stood at the door, watching until the chocolate candy—I mean, Amber—was out of sight.

I stepped back inside and closed the door. Of course, I was doing the right thing. I'd stuck by my reverse world commitment. I was doing something that was good for me

I hate it when I have to do things—especially if they're good for me.

Ty stood in the middle of my living room watching me.

He didn't have that have-you-lost-your-mind look on his face anymore. This was something different. Something I'd never seen before.

Yikes! What was going on?

"Haley, I really need to talk to you," he said.

My stomach jumped, sort of like it does when I learn a totally cool handbag is out of stock—and won't be re-ordered.

"Something happened," Ty said.

How was I supposed to get through a conversation like this without chocolate? Jeez, what had I been thinking?

"I know things have been rough between us at times," Ty said.

Had Amber gotten to her car yet?

"And I know it's been hard on both of us," he said.

Could I catch her before she left the parking lot?

"So I've come to a decision," Ty said.

She'd stop if I threw myself on the hood of her car, wouldn't she?

"I want to explain everything to you, completely," he told me.

Jeez, why does he want to talk about something *now?* It's Friday night. Can't we just roll around in bed for a while, then order pizza?

Ty crossed the room and placed his hands on my shoulders. I braced myself for the worst.

"This car accident has been a real wake-up call for me," Ty said, gazing into my eyes.

Oh my God. Ty was breaking up with me.

"I've done a lot of thinking," he said.

How would I explain it to Mom that totally-hot-and-super-successful Ty and I broke up?

"I need to make some changes in my life," he said.

Could I keep this a secret from Jeanette at Holt's so she'd still be afraid to fight me on the work schedule I requested?

"I've been the worst boyfriend imaginable," Ty said, gazing into my eyes. "I'm changing that. Starting right now."

Oh my God. I'll definitely have to buy myself that Temptress bag—just to get over the breakup, of course. How else will I get through it?

"You've been understanding and kind and generous. And I've been none of those things," Ty said. "From now on, I'm going to devote myself to you."

He's going to—what?

"I'm not going back to the office," Ty said. "I'm going to stay here with you, and be the kind of boyfriend you deserve. I'm going to show you exactly how much you mean to me."

Huh?

Ty pulled me closer. "Please let me do this, Haley. Will you?"

Oh my God. *Oh my God.* I could tell by the expression on Ty's face that he was serious. He really wanted to be the kind of boyfriend I've always wanted him to be. This was great—super great.

He wasn't breaking up with me at all.

But I was still getting that Temptress bag, of course.

CHAPTER 10

A ringing cell phone woke me way too early. At first I thought it must be Ty's, then managed to rouse enough brain cells to recall he'd turned his phone off, a key element in the completely-devoted-to-*me* plan he'd announced last night.

I rolled over and grabbed my phone. It was Mom. What the heck was she doing called me this early on a Saturday morning?

"Haley, it's Juanita," Mom said, when I answered. "She's been kidnapped."

I shot straight up in bed. "She's *what?* Kidnapped? How do you know—"

"I just received a ransom demand," Mom told me.

"I'll be right there."

I ran through the shower, put on makeup, styled my hair in an I'm-fun-but-still-paying-attention updo, then threw on khaki capris, sandals, and my favorite don't-my-boobs-look-great scoop-neck T-shirt. I mean, really, I was heading to a potential crime scene. Cops would be there, of course, but maybe some firefighters, too—and you know how hot those guys are. Not that I was interested, of course, since I have an official boyfriend, but still.

I got to my front door and stopped short. Oh, crap. I forgot Ty—again. I rushed back to my bedroom, saw that he was still sleeping—he's saving himself for a full day of catering to my every whim, I'm sure—then hustled back to the kitchen, dashed off a quick note, and left.

I rushed downstairs to the parking lot searching for my car keys in my purse—a totally fabulous Fendi—when it hit me. Oh my God. That Temptress bag would look perfect with this outfit. I absolutely had to—

A guy on a bicycle shot right in front of me. I jumped back.

"Hey!" I shouted.

He didn't look back. He didn't even slow down. Jeez, he nearly hit me.

I watched as he pedaled furiously through the parking lot, then looped around another row of parked cars. He had on a helmet and full cycling gear, so I couldn't get much of a look at him, but he wasn't a kid. He looked old enough to be more careful.

I kept an eye on him until he rode out of the parking lot into the street. A yellow VW bug pulled out behind him. They both disappeared. I hurried to my car.

I hauled out to Mom and Dad's house, berating myself the whole way. Why hadn't I taken Mom's concern over Juanita's absence more seriously? Why hadn't I investigated sooner, more thoroughly? Why hadn't I called Detective Shuman for help?

And now Juanita had been kidnapped. The family had received a ransom demand. Days had gone by when the police could have been searching for her.

I whipped into the driveway and skidded to a stop. No police cars, no plain vanilla Crown Vics the detectives drove, no news crews, no helicopters circling overhead, no firefighters—not that I was really anxious to see them, of course.

I hurried into the house. Everything was silent. I didn't

bother checking in the kitchen—why would Mom be in there?—but caught sight of her through the patio door.

Mom sat under an umbrella table by the pool wearing a bathing suit—maybe she expected firefighters, too—sipping a fruit drink. She had on a loose wrap, two-inch heels, sunglasses, and full-on jewelry.

As I walked outside, Mom gestured to her cell phone and day planner on the table in front of her.

"Don't worry. I have everything under control," she said.

If my mom has everything under control—that's the best time to worry.

"Everyone will arrive this afternoon at two," Mom said.

Police detectives were scheduling appointments now?

"Mom, what's going on?" I asked. "What are you talking about?"

"The caterer, of course," she said. "For this evening's dinner party."

"What about Juanita?" I might have yelled that.

Mom bristled slightly. "This entire incident is very disconcerting," she said. "It's nearly taken all the joy out of my dinner party."

I drew in a big breath and forced myself to calm down.

Where was my *real* family when I needed them?

"Mom," I said. "You told me Juanita had been kidnapped. You received a ransom demand."

"Yes. A rather disagreeable young woman showed up here this morning jabbering incoherently about Juanita and money," Mom said.

"What did she say—exactly?" I asked.

Mom waved her perfectly manicured hand. "I have no idea. She must have been speaking some arcane language, because I understood only a few words. And you know how fluent I am."

Mom's idea of fluent was knowing how to ask, "Do you take American Express?" in multiple languages.

I got a weird feeling.

"Like maybe Romanian?" I asked.

I'd had a run-in with a Romanian woman—long story— a few weeks ago. It hadn't turned out so great.

"Perhaps," Mom said.

My weird feeling got weirder.

"Or Russian?"

Around that same time, a maybe-or-maybe-not Russian mobster had vowed he wouldn't forget me—or what I'd done.

"Possibly," Mom said.

"What did you do?" I asked.

"I insisted she leave, of course, and assured her I would call the authorities if she came here again," Mom said.

"Did you call the police?" I asked.

A few strands of her hair fell across her cheek. She spent a full minute—which seemed like an hour—smoothing them back into place.

I thought she'd forgotten my question, then she finally said, "I didn't call the police. Why would I? I called *you.*"

Mom rose from her chair and gathered her phone and day planner. "The important thing is that my dinner party will be handled properly this evening."

Chin up, shoulders back, Mom pageant-walked into the house.

I left.

I drove to Juanita's house. When I'd been here before, the place had looked empty. Now it looked deserted.

I got a yucky feeling in my stomach.

I rang the bell and knocked on the front door. No response.

I raced around back. Her car was still in the garage. In the kitchen, dirty glasses still sat on the counter.

These things had seemed so normal. Now they looked sinister. The Chevy in the garage meant Juanita hadn't left on her own. The dishes on the counter told me she'd left in a hurry.

The yucky feeling in my stomach got yuckier.

I walked around to the front of the house and stood under the covered porch. Already, the day was heating up. The neighborhood was coming to life. Down the block, a guy was washing his car. A few kids were playing across the street.

How could everything look so normal?

Of course, there could have been a lot of reasons Juanita left dirty dishes in her kitchen and her car in her garage. But why hadn't she called Mom saying she wouldn't be at work? And who had showed up at Mom's place this morning demanding money?

Juanita had worked for our family for years, and I'm sure she'd shared some choice stories about Mom—not that I blamed her, of course—with her friends and family members. So most everybody knew who Juanita worked for and that our family was somewhat well-off.

Was this some kind of new kidnapping scheme? Take the servants instead of the children? The servants would be less trouble, and some families probably liked their help better than their kids.

I mean that in the nicest way, of course.

Stepping off the porch, I crossed the front yard and went out the gate. I had to call Detective Shuman. Yeah, okay, I knew there could be a reasonable explanation for Juanita's disappearance, but I couldn't wait any longer to figure it out.

Jeez, I really hope I hadn't waited too long already.

As I rounded my car to get in on the driver's side, I pulled out my cell phone.

"Hello? Excuse me," someone called.

A young woman pushing a baby in a stroller waved from across the street, then checked traffic and crossed.

"Excuse me," she said again. "Are you a friend of Juanita's?"

I figured her for about my age. Her blond hair was in a ponytail and she had that I-didn't-put-on-makeup-and-I-don't-care look.

I didn't want to get into the whole maybe-she-was-kidnapped thing with her, so I said, "She's been a friend for years."

"I'm worried about her," she said. "Maybe it's nothing, but, well, I live across the street, and the other night I was up with Riley."

She gestured to the little girl in the stroller, who was smiling and chewing on the toe of her shoe.

"I saw Juanita leave," she said. "Two men were with her. She was crying."

Oh my God. Juanita really had been kidnapped.

Oh my God. Mom was right.

"Listen, if you should see her, or anything else weird going on, would you let me know?" I asked.

"Sure," she said.

I got her name, and we programmed each other's numbers into our cell phones.

"Do you think we should call the police, or something?" she asked.

"I'll handle it," I told her.

I jumped into my car and drove away.

I didn't know what was going on, exactly, but that maybe-Romanian-or-maybe-Russian woman at Mom's house this morning weirded me out big time.

I only knew one thing for sure.

The cops wouldn't do.

I needed the Russian mob.

* * *

"I want another one of these," the woman across the counter from me said.

I stood behind register number three, two hours and forty-six minutes into my four-hour shift at Holt's—not that I was counting, or anything—providing my own personal brand of customer service to the shoppers who passed through my line.

This particular shopper was a woman who appeared to be already over the hump and on the downhill side of sixty. She had that I've-hurried-for-decades-and-now-I'm-taking-my-own-sweet-time look about her.

Maybe when I get that old—eek!—I'll feel the same. Right now, I just wanted to keep my line moving.

She opened her massive handbag—a brocade satchel that had probably arrived in California via wagon train—and rooted around, finally pulling out an ink pen.

"I bought this here the other day," she said. "I want another one."

I glanced at my line. Customers were stacked seven deep.

In a totally screwball how-crazy-is-this moment, I recalled seeing that particular pen in our Back To School aisle last week. *Someone* had ripped open the package and taken the pen.

"They're in aisle five," I told her, using my move-along-lady voice.

She didn't move, except to look down at the pen and roll it around in her fingers.

"Aisle five," I said, and amped up to my stop-holding-up-my-line voice.

"Those pens are in packs of three," she said. "I only need one."

Two more customers got in my line.

"The single-pen package was a special promotion. They come in three-packs now," I told her.

I have no idea if that's true, of course.

The woman studied the pen in her hand for another few minutes, then said, "I only need one."

"They only come three to a pack now," I told her again.

A mom and baby got in my line. The baby started screaming.

"I don't think I should be forced to buy three when all I need is one," the woman told me.

The man in line behind her rolled his eyes—not that I blamed him, of course. The next three people back shuffled impatiently—not that I blamed them either. I had to get my line moving. Something had to be done.

"Let me see it," I said, and plucked the pen from her hand. I studied it for about a half-second, then said, "We can probably special order this for you. Just ask them back in our customer service booth."

Yeah, okay, it was a total lie, but what else could I do?

The woman still didn't budge, and finally said, "Could you call them for me so I don't have to walk back there?"

I hate my life.

I spotted Colleen wandering through the racks of workout clothes near the registers. She'd worked for Holt's longer than I had but never seemed to realize what a crappy job it was. To be generous, I'll say Colleen is a little slow.

Slow worked for me right now.

"Colleen!"

About thirty seconds passed before her own name seemed to register with her. I waved her over.

"You need to take over for me," I said. "I have training."

Yeah, okay, it was another total lie.

"Training?" Colleen asked, looking lost.

"Yeah," I said.

I punched in what I like to think of as the thank-God-I-can-leave-this-boring-job-now code into the register, and headed for the stock room.

Since leaving Juanita's house this morning and realizing I had to call my was-he-or-wasn't-he-connected contact, Mike Ivan, I knew I'd been putting it off. I mean, jeez, phoning up somebody rumored to be in the Russian mob wasn't to be taken lightly. Sort of like making an impulse purchase at a department store handbag section—yeah, sure, you could pick up a mini skinny or a wristlet with little thought, but a satchel or hobo required considerable contemplation.

But I had to do it. I knew I did. Juanita's life was—maybe—on the line. If anybody could find out who the mystery woman was at Mom's house this morning, it was Mike Ivan.

I hurried through the store, past the lingerie department—keeping my gaze focused straight ahead so as not to encourage customers to actually ask me for help—and went through the doors into the stock room.

It's usually quiet back here, but today I heard voices and all kinds of racket. I followed the sounds and saw two big rigs backed up to the loading dock, and the truck team busy unloading zillions of boxes.

"Hey, girl," somebody called.

I spotted my Holt's BFF, Bella, lounging on an empty U-boat surrounded by a forest of hanging plastic-wrapped dresses. Beside her was Sandy, my other Holt's BFF.

"What's up?" I asked, as I walked over.

Bella gestured to the dresses. "I'm getting a red thirty-six C underwire for a customer."

"I'm restocking towels," Sandy said.

"I'm in training," I said. I grabbed another U-boat, dragged it over, and sat down.

"Want to hear some crap?" Bella asked.

I always want to hear some crap.

"Holt's is cracking down on training," Bella said, shaking her head. "They're keeping a log of who goes and who doesn't."

Holt's was going to make sure we actually attended the training meetings?

Yeah, that was some crap, all right.

"I heard the corporate office is sending someone to the store to monitor attendance," Sandy said. "No more skipping training for you, Haley."

This could seriously impact my day here.

The noise level from the receiving department picked up a little. I saw the guys on the truck team closing up one of the big rigs. The engine fired up and it pulled away. Gorgeous Southern California sunshine beamed into the stock room.

"I need a new life," I said.

"Yeah," Bella said. "I need a condo on the beach."

"I wish I was dating a vampire," Sandy said.

"Now's your chance," Bella told her.

By the tone in her voice, I knew instantly that I'd somehow missed out on some totally major news.

Bella gestured to Sandy. "Her boyfriend dumped her."

"It wasn't a dumping," Sandy insisted. "He thought we should break up and I agreed to it."

"It was about damn time," Bella said.

I couldn't have agreed more. Sandy's tattoo artist boyfriend treated her like all-out crap, and she was such a nice person, she totally put up with it. I couldn't imagine what had happened that she'd finally agreed to their split.

Then it hit me.

"Tat-boy has a new girlfriend, doesn't he?" I said.

Sandy squirmed for a few seconds, then said, "Yes, he's seeing someone. But they only just met. He swore to me that absolutely nothing was going on between them until after we broke up."

Bella rolled her eyes. "That's b.s., if I ever heard it."

"You could definitely do better," I said.

Bella glanced at her watch and stood up. "I've got to go. It's time for my break."

"See you," Sandy called with a little finger wave as she, too, headed back into the store.

I knew I had to call Mike Ivan. And I would. Really. But I couldn't bring myself to do it quite yet.

One of the men from the truck team walked to the control panel beside the big rollup door, ready to throw the switches that would bring it down and shut off my view of freedom.

"Hang on a second," I called.

I hurried over and stood on the loading dock. It was only a view of the back parking lot and the Dumpsters—which was kind of pathetic, I know—but I wasn't ready to let go of it yet.

A yellow VW Beetle shot out of a parking space, whipped past the big rig, and disappeared around the corner of the building.

Hey, wait a minute.

Were there a couple quad-zillion yellow VW bugs on the road these days, or was I being followed?

I pulled out my cell phone. Not only did I need the Russian mob—I needed a smoking-hot private detective.

CHAPTER 11

I'd never actually been in a beauty pageant or walked a runway, but I could strut it with the best of them—as long as I was in a dressing room and the clothes were for me, of course.

Marcie had met me at Nordstrom at The Grove after my shift ended at Holt's and we were shopping for business suits. I couldn't possibly show up at work on Monday still wearing my old ones from last fall.

"This will look great on you," Marcie declared, pulling a suit off the rack.

I'd already picked out about a half-dozen black ones and, really, they were all starting to look alike. But Marcie was almost always right about things so I nodded. The sales clerk who'd been following us around took it and headed off to the dressing room she'd reserved for us.

"How's Ty feeling since his car accident?" Marcie asked, turning back to the rack.

"Okay," I said, flipping through the suits again. "Except, well, something kind of weird happened."

"With Ty? Ty's never weird," Marcie said.

See how Marcie's right about things?

"He told me the accident was kind of a wake-up call for him. He's not going back to work," I said.

"Ever?"

"And he said he knew he'd been a crappy boyfriend, and that from now on he was going to devote himself to being the kind of man I deserve," I said.

"Oh my God. Are you kidding?" Marcie spun around to face me. "Did he sustain a head injury in the crash, maybe?"

"I told you it was weird," I said.

"So what's he done for you to prove he's a great boyfriend?" Marcie asked.

"Well, nothing yet," I admitted.

"It must have been nice to hear him say those things, especially after what you've been through with him," Marcie said. "Ty is sort of closed off—to everything but his job, of course."

Everything that had happened with Ty since I'd gotten the call from the emergency room flashed in my head. Marcie read my expression, as only a best friend can.

"What? What is it?" she asked.

"The whole car-crash thing," I said. "It was kind of strange."

Marcie didn't say anything. She didn't have to. She just stood there with a charcoal gray, single-breasted crop jacket and matching swing skirt in her hand, waiting. The sales clerk started to take it from her, then saw our expressions and backed off. *That's* the kind of service you get at Nordstrom.

"The accident was near Palmdale. Holt's doesn't have a store there and doesn't plan to open one—that I know of, anyway. So why was he there?" I said. "And another thing: when I picked him up, he had on jeans and a polo shirt."

"It was the middle of the day—a work day—and he wasn't wearing a suit?" Marcie asked.

I shook my head. "Amber told me he'd asked her to cancel all his afternoon appointments, then left."

Marcie didn't say anything.

"I found a receipt from a convenience store in his pocket," I said. "Like maybe he'd stopped there and changed out of his suit."

Marcie still didn't say anything, which didn't make me feel all that great. She can most always think of a logical explanation for just about anything.

"And he was driving a rental car," I said.

"Oh, wow," Marcie mumbled.

I really wished she could come up with some simple solution to this whole puzzle. The pieces had been swirling around in my head since I picked Ty up from the emergency room, but nothing had fallen into place—nothing that I liked, anyway.

"Do you think he was sneaking off to meet somebody?" Marcie asked. "Another woman, maybe?"

Only a true BFF would have guts enough to broach the subject, and as much as I didn't want to consider the possibility, I knew I had to.

I let the thought sit on my brain for about three seconds, then rejected it like a house-brand purse on a clearance rack.

Ty hadn't been the best boyfriend and we'd had our problems. But no way would he cheat on me. He just wasn't that kind of man.

"He wouldn't do that," I said.

"Not his style," Marcie agreed. "So did you ask him about the whole thing?"

I'm not big on suspense, so flat-out asking about something wasn't a problem for me. But between my new job, Violet's murder, Juanita's disappearance, and all the car-crash sex, I just hadn't had time.

"You have to ask him," Marcie told me.

"I know. And I will," I said.

Marcie gave me best-friend stink-eye.

"I will," I swore.

We turned our attention back to shopping. I bought eight suits—four black, two gray, one brown, and a navy blue—then matched up accessories. I couldn't possibly leave the store without shoes, of course, so I found three pair of sassy-but-kind-of-sensible pumps that were actually comfortable. We saved the best—the handbag department, of course—for last.

"You absolutely have to have a good tote for working downtown," Marcie declared. "Oh my God, the Temptress would look perfect with all of those suits."

"Sorry, we're out of stock," our sales clerk, who was still trailing us, said. "I'll put you on the waiting list."

Just because I couldn't get the *it* bag of the season today, I saw no reason not to buy *something*. I picked out a Michael Kors and a Chanel, and Marcie got a fabulous Betsey Johnson. My graduation gift cards covered everything—well, okay, I did have to break out a credit card or two—and we called it mission accomplished. I'd look great at the office now.

I just hoped I got to keep my job.

My cell phone rang just as I swung into a parking space at my apartment complex. Jack Bishop's name appeared on my caller I.D. screen and my heart did a quick double-beat—which was bad of me, I know, especially with my official boyfriend upstairs waiting for me.

But, jeez, Jack was a smoking-hot guy. I wouldn't be a red-blooded American female if I didn't have that kind of response to him. Not only was he absolutely gorgeous, with a great body, thick brown hair, and fabulous blue eyes, but he also had a supercool job.

Jack was a private detective. We met last fall at the Pike Warner law firm. While I toiled away in accounts payable, Jack conducted investigations—discreet and otherwise—on cases involving the firm's wealthy, well-connected, sometimes pompous, and pampered clientele.

Jack also handled cases on the side and—lucky me—I'd helped him out with some of them. We'd always shared some kind of attraction, but neither of us had moved on it. I had an official boyfriend—I was a stickler for that sort of thing—and Ty's family was a lifelong client of Pike Warner.

"What are you wearing?" Jack asked, when I answered my phone.

"Leopard-print boots and a clown wig," I said.

"I'll be right over."

He said it in his Barry White voice. My belly felt all gooey inside.

"I only want to use you for my personal gain," I said.

"I wouldn't want it any other way," Jack said. Then he switched into private detective mode. "So what's up?"

"I need you to look up a license plate for me," I said.

"What's the story?" he asked.

Jack and I had been friends for a while and we'd helped each other out a number of times, but that didn't mean he'd jump blindly into something just because I asked, which was kind of annoying, but there it was.

"I think I'm being followed," I said. "I keep seeing a bright yellow VW Beetle everywhere I go."

"A yellow Bug, huh? I hear that's what all the international terrorist groups are driving now. Did you notify Homeland Security?" Jack asked.

"I thought you'd like first crack at breaking the case," I said. "Look, it may not be anything, but there's this other thing going on and it may be connected."

"Are you talking about Mike Ivan?"

Hearing Mike Ivan's name gave me a little jolt—and not in a good way. First, because the man just had that effect on me and, second, because he was Jack's first thought when I said the word "connected."

"Don't call Mike Ivan." Jack's tone changed to don't-screw-with-me-on-this serious.

"I need his help," I said.

"Don't call Mike Ivan."

"He told me I could, after that whole thing in Vegas a few weeks ago," I said. "And I need to find out—"

"*Don't call Mike Ivan.*"

It was the closest Jack had ever come to yelling at me, which didn't suit me, but I understood his concern.

"Okay, look," I said. "I've got this friend Juanita—she's a friend of the family, really. She's missing and there's a possibility she was kidnapped by Romanians or Russians, or something. I figured if anybody can help me learn the real story, it's Mike."

"Call the police," Jack said.

"I don't want to involve them yet," I said. "The whole thing may be nothing."

Jeez, I really hope the whole thing is nothing.

"How does the yellow VW fit in?" Jack asked.

He was in big-time private investigator mode now. I imaged him sitting somewhere, taking notes and making plans. It was way hot.

"The VW is a whole other thing," I said. "Maybe."

"How many *things* are you involved in?" Jack asked.

He was starting to sound a little testy now—which was still way hot, of course—but I didn't want to get into everything with him.

"Just run the VW plate," I said, and gave him the number I'd memorized when I saw it barrel out of the back parking lot at Holt's.

"Don't make a move on Mike Ivan until I get back to you," Jack said, and hung up.

I stared down at my phone for a minute, a little ticked off. Jeez, what was the big deal? Yeah, Mike Ivan probably had some connection to the Russian mob and staying away from him was a good idea. But I knew all that. I didn't need Jack ordering me around over it—no matter how hot he looked.

So what could I do but turn into the hardheaded, determined person I'm often accused of being?

I scrolled through my phone book and punched in Mike Ivan's number. It rang once and a shock wave of what-the-heck-am-I-doing shot through me. I hung up.

Okay, so maybe Jack was right. Involving Mike Ivan might not be the best thing to do—right now. I still had other avenues to check out.

I sat in my car and Googled all the hospitals and morgues in the Los Angeles area, then called each one and asked about Juanita. Most of the people I talked to weren't all that pleasant, and it took forever. But no way was I going up to my apartment—with Ty there—and make these calls.

When I got through the list, annoying as it was, I was relieved to learn that Juanita wasn't dead or hospitalized. I sat there for another few minutes, thinking. Mom's accountant's secretary, who'd given me Juanita's address and contact info, hadn't had any phone numbers for family members, so I couldn't think of anyone else to call—except Juanita herself. I called her home and cell numbers and left messages again. Hopefully, even if Juanita was unable to return my calls, some family member might.

I got out of my car, gathered my shopping and garment bags, and trudged up the stairs to my apartment. I was tired and more than a little annoyed—at just about everything in my life.

In the middle of my mental image of me sinking into my couch with a package of Oreos in one hand and a frozen Snickers bar in the other, Ty popped into my head. My official boyfriend was waiting for me in my apartment ready to devote himself to showing me what a great guy he was, and making up for all the crappy things he'd done in the past. My spirits lifted a little.

I wrestled with my bags trying to get my front door open, and finally made my way inside.

Ty sat on the couch. He had on jeans and a henley shirt, and was barefoot. A beer bottle was on my coffee table—no coaster—and a baseball game played on TV.

He hopped up and smiled—Ty's got a killer smile—and took all the bags from me.

"I guess the shopping went well. I want to see every-thing you bought," he said, and gave me a quick kiss. "But first, I want to show you what I did for you today."

He dumped all my bags on the couch, took my hand, and led me into the kitchen.

Immediately, I could see that what he'd done for me *wasn't* loading the dishwasher, wiping down the counter-tops, or scrubbing the pots and pans he'd obviously used to make himself breakfast.

Ty stood up straight and gestured around the room, then announced, "I cleaned out your cabinets for you."

He—what?

"You said you wanted a whole new you, and you wanted to eat better," Ty said, nodding and smiling. "So I threw away all your bad food."

He threw away my—what?

"Haley, you wouldn't believe what I found in your cab-inets," he said, shaking his head. "Some of your spices had expired."

Spices had an expiration date?

"There was an open package of Oreo cookies," Ty said.

Oh my God, my emergency Oreos.

"It was hidden up on the top shelf," Ty said. "I knew you didn't want that stuff anymore."

Oh my God, he didn't throw them away?

"So I tossed them out," Ty said.

Oh my God!

"You—you threw them out?" I might have yelled that.

Ty put his arms around me and drew me closer.

"You bet I did. What kind of boyfriend would I be if I didn't support you in this new direction your life is taking?" he said. "And don't worry, Haley, you can count on me to do this kind of thing from now on."

Great.

Chapter 12

Smoking-hot Jack Bishop called me the next morning at the exact moment my smoking-hot boyfriend stepped into the shower. Do I have the coolest life of anyone on planet Earth, or what?

I answered my cell phone as I stood in my kitchen searching for the sugar in the cabinets Ty had so thoughtfully rearranged for me yesterday.

"Any luck with my DMV search?" I asked, opening yet another cabinet door.

"I don't need luck," Jack told me in his I'm-way-hot voice.

I love that voice.

"So what's the story?" I asked.

"Meet me," Jack said. "Your favorite place in an hour."

Oh my God. Private detective lingo was so cool.

"I'm buying," I told him.

"Damn right you are," Jack said, and hung up.

I turned and ran smack into Ty standing in my kitchen wearing sweatpants and a T-shirt. His hair was damp, and that freshly shaved smell wafted from him.

"I made coffee," he said.

"Yeah, I saw," I said. "I can't find the sugar. Where'd you put it?"

"I threw it out."

"You—you what?"

"Sugar's really bad for you, Haley," he said. "And it's certainly not part of your better-eating commitment."

Ty moved around me and opened the drawer beneath the coffeemaker—the one that *used* to have take-out menus in it.

"I bought you these," Ty said, proudly pointing to a stunning array of tiny pink, blue, and yellow packets stacked neatly in the drawer. "Sugar substitutes."

"You bought sugar . . . sub—sub—"

I couldn't even say the words "substitute" and "sugar" in the same sentence.

"Wait until you taste this coffee," Ty said. He pulled two mugs from the cabinet, filled them from the pot he'd put on earlier, and presented one of them to me. "Try it black. It's great."

I took a sip. Yikes! It tasted like liquefied chewing gum scraped off the sidewalk outside a Middle Eastern sushi restaurant, or something.

"I bought it for you," Ty said, sipping his. "It's a special blend of zinc, magnesium, and folic acid, and has lots of great health benefits."

"Wow, that's really something," I said, setting the cup aside. "Listen, I have to go out for a while."

Ty sipped more of the coffee. "No problem. I have some things to take care of this morning."

I was tempted to ask him what kind of things he was taking care of, but then I'd be obligated to tell him what I was doing, and I didn't think mentioning that I was getting info on a car that I suspected had been following me was the right move to make.

And I wasn't using that as an excuse not to tell him I was meeting Jack Bishop. Really.

"We'll have dinner together," Ty said. "I heard about a new place I know you'll love."

"Sounds great," I said.

I dashed into the bedroom, threw on a sundress and sandals, freshened my makeup, twisted my hair into an oh-so-casual updo—none of which had *anything* to do with my meeting Jack Bishop—grabbed a totally awesome Fendi bag, and left.

My favorite place, which Jack had so cryptically mentioned on the phone, was the Starbucks about a half-mile from my apartment. It was a great Southern California morning and sitting on their patio sipping a mocha frappuccino would be awesome—not to mention having hot, hot, hot Jack beside me, making everyone who saw me totally jealous.

Yeah, okay, I knew a mocha frappuccino was a total no-no in my whole-new-me plan, but, jeez, I couldn't sit at Starbucks and drink water. It went against everything Starbucks—and I—believe in.

Since Jack wouldn't be there for a while, I had some time to kill. My first thought was to go to the mall, of course. But the stores weren't open this early—which was just plain crazy, if you ask me. I mean, really, was that any way to do business? Why couldn't they stay open 24/7? Where was their concern over a customer with a fashion crisis?

Anyway, I decided this was a good time to check out another suspect in Violet's murder. I pulled out of my apartment complex and hung a right on Via Princessa as I accessed the info on my cell phone.

Tina Sheldon lived in Canyon Country, an area just a few miles from my apartment. I figured I could run by her place, perhaps find evidence of Violet's murder lying on her lawn, or something, and still have plenty of time to meet Jack.

I punched her address into my GPS and took Whites Canyon Road past Soledad Canyon Road—*everything* out here was some sort of a canyon—to Stillmore Avenue.

It was an older, settled neighborhood with most of the houses in okay condition. Some peeling paint here, an overgrown planter there, but generally a nice place to live. It was early on a Sunday morning so not a lot of people were outside, and there was little traffic on the street.

I cruised down the block until I found Tina's place. Her house looked a little better than those around it. Somebody had put in a lot of time on the shrubbery and intricately planted flower beds. A gnome garden and a birdbath sat in her front yard.

No evidence of Violet's murderer in sight.

Darn. I hate when that happens.

I rode past her place, hung a U at the corner, and pulled in at the curb about four houses down, angled so that I had a good view of Tina's front yard and driveway. I scrunched down in the seat a little—I'm pretty sure that's mandatory in the private detectives' handbook—and waited for something incriminating to present itself.

Nothing presented itself—incriminating or otherwise.

A couple of cars drove past me, a guy fired up his motorcycle across the street and took off, and that was about it. I figured I could devote forty-five minutes or so to my stakeout, then I'd have to leave to meet Jack. About ten minutes in, I was done.

I just don't have the patience for this sort of private detective work.

Maybe I could go to the mall instead.

My spirits lifted. Yeah, that was way better. I could run by Macy's, even though they weren't open yet. Their handbag department was near the entrance. Maybe I could spot a Temptress in a display case.

No wait, even better—maybe employees would be in the store getting ready to open, and they'd see me and let me in early. Wow, I can picture it now. The whole store to myself. A new, huge shipment of Temptress bags just arrived. Me touching the buttery leather, gazing at the silk lining, trying on bag after bag, having my pick of them all until I—

The garage door at Tina's house rolled up. A white panel van backed out into the street and I spotted Tina behind the wheel—completely shattering my fabulous Temptress fantasy.

I hate it when that happens.

The van headed straight toward me. Yikes!

I slumped farther down in my seat and was considering diving into the floor—a hot private detective move, I'm sure—as the van rolled closer to me. Oh, yeah, it was definitely Tina behind the wheel. My heart rate picked up, as I bordered on total-panic mode.

Oh my God, she'd recognize me for sure. My covert op would be blown to bits. And what would I tell her when she hit the brakes, rolled down her window, and gave me a what-the-heck-are-you-doing-here look? How would I explain why I was here?

I've got to get better about thinking things through.

But Tina didn't notice me. She was gazing down at something, like she was adjusting the radio or maybe fooling with a GPS, and didn't even look my way as she passed my car. Whew!

I watched in my side mirror and saw her turn left at the intersection, and my wanna-be private detective gene kicked in. Oh my God, I could follow her. I swung away from the curb in hot pursuit.

My undercover operation was suddenly cool again—not as cool as having alone time with an entire shipment of Temptress bags at Macy's, of course—but still pretty darn cool.

Tina might have been going out for the Sunday newspaper or to pick up doughnuts for the family, but I followed her anyway. I caught up with her as she took Whites Canyon to Via Princessa, then hit the 14 freeway south. I followed as she merged onto the southbound 5 a few minutes later.

The 5 freeway ran east of Los Angeles, through Orange County, and ended in San Diego, about two hours away. I stayed a few car lengths behind her and changed lanes a couple of times, so as not to look suspicious. Tina drove in the middle lane and kept her speed steady at just two miles over the speed limit—which was kind of annoying—so I figured she must have set her cruise control.

Not exactly the kind of behavior of someone who had a lot to hide.

I hung in there for a while, then gave up and headed back to Santa Clarita to meet Jack.

I swung into the parking lot of the little shopping center that included Starbucks, some fast-food restaurants, doctors' offices, and mom-and-pop shops, and did a quick check of vehicles already there. No sign of Jack's black Land Rover or the way cool convertible BMW he'd offered to let me drive back from Las Vegas a few weeks ago—long story.

I pulled into a space, killed the engine, and flipped down the mirror in my visor. Yeah, okay, I knew it was kind of bad to worry about my appearance before meeting Jack, since I have an official boyfriend, but, well, there it was. I dug a brush from my purse and ran it through my hair, thinking I could use a touch of lipstick, when my passenger-side door opened and a man got in.

For a second I thought it was Jack.

It wasn't.

My heart nearly flew out of my chest and I almost launched myself through the roof.

It was Mike Ivan.

Now I was even more scared.

Oh my God. What was he doing here? In my car. Outside my favorite Starbucks.

Had he simply been here? He didn't really look like a frappuccino-cappuccino-latte kind of guy.

Was he in one of the other stores and saw me? Had he just wanted to be sociable and walked over to say hi?

I doubted it.

"Did I scare you?" Mike asked.

I guess that in Mike's maybe-connected-to-the-Russian-mob world, springing unannounced into someone's car was no big deal. But I was clutching my chest, breathing like I had a front row seat at every Milan Fashion Week show, thinking I was about to be killed and that Marcie darn well better find a Temptress to bury with me.

"Yeah . . . you . . . scared . . . me."

"Oh. Sorry."

I panted for a few more minutes, then forced myself to calm down.

Mike sat beside me, his gaze scanning the parking lot. To look at him you'd never think mobbed-up. Mike was nice looking, with brown hair and eyes. I figured him for mid-thirties, about my height, with a good build. He wore khaki pants, loafers, a blue short-sleeve shirt, and a necktie.

He looked like a claims adjuster.

"You need something," Mike said. It wasn't a question.

I got the feeling he wasn't referring to the items on the Starbucks menu.

My mind was spinning, trying to figure out how Mike knew I wanted his help with Juanita's disappearance and the woman who'd showed up at Mom's house speaking what I was afraid was Romanian or Russian. I'd mentioned it to Jack Bishop, but he'd been adamant about not approaching Mike. No way had I mentioned it to Detective Shuman, the only other connection to Mike I could think of.

"How did you know?" I asked.

"You called me," Mike said.

Then I remembered calling him from my cell phone, but hanging up after just one ring. Now I realized he'd seen my name on his caller I.D. screen.

"I told you," Mike said. "I don't forget a favor."

When I met Mike for the first time a few weeks ago in Las Vegas, he'd insisted that, though his family was rumored to be in the Russian mob, he was not. He claimed he ran a completely legitimate import-export business. Still, when it all hit the fan in Vegas, I'd made sure Mike Ivan's interests were protected. He said he wouldn't forget what I did, and I could see now that he meant it, but, jeez, did he have to give me a heart attack to prove it?

"How did you find me?" I asked.

Mike glanced out the window. "I didn't want to bother you at your apartment."

Oh my God. Mike Ivan knew where I lived.

"Not with your boyfriend up there," he added.

Oh, jeez, he knew about Ty, too?

"So I found you here instead," Mike said.

He *found* me? No way. He must have followed me.

Oh, crap.

"So what do you need?" he asked.

At this point I figured I was in too deep to hold back.

I'm not great at holding back.

"A friend of mine has disappeared," I said. "She may have been kidnapped."

I gave Mike all the info I had about Juanita's possible murder/possible kidnapping, and the possible ransom demand Mom had received from the possibly Romanian/possibly Russian woman who'd come to her house. I didn't mention Mom, specifically.

Not even the Russian mob should be subjected to my mom.

Mike listened, then nodded. "I'll get back with you."

"You can just call me," I offered.

He threw me a little grin, then got out of my car and left.

I collapsed against the seat and closed my eyes.

Oh my God. What had I done? Was it the right thing? Should I have just told Mike—

A fist pounded on my window. My eyes flew open and I bolted upright in the seat.

Jack Bishop stared in at me.

I flung open the door, forcing him to step back, and jumped out of my car.

"Don't ever do that again." I'm pretty sure I shouted that.

I flattened my hand against my chest and told him, "You could have given me a heart attack."

Jack gave me a smoking-hot grin. "A rapid pulse and pounding heart are all part of the service."

Lucky for Jack, he looked so great. Otherwise, I might have ripped his head off and thrown it in his face.

Today he had on gun metal gray cargo pants, black CAT boots, a snug—and I mean *really* snug—white T-shirt, and aviator sunglasses. Way hot.

He nodded toward Starbucks. "Want something?"

Screw this whole-new-me thing. I pushed past Jack, went inside, and ordered a venti mocha frappie, with extra whipped cream and a double shot of chocolate. By the time Jack ordered a coffee and we settled at an umbrella table on the patio, I'd calmed down. I mean, jeez, what else could happen today?

"I got the info you wanted," Jack said.

Oh, yeah, the DMV report on the yellow VW Beetle that had been following me. I'd been so rattled I'd almost forgotten why I was here.

Jack pulled a slip of paper from his shirt pocket but didn't hand it over.

"You owe me," he said.

"Just tell me what you want," I said.

"I will," Jack said. "I'll tell you—when I want it."

He'd told me that before, several times. So far, he hadn't asked for payment of any sort, but when he did—well, best not to think about what might happen between us, as long as I have an official boyfriend, anyway.

I plucked the paper from his hand—honestly, I was starting to shake again, but for an entirely different reason.

I unfolded the paper and read the name of the VW's registered owner.

Evelyn Croft.

Oh, crap.

Chapter 13

Evelyn and I met last fall when I started working at Holt's. She was an assistant department manager whose appearance was so demure and conservative she was continually mistaken for a librarian married to a minister who worked as a museum docent. Evelyn was also the sweetest, most gentle person I've known in my entire life.

Which, in a way, was kind of annoying.

I mean that in the nicest way, of course.

All sorts of stuff went down at Holt's last fall, some of it involving Evelyn. She'd recovered from her physical injuries but couldn't climb out of the emotional pit she'd fallen into. She wouldn't even talk about it. She referred to the whole thing as "the incident" caused by "that certain someone."

But the really troubling part of the whole thing was that she wouldn't come out of her house. Hardly ever. Really.

I'd visited her—it's like entering Fort Knox to get through her front door—and I'd tried coaxing her out into the real world, but she'd wanted no part of it.

For a while, I'd thought Evelyn had a boyfriend, a stuffy gray-haired gentleman who was a vice president of the equally stuffy Golden State Bank & Trust. But I'd never actually seen them together or gotten Evelyn to admit to the relationship—I hate it when people don't dish on the cool stuff—so I couldn't say for sure what was going on there.

A few weeks ago, Evelyn had almost gone to a party. I say almost because she'd actually left her house—courtesy of yours truly, of course—and gone shopping for a new outfit. I was pumped, not only because Evelyn had finally made the giant leap to get out socially, but because I got to take her shopping.

There's something way cool about spending someone else's money.

But in the end, Evelyn had canceled on the party. If she'd been out of her house since our big shopping trip, I wasn't aware of it.

That's why it was weird that her name had come back on the DMV registration of the yellow VW Beetle I'd seen at my apartment, at the Holt's store, and near my mom's house.

Plus, it was weirder than weird that she owned a yellow *anything*—much less a Beetle. I mean, come on, a woman who's afraid to leave her own home wasn't likely to bat around town in a flashy car.

I parked at the curb in front of Evelyn's house—a conservative home in a conservative neighborhood—and walked up to the front door. The blinds covering the living room window moved a millimeter so I knew Evelyn had seen me arrive. I'd called ahead, of course, not to make sure it was a convenient time to visit, but because an unexpected knock on her door sent Evelyn into full-on panic mode.

Even though I'd called ahead and I'd seen the blinds move at the window, I knocked on the front door and rang the bell.

"It's me," I called. "Haley."

I stood in front of the peephole and gave her my big

there's-nothing-to-be-afraid-of smile, which I had perfected solely to visit Evelyn.

Chains rattled, locks turned, and the door opened a couple of inches. Half of Evelyn's face appeared in the crack. Then she jerked the door open, I rushed inside, and she secured the door again.

"Well, Haley, it's good to see you," Evelyn said, twisting her fingers together.

I was never sure how old Evelyn was, somewhere between mid-thirties and early forties, I thought. Though she seldom left her home, she always kept her dark hair looking nice, her nails done, and makeup on. I wasn't so crazy about her style of clothing. Today she had on a long print skirt, a beige blouse with a ruffled collar, and loafers.

She looked as if she were auditioning for a remake of *Little House on the Prairie*.

"Come in," Evelyn said, gesturing toward her living room. "I've made us some refreshments."

Oh, crap. I'd forgotten about Evelyn's refreshments.

I took my customary spot on the sofa in the living room. The place looked like a florist had exploded in here. Blue and yellow floral prints were everywhere. Evelyn had made slipcovers not long ago, covering the pink and mint green florals with these newer florals.

She came in from the kitchen carrying a tray with a tea service and a plate of cookies—and believe me, these things were not Oreos. Honestly, I didn't know what kind of cookies they were, but I suspected the box they came in would taste better.

"Have you registered for your fall classes?" Evelyn asked, pouring.

No way was I getting into the whole University of Mixology/University of Michigan thing with her.

"Not yet," I said, accepting the tea cup she passed me.

She held out the plate of cookies. I took three—just so she wouldn't think I didn't like them, of course.

"Hasn't this weather been something," Evelyn said, sipping from her own cup. "Those poor farmers in the Midwest are having such a terrible time this year."

Evelyn loved the Internet. She had newspaper and magazine subscriptions. She stayed informed about absolutely everything going on, everywhere on the planet.

Most of the time, I didn't know what she was talking about.

I crunched my way through all three cookies and finished my tea while she chatted about—well, I don't know exactly what she talked about. I drifted off.

Silence got my attention, and I realized Evelyn was gazing at me expectantly. Jeez, had she just asked me a question?

I didn't want her to think I wasn't interested in what she was saying—I wasn't, but I didn't want her to know that—so I set aside my teacup and acted like I'd just thought of something.

"That reminds me," I said. "Did you get a new car?"

Evelyn gasped and lurched back a little. The teacup rattled in her hand. Her cheeks turned pink.

Jeez, I really hope Evelyn never tries to take up poker.

"Well, Haley, actually I—I did," she said, her gaze bouncing everywhere in the room but on me.

For about a half-second, I considered that she might have bought the yellow Beetle for a niece or nephew, or something. Evelyn certainly had plenty of money, thanks to the generous settlement Ty had insisted on after "the incident" last fall. But that didn't explain why I was being followed.

"Is it a Volkswagen Beetle?" I asked. "Bright yellow?"

"Well, yes." Evelyn's gaze dropped to the floor for about a minute, then she drew in a breath and looked at me again. "I guess you saw me."

I thought it might alarm her to know that I'd had a private detective access her DMV records, so I didn't say anything.

Evelyn pressed her fingertips to her lips. For a moment I thought she might cry but—whew!—she didn't.

I'm not good with a crier.

"I want to start working again," Evelyn said.

"You *do?*" I might have said that louder than I meant to.

Evelyn nodded. "I think it's time. So I bought a new car."

"A yellow Bug?" I might have said that a little too loud also.

"I wanted something bold," Evelyn said. "I thought driving it might make me feel . . . bold."

I doubted Evelyn had ever done anything *bold* in her entire life, but this hardly seemed the time to say so.

"I hope you don't mind that I drove by your apartment and the store, and that I followed you to that lovely house out in La Cañada Flintridge." Evelyn twisted her fingers together. "But I thought that if I was out and I got too upset, well, you'd be nearby and maybe . . ."

I don't know what it is about Evelyn. But for some reason, I can't stop wanting to help her.

"It's fine," I said. "If you need me—anywhere, anytime—just call."

"Thank you, Haley," she said softly.

Then it hit me that Evelyn had said she wanted to start working again. Yikes! I couldn't imagine her dealing with crabby, backstabbing coworkers and demanding, insulting, overbearing supervisors.

I might have to get a job at the same place just to protect her.

"When you get to the new job," I said, "you'll have to stand up for yourself."

Evelyn looked surprised.

"I know it will be hard because you haven't been out

much lately," I said, using my pay-attention-I-know-what-I'm-talking-about voice. "But you can't let other people take advantage of you. You have to be tough."

Evelyn cringed. "Really? Do you think so?"

"Yes, absolutely," I said. "And you can do it. You're stronger than you think."

She seemed to process my words for a minute or two, then sat up a little straighter. "You're right, Haley. I am stronger now."

"You bet you are," I said. "You bought that really cool Beetle."

"I did, didn't I," she said, as if she just realized it.

"And you're driving it all over the place."

Evelyn nodded. "Yes. Yes, I am."

"You're going to be great at work," I told her. "Just remember, no matter what other people say, you have to stick by what you know is right."

She made a fist and bounced it off the coffee table. "I will."

Cool.

It was a Gucci day. Definitely a Gucci day.

Bright and early the next morning, I nosed my Honda into a spot in the Dempsey Rowland parking garage and moved with the crowd into the lobby, then took the elevator up to the fifth floor.

I felt like I really fit in today. I had on one of the new suits Marcie had helped me pick out—I went with classic black—and teamed it with some of the conservative-yet-sassy accessories, and a pair of the I-refuse-to-take-this-job-seriously shoes I'd also purchased.

The only thing needed to complete the look was a Temptress bag. I'd searched everywhere for one, and even put myself on a waiting list at a couple of stores, but no luck yet. I wasn't deterred. I'd been down this road many, many times.

Even though I'd only worked here a short while, I recognized some of the people moving along the Dempsey Rowland halls with me. Lots of men, young and old. A few women, all old.

I smiled and said hi. I got a few smiles in return and a couple of good mornings, but nobody seemed all that friendly. It made me wonder if that whole Violet-was-murdered-and-the-cops-questioned-me thing had something to do with the cool reception I was receiving.

But maybe I was just being paranoid. It was, after all, Monday morning.

I turned a corner and saw Max Corwin headed my way with a cup of coffee in his hand.

"Morning, Max," I said.

He stopped, glanced around, then leaned in a little.

"Bad news," he whispered.

Jeez, I didn't want to hear bad news first thing on a Monday morning—not when I had on a brand-new outfit.

Max glanced around again, then whispered, "I heard they turned over our background investigations to someone. I didn't get a name."

He looked at me as if he expected me to say something profound.

I couldn't think of anything—not this early on a Monday.

"But whoever this person is, they're just doing the preliminary workup," Max said.

He nodded his head, as if this was significant and I should be as relieved as he seemed to be.

I figured that the longer our background checks were delayed, the better. But I decided to keep that to myself. Besides, Max seemed to be worrying enough for both of us.

"I'll keep you posted," he whispered, and hurried away.

I went to my office—it was easy to find since the yellow

crime scene tape was still strung in front of Constance's door—and went inside.

So much to do. Time to buckle down, get organized for the day, make plans for the week. My schedule popped into my head. First, update my Facebook page. Second, check my horoscope, e-mails, bank balance, and available credit on my credit cards. Next, make lunch plans. After that, I would check the Internet for the Temptress bag.

But before I got too deep into my morning routine, I decided to grab a cup of coffee. Really, I could hardly be expected to tackle such a demanding schedule without benefit of caffeine.

I went to the breakroom. Only two other people were there, older men I didn't recognize, helping themselves to coffee. They talked between themselves, ignoring me, which I thought was super rude, especially since I had on a killer outfit today.

They left and I poured myself a coffee. My spirits lifted when I saw packets of actual sugar at the ready. I dumped two into my cup—which I know was bad, especially since Ty went to all the trouble to buy those sugar substitutes and had even bought that special coffee, and was being so helpful in my whole-new-me quest.

Yes, Ty was being way helpful. I mean, *way* helpful.

He'd promised me dinner out last night at a place he'd found on the Internet, a restaurant he said he knew I'd love. My vision of crab-stuffed lobster, baked potato all-the-way, and triple chocolate cake at a romantic restaurant overlooking the ocean was shattered all to heck when we pulled up in front of some health food place in Sherman Oaks.

I didn't even know what most of the food on their menu was and, frankly, if I never found out, it would be okay with me. Ty had seemed to enjoy his meal. I ate a little and pushed the rest around my plate until it was time to go.

He was setting a good example for me, being supportive

and all—thank goodness he had been asleep when I left this morning so I didn't have to drink any more of that coffee—but, jeez, it was Monday morning. I definitely needed a boost.

The breakroom door swung open as I stirred some French vanilla–flavored cream into my coffee. Tina walked in and joined me at the counter.

"Good morning," I said, and managed to put a lot of enthusiasm into my greeting, even though I hadn't had the coffee yet.

"Yeah, hi," Tina mumbled, as she found a mug in the cabinet.

Tina looked a little weary today. But, oh well, most people did, after two days off.

"How was your weekend?" I asked, sipping my coffee. Wow, real coffee. And real sugar. Yummy.

"It was okay," Tina said, filling her cup from the carafe.

Hum. Maybe it could be a little yummier. I ripped open another sugar packet and stirred it into my cup.

"Mostly, it was boring," Tina said, stifling a yawn.

I sipped. Oh, yeah. Now I was onto something.

"All weekend I was at home with sick kids," Tina said, adding a touch of cream to her coffee.

Maybe a little more French vanilla—just to balance out the sugar. I added a dash, then sipped again. Oh, yeah, this was something—

Hang on a second.

"You were at home all weekend?" I asked Tina.

"Yeah, that's what I said." There was a slight edge to her voice.

"You didn't go out at all?" I asked. "You didn't leave your house for medicine or anything?"

"That's what you do when you have sick kids," Tina told me. "You stay home with them."

She mumbled something under her breath, and left the breakroom.

Okay, that was weird.

Why would Tina lie to me about staying home all weekend? When I'd followed her down the 5 yesterday, I'd figured she was visiting family or going shopping, or something. No big deal.

But maybe it was a big deal. Maybe, if I was lucky, it somehow tied to Violet's murder. I didn't know how it possibly could, of course. But at the moment I had only three suspects, and two of them weren't looking all that guilty.

I hate it when that happens.

Max Corwin seemed a little paranoid—aren't most people who work for years in an office setting?—but I'd discovered nothing about his life that made him a likely murderer, except that he'd changed jobs a few times. Even though Detective Shuman thought that was somehow suspicious, I didn't.

Ray Boyd, the other new hire, didn't have much going for him in the I'm-a-murder-suspect category either. A guy who probably spent his evenings and weekends playing World of Warcraft didn't rate high on my personal I-could-kill-an-actual-human-being scale.

That left Tina. Not much to go on there, but why should that stop me?

I dumped another packet of sugar into my coffee and went back to my office.

CHAPTER 14

I needed an old lady.

With the brain boosting effect of my real-sugar-flavored, cream-added, loaded-with-caffeine coffee, I sat in my office plotting my next move in Violet's murder investigation. Luckily, a flash of brilliance shot through my head almost immediately.

An older woman was who I had to talk to. One who had worked here at Dempsey Rowland for a long time, had known Violet, and hopefully had been friends with her.

Since most of the women I'd seen so far in this place surely had age-defying and anti-wrinkle written on every jar in their bathroom cabinets, I figured I had plenty to pick from.

I searched the desk and cabinets until I found a black leather portfolio with the Dempsey Rowland logo on the front and a pad of yellow legal paper inside, then chugged the last of my coffee and left my office.

Though I didn't really want to, I knew I had to start at the reception area. Camille, whose appearance screamed office-of-the-living-dead, would likely know everyone who worked here, plus a lot of gossip.

Still, I didn't want to spend too much time with her. She creeped me out big time. So I came up with a perfect cover story, thanks in no small part to that supercharged cup of coffee I'd downed.

I approached the reception desk trying not to look Camille directly in the eye, afraid she might put the whammy on me, or something. She had on a fuchsia suit today, which made the blotches on her thin, overtightened skin appear fuchsia, too.

Not a look likely to be featured in *Glamour* anytime soon.

"I'm planning Violet's memorial service," I said to Camille, flipping open the portfolio.

She turned to me—I'm pretty sure I heard bones rattling—and said, "A memorial service?"

"It's the right thing to do," I said.

"Does Mr. Dempsey know you're doing this?" she asked.

"Of course," I said.

"Are you certain?"

"Absolutely."

I kept my gaze down hoping Camille would think I looked sorrowful over Violet's death, rather than simply afraid to make eye contact with her.

After nearly a full minute passed with no response from Camille, I chanced a quick glance up. I got the impression she wanted to frown, but since none of the muscles in her face could actually move, I wasn't sure.

"Violet was a wonderful woman," Camille said. "This place couldn't have run without her."

I pretended to jot that down.

"I want to get some input for the service and some background on her," I said. "Can you give me the name of someone she was close to here?"

"Beatrice," Camille declared. "Talk to Beatrice. She's an admin assistant in contracting."

"Thanks."

I snapped my portfolio closed and headed down the hallway, just as if I actually knew where the contracting department was located.

I channeled my mom's pageant walk and morphed it into my own I'm-not-lost walk, and wandered the corridors for a while. Then it hit me that the contracting department was probably in the Support Unit.

My spirits fell a little. I didn't really love the idea of going back into that snake pit again but didn't have a choice.

I can make the hard decisions when I have to.

I turned a corner and found myself in a totally different part of the office complex. Jeez, how did that happen?

A small sign over the entrance read ENGINEERING UNIT.

Engineering Unit?

I'm really going to have to find out what the heck this company does.

My dad was an aerospace engineer, and I'd actually dated an engineer a few months ago—long story—so I knew the atmosphere in this unit would definitely be less hostile than in support. Maybe somebody here could tell me where to find contracting.

Engineers were brilliant. They'd taken us off this planet, designed behemoth aircraft, ships, and buildings, and given us more gadgets, gizmos, apps, and downloads than most of us knew how to operate. But no way were any of them the first invited to a party.

Let's face it: not *everyone* is good at *everything*.

The cube dwellers here were all men. Young men, mostly, dressed in what I'd come to think of as the engineer's uniform: khaki pants and a pale blue oxford shirt. They were all hunched over computers and calculators, working feverishly while, I'm sure, "Highway to the Danger Zone" played in their heads.

I walked past the cubes trying to catch the eye of one of

the guys—which you wouldn't think would be difficult since I am, after all, *me*, plus I had on a killer new outfit—but all of them kept working. Kind of depressing.

Then I spotted another hallway with a sign that read CONTRACTING DEPARTMENT.

Do I have fabulous luck, or what?

A brilliant idea exploded in my mind. Adela had told me when I was hired that I would be assigned to the contracting department. On the off chance—and I'm talking a real long shot here—that I passed the background investigation and got my security clearance, I would actually work there.

It would help if I knew what that department did, of course. Maybe I could use my super-stealthy-private-investigator-while-looking-totally-hot skills to find out from Beatrice exactly what it was, plus solve Violet's murder at the same time.

Am I not truly awesome? Wow, maybe I should wear a cape.

I passed yet another cube farm, this one much smaller than the one I'd seen in the Engineering Unit. I found Beatrice's cube along the perimeter of the room outside a glass-walled office where I supposed her supervisor worked. No sign of the supervisor.

"Beatrice?" I asked, standing in the entrance of her cube.

She jumped as if I'd startled her, and slammed her desk drawer shut. Before it closed I spotted an open box of candy inside.

So far, Beatrice was my kind of gal.

"Hi, I'm Haley Randolph," I said, giving her my biggest I'm-completely-nonthreatening-and-you-can-trust-me smile. "I took over for Constance in the Executive Unit. I'm handling all the corporate events. Can I talk to you for a minute about Violet Hamilton's memorial service?"

Beatrice covered her mouth with her palm as if I couldn't

see that she was chewing, and made a sound I decided meant sure, come in, so I did.

She looked like a lot of the other women I'd seen at Dempsey Rowland. Fiftyish, chunky, gray haired, with clothing, shoes, hair, makeup, and accessories that were in style around the time of the *When Harry Met Sally* premiere.

I settled into the chair beside Beatrice's desk. I needed to get her take on Violet's death, but I saw no need to rush into it immediately. Better to open with something that benefited *me*.

"So, how's it going?" I asked, and nodded toward the nearby cube farm.

"Fine," she said.

She looked a little uncomfortable, as if someone from the Executive Unit showing up at her cube and asking questions was completely out of the ordinary—and not in a good way.

"What is it you do here in contracting?" I asked. "Exactly."

Beatrice didn't answer right away. Her gaze zipped around the cube as if she thought this might be a trick question, so she wanted to think about it before responding.

"Contracts," she said.

Okay, obviously I was going to have to push a little harder for info.

"By contracts, do you mean . . . ?"

I deliberately left my question hanging so she could jump in with a full explanation.

She didn't jump in.

"I mean contracts," Beatrice said, looking slightly alarmed now.

Apparently, she wasn't going to work with me on this whole contract thing. I decided to move on.

"So, about Violet's memorial service," I said, and opened

the portfolio. "I'd like to get a little background on her. I understand you two were friends?"

"Well . . . yes," she said. "You might say that, I suppose."

"Had you known her long?" I asked.

"Years," Beatrice said.

"And what did you think of her?" I asked.

"She was nice."

Beatrice seemed to be one of those employees who just want to put in their time, mind their own business, and go home at the end of the day. No gossiping, no rumor spreading, no talking crap about anybody, no interest in office politics. I grasped the concept, of course, but that sort of attitude sure as heck took all the fun out of working in a big office.

"Does Mr. Dempsey know you're doing this?" she asked, her eyes looking a little wild now.

"Of course," I said. "I spoke with his secretary, Ruth, about it."

I saw no need to mention that Ruth looked as if she might taser me if I didn't jump on planning the service immediately.

"I'm not trying to trip you up here, Beatrice. I just want to do the right thing by Violet at her memorial service," I said.

She hesitated another minute, then leaned forward just a little and lowered her voice.

"Violet was a wonderful person. She started this company alongside Mr. Dempsey, you know. Built it from the ground up. He couldn't have done it without her," Beatrice said. "She knew this place inside out. Nothing got past her. Nothing."

"It's hard to imagine that somebody would kill her," I said, because, really, it was.

"In the last year, Violet mostly kept to herself because of

the security work she was doing," Beatrice said. She shook her head. "Everybody liked her. Well, I guess everybody but one person. The person who . . . murdered her."

Camille and now Beatrice had told me what a great person Violet had been. So who would have killed her? And why?

"Do you have any idea who might have wanted to harm Violet?" I asked.

Beatrice pressed her lips together, as if forcing herself to not say anything. A few seconds crawled by and finally she whispered, "Something happened with her granddaughter."

Whoa. Where did this come from?

"Her granddaughter?" I asked, then added, just to make sure, "Violet's granddaughter?"

"She was supposed to come to work here, but something happened and she didn't. It got ugly, very ugly," Beatrice said. "Violet was furious over the whole thing. Her granddaughter was furious with Violet."

"Furious enough to kill her?" I asked.

Something outside her cube caught Beatrice's attention. She sat up straight and grabbed a stack of papers from the corner of her desk. I turned and saw a man—her supervisor, I guessed—walking toward us.

"Talk to Iris in payroll," Beatrice whispered. She turned away and started shuffling papers. I left.

Hearing that things had gotten ugly between Violet and her granddaughter boosted my day considerably. As I wandered the corridors searching for my office, it occurred to me that if things had gone sour between the two of them and Violet's murder had nothing to do with the background investigations she was conducting, then Detective Madison would be forced to cross me off his suspect list.

That was some good news I could sure stand.

My thoughts raced ahead.

Maybe Violet's granddaughter had killed her over some family thing. Of course, I had no idea what had really gone on between Violet and her granddaughter. I was short on suspects—not to mention motives—so what could I do but speculate about both and hope for the best?

I'm pretty sure that's the way all the great investigators do it.

By the time I found my way back to the Executive Unit, I realized it was nearly lunch time. I decided to see if Marcie wanted to meet somewhere.

I walked into my office and froze.

A huge arrangement of yellow roses sat on my desk. I opened the little envelope almost hidden in the greenery. It read, *Just wanted you to know I was thinking about you. Ty.*

Ty had sent me flowers? Wow.

I studied the handwriting and—oh my God—he'd actually signed the card himself. That meant he'd gone to the florist in person, picked out the flowers, stood at the counter, and composed the message to write on the card.

My heart fluttered and my stomach got all gooey, just like it always did when Ty did something nice for me—which really wasn't that often, but still. Maybe this was all part of his plan to show me what a great boyfriend he could be.

So far I liked this a heck of a lot better than his help-me-with-the-whole-new-me thing.

I got my cell phone and called him. His voicemail picked up. I left a message thanking him for the flowers, telling him how they'd boosted my day, and that I was thinking about him, too.

Immediately, I called Marcie. She was duly impressed by the flowers and agreed we had to have lunch. No way could we let an unexpected flower delivery pass us by without discussing it in depth to determine a hidden meaning. She had a meeting or something and couldn't go until later, so we decided to meet at a restaurant down the block near 8th Street.

I saw no need to perform the work Dempsey Rowland was paying me for this early in the day, so I decided I'd talk to Iris in payroll. I grabbed my portfolio and left my office.

CHAPTER 15

Payroll was buried deep in the Support Unit. I figured that most of the girls who worked there would be at lunch right about now so fewer of them would be around to give me a hard time. It made me kind of sad, though, because I wished some of them could be my friends; it was always cool to have lots of friends to go to lunch with.

When I got to the Support Unit I saw a friendly face. Shawna was standing in her cube and waved when she spotted me.

"How's it going?" I asked, as I stopped outside her cube.

"Cool," she said.

Today Shawna had a retro-fifties thing going on, with a full skirt and white blouse. She'd jazzed it up with flaming red accessories that really pulled the look together.

It sure as heck looked like an outfit that was way more fun than my black business suit, and that meant Shawna would probably be fun, too. Maybe she'd be my friend, despite the fact that we worked in two different units.

"Love your clothes," I told her. "We should go shopping together on our lunch hour sometime."

"Sounds great," Shawna said, then gave me a sad smile. "But I gave my notice. I'm leaving at the end of next week."

Darn. I finally found a friend here and she was leaving?
"How come?" I asked.

Shawna shrugged. "It's grim here. No future."

I remembered she'd mentioned before that promotion out of the Support Unit was nearly impossible, even though lots of the girls here were qualified to do more.

"I can't say that I blame you," I told her.

"And that old guy Dempsey." Shawna shook her head. "What a creep."

Okay, this was new. I hadn't heard anyone say anything bad about the founder of the company.

"He is?" I asked.

She uttered a disgusted grunt. "Why do you think no young women work in the Executive Unit?"

I'd noticed that everyone over there was either old or male, but I hadn't devoted too many brain cells to figuring out why—not when I had a murder to solve, new clothes to buy, and a smoking-hot handbag to track down. But maybe I should.

"Lunch and shopping later this week, for sure," Shawna said, and picked up a stack of papers from her desk. "Got to run."

I wound my way to the payroll department and searched the cubes outside the glass-walled offices until I found the one that bore Iris's nameplate. A clone of almost every other woman I'd seen in this office complex sat at the desk—fiftyish, gray haired, short, heavyset.

"Iris?" I asked.

She didn't look up from her work. "If you have a problem with your paycheck, get a form from your immediate supervisor and route it thought interoffice mail."

I got the feeling she'd said that same sentence about a zillion times.

"I'm here to talk with you about Violet Hamilton's memorial service," I said, and introduced myself.

"Oh." Iris looked up at me, startled, or like maybe she

was concerned for my safety. "Does Mr. Dempsey know you're doing this?"

"I cleared everything through Ruth," I said, which wasn't exactly the truth, but, oh well.

Before she had a chance to question me further, I pushed ahead.

"I understand you and Violet were friends," I said. "I want to consult with her family, of course, about the service. Would you suggest I contact her granddaughter?"

Iris drew back, as if I'd slapped her. I shifted immediately into concerned-friend mode—which I'm not all that great at, really—and dropped into the chair next to her desk.

"Did something happen between Violet and her granddaughter?" I asked, and luckily it came out sounding like I didn't really already know the answer.

Iris pressed her fingers to her lips and for a moment—eek!—I thought she was going to cry.

What was with all the women who worked here that they acted like they were going to cry all the time? No wonder none of them were getting promoted, if they were boo-hooing at the drop of a hat.

I figured it was best to just wait her out—not something I have the patience for, usually, but I needed to learn what was going on with Violet and her granddaughter, and I didn't think I could handle questioning another old lady today.

Finally, Iris pulled herself together.

"Violet adored her granddaughter. Absolutely adored her," Iris said. "Violet's daughter—Dale's mother—died when Dale was in her teens. Well, you can just imagine what that did to their relationship."

I couldn't, but I didn't say so.

"Dale's dad was a nice fellow, but not well-off. Violet wanted nothing but the best for Dale," Iris went on. "She paid for her college, every cent of it. She even paid for

Dale to get her master's degree from Harvard. Violet flew her out for visits, took her on vacations, bought her a car—everything. Violet was there a few months ago for her graduation. She said they had a lovely time together."

"So what went wrong?" I asked.

Iris shook her head. "I don't really know. Violet wanted Dale to come to work here. Violet practically considered it her birthright, since she'd started the company alongside Mr. Dempsey. And Violet wanted Dale close to her—which was understandable. She'd paid for Dale's MBA, and I think she wanted to show her off. Violet was so proud of the way she'd turned out."

"But Dale didn't want to work here?" I asked.

"I thought she did. She filled out an application, submitted her résumé, and started the interview process," Iris said. "Then, out of the blue, the whole thing was called off."

"Dale changed her mind?" I asked.

"I suppose so, but I don't know why. Violet refused to talk about it—even to me, and we'd been friends for years," Iris said. "Violet was bitterly disappointed, and things just weren't the same between her and Dale after that."

Okay, that was a sad story, but I didn't see how it could cause Dale to kill Violet, which blew my whole the-granddaughter-did-it theory. Still, I saw no reason to give up on it.

"Do you think things were bad enough that Dale might have attacked Violet?" I asked.

Iris's eyes widened and she gasped aloud. "Oh, dear, I hadn't thought about that."

"Well . . . ?"

She shook her head. "Violet had plenty to be upset about—I mean, who doesn't working *here?*—but especially Violet. She really hadn't been herself for the last month or so before she . . . died. Still, I can't imagine she and Dale would get physically violent."

I waited for a minute or two, hoping Iris might think of something new to add, but she didn't.

"Well, thanks," I said.

Iris touched my arm and gave me a gentle smile. "It's really sweet of you to plan this service for Violet. It's the least the company can do for her, after all the years she worked here."

Iris sounded sincere, and it was nice to know somebody appreciated what I was doing.

"From everything I've heard, Violet was a really nice lady," I said. "She sure gave a lot of years to this place."

"You have no idea," Iris said softly.

She gazed off into nothing, and I guessed she was remembering Violet and some of the things they'd been through working here together. I wanted to ask her if she had any idea who might have killed Violet, but didn't. I couldn't spoil the moment, which was weird of me, I know, but there it is.

"You're here at a good time," Iris said quietly. "Things are changing. They'll be different now, with Mr. Dempsey retiring. They'll be better. Too bad those of us who hung in here for so long won't benefit from it."

"Especially Violet?" I asked.

Iris's expression hardened, as if she'd mentally shifted gears. "I have to get back to work."

She turned back to her computer, so I left.

I headed back to the Executive Unit and stopped by H.R. on the way. Adela was in her office, seated at her desk. She caught me out of the corner of her eye and waved me inside.

"I'm planning Violet's memorial service," I said. "I'd like to get the contact info for—"

Adela bolted out of her chair, her eyes all wide and

crazy, as if she'd just seen a sneak preview of the Marc Jacobs fall line or something.

"Does Mr. Dempsey know about this?" she demanded.

Jeez, was this Groundhog Day or something?

"Yes, he knows," I told her. "I'm coordinating with Ruth."

Adela just glared at me, like I'd suddenly grown another head or something.

"So anyway," I said. "I need to invite Violet's family. Can I get her granddaughter's contact info from you? She applied for a job here a couple of months ago, so it must be on her employment application."

Adela's expression soured. "Oh, yes . . . *that*."

I expected Adela to take her seat again, access a file on her computer, and e-mail me the info, but instead she pulled a folder from the bottom drawer of one of the big file cabinets, opened it, and jotted down a name and number. Like most of the older ladies here, she didn't seem all that crazy about using the latest technology.

She handed me the slip of paper without a word. I went back to my office. When I stepped inside, I froze in place again.

A huge bouquet of white roses sat on my desk, next to the yellow ones delivered earlier today.

Okay, this was weird.

I dug out the card and saw Ty's handwriting on it. It said, *Still thinking about you.*

Hum. Did he go to the florist again? Or had he just stood at the counter during his first visit and filled out both cards?

Oh well. I guess that didn't matter. Not really. Well, okay, maybe kind of. A little. No wait. It mattered a lot. I had to call Marcie immediately and get her take on it.

Just as I was reaching for my phone, the wicked witch of the west—I mean, Ruth—stormed into my office.

"Miss Randolph," she said, which came out sounding like "you idiot."

Her back was rigid and her eyes bored into me like she had X-ray vision or something.

"I specifically instructed you to have the plans for Violet Hamilton's memorial service on my desk first thing this morning," she told me. "And they weren't there."

Okay, this old gal was ticking me off big time. I'm great at confrontation—I should probably list that as an asset on my résumé—and Ruth was about to find out that my skills bordered on superpowers.

Still, I wasn't in the mood to get fired today, so I held my temper.

"The plans aren't completed yet," I told her in my I-can-be-as-big-a-bitch-as-you-can-be voice. "I have to contact Violet's family, her granddaughter, specifically, and when I've done that I'll—"

Ruth's eyes bulged. Her arms flattened against her sides. For a couple of seconds, I thought she was going to come at me.

"You will do *no such thing*." Ruth hissed the words at me through pressed lips. "This is *exactly* why you are to clear everything *with me*. This memorial service is for *employees* only. You are *not* to contact *anyone* in the family. *Anyone!*"

What was with this woman? She'd gone all crazy on me over a memorial service?

Ruth narrowed her eyes at me. "And don't even *think* about inviting former employees who have *retired*."

Okay, now I was going to definitely have to hunt up some retired employees to invite.

"Do you *understand* me?" Ruth demanded.

"It's kind of complicated, so I'm going to jot it down so I don't forget," I told her, then gestured to the tablet on my desk, which I didn't bother to pick up, of course.

We glared at each other for a few more seconds, then Ruth gave me what I guessed was the executive secretary version of stink-eye.

"Mr. Dempsey will hear about this," she told me, then whipped around and left my office.

Jeez, what was the big deal about calling Violet's granddaughter? It was the woman's memorial service. Who ever heard of a memorial service that *excluded* the family?

And why wouldn't retired employees who'd known Violet be included on the guest list? She'd probably had friends here for decades.

Ruth was sure as heck riled up about it, absolutely adamant that I not contact Dale or any of Violet's family or friends. If I did, Ruth might actually have a stroke.

Jeez, wouldn't that be a shame.

This whole memorial service was working my nerves big time. Dropping into my desk chair, I leaned back and closed my eyes, letting the delicate scent of Ty's roses wash over me, waiting for the natural therapeutic qualities of the flowers to calm me.

They didn't calm me.

My eyes popped open. I desperately needed a Snickers bar.

I rifled through the desk drawers, the file cabinet, and my purse, but came up empty. Damn. Nothing left to do but head for the vending machine in the breakroom.

Yes, I know I'd sworn not to eat chocolate anymore. But this was an emergency.

I headed down the hallway focusing on the chocolate fix that awaited me, but I couldn't get that whole don't-call-Dale thing out of my head. Okay, so maybe Ruth wouldn't want retired employees at the service, talking trash about how things were back in the day.

But why had Ruth gone off on me when I mentioned Dale? Why had she insisted I not contact anyone in the family?

It was crazy. Like having Dale at the memorial service would cause some huge problem. But what sort of problem?

I stopped in the hallway.

I definitely needed to find out.

I whipped around and went back into my office, pulled out my cell phone, and dialed the number Adela had given me for Dale.

This was better than a Snickers bar.

Almost.

CHAPTER 16

Somehow, it was still Monday.

My days of working at Dempsey Rowland, then pulling my evening shift at Holt's, made for a lot of hours in service to others—something I wasn't all that crazy about. So what could I do but compensate by taking longer breaks at Holt's?

I sat at the table in the breakroom, leafing through *People* magazine. Bella sat across from me flipping through *Elle.* Her tropical phase of hair design continued. Tonight, it looked as if a hula dancer were perched atop her head.

Around us, other employees came and went, heating up food in the microwave, eating snacks from the vending machine. A new addition to the breakroom was a television, which sat on the counter near the refrigerator, tuned to a news channel that nobody was watching.

"It's b.s.," Bella said. "Nothing but b.s., pure and simple."

At first I thought she was talking about something she'd spotted in the magazine—which, of course, I'd want to see immediately—then realized she was looking at the notices pinned to the bulletin board across the room.

"Training reviews," Bella grumbled. "Starting today."

I remembered somebody mentioning that Corporate was cracking down on training, assigning an employee to make sure we attended every butt-numbing, sleep-inducing session they came up with. And now they'd actually done it? Okay, this was really annoying.

The breakroom door swung open and Sandy walked in. She got a soda from the vending machine and sat down at the table with us.

"Have you had your b.s. training review yet?" Bella asked.

"No," Sandy said. "Your review is tonight, Haley."

I was having a training review?

"You're on the schedule," Sandy said, gesturing toward the bulletin board.

There's a schedule?

"Let us know how it goes," Sandy said.

"It'll be b.s.," Bella said. "Everything Corporate does is b.s."

Neither of us could argue with that.

"Look at those women," Bella said, gesturing toward the television. "When I finish beauty school, I'm going to run my own salon, and you're going to see all the celebrities flaunting themselves with my hairstyles. And then— hey, what the hell? Look at that."

Sandy and I both turned to the TV. A shampoo commercial was playing. A blonde with super long hair wagged her head back and forth, showing how full and lustrous it was. I'd seen this kind of advertisement a zillion times, but something looked different about this one. Something about the girl with the long hair.

Then it hit me.

"Oh my God," I said. "Is that—"

"No way," Sandy insisted.

"Yeah, it is," Bella declared.

We all sat glued to the TV set, watching the commercial run.

"It *is* her," I realized.

"Definitely," Sandy agreed.

It was that girl whose name I can never remember. She used to work here at Holt's and stink up the breakroom with those diet meals she ate all the time. She'd lost like a hundred pounds, or something, dyed her hair blond, ditched her glasses, and quit Holt's. I'd seen her modeling for a clothing print ad not long ago. And now she was in a commercial on TV?

"She looks great," Sandy said.

"I saw her last week in a Pepsi ad," Bella said. "She was holding a baby and yelling at her husband."

"Wow," Sandy said.

"I hate her," Bella said.

I hated her, too, of course.

We all just sat there for a few minutes after the commercial ended, jealous and envious but not wanting to admit to it. Then finally Sandy said, "I went shopping with my ex-boyfriend today."

Like this was supposed to cheer us up?

"Tat-guy?" Bella asked. "You went shopping with him?"

"You two broke up," I said.

"What the hell is the matter with you?" Bella asked.

"He needed my help," Sandy said. "He called and said he had to go shopping for clothes to take to Hawaii and didn't know what he should buy."

"He's going to Hawaii?" Bella asked. "Let me guess, he's taking the new girlfriend."

"I think it might be serious between them," Sandy said. "While we were in the mall, he stopped at a jewelry store and bought something."

"An engagement ring?" I asked.

"I don't know for sure," Sandy said. "I was carrying the bags and they were kind of heavy, so I sat on a bench to rest a bit."

"I'm out of here," Bella declared, and shoved to her feet. "There's only so much b.s. I can take."

I was with Bella on this one.

"Later," I said to Sandy, and left the breakroom.

I headed through the store aisles toward the shoe department, my assigned corner of retail hell for the evening. I liked working in shoes—not that I actually performed much *work* while I was there. But it wasn't my fault. Really. The shoe department had its own stock room, so what could I do but spend most of my time in there texting friends and handling my personal business?

Still, showing up in any department didn't seem all that appealing right now. Sandy had mentioned I was on the schedule to meet with the person destined to become known as the Training Nazi—not that I would ever start that kind of rumor myself, of course—so I decided to swing by the store offices and see what was up.

A position in the corporate training department monitoring training class attendance seemed pretty lame to me. I figured they must have hired somebody fresh out of college and stuck them with the job. Major yawner, if you asked me.

Personally, I was proud of my training record. Over the past few weeks I'd managed to ditch five out of the last six training sessions, thanks to my superior training avoidance tactics. I was on a hot streak, and I sure as heck wasn't going to let some corporate newbie ruin it for me.

I walked past the customer service booth and the breakroom, down the hallway where the stores offices were, and spotted—oh my God—Evelyn Croft standing outside one of the offices. She saw me at the same instant.

"Hello, Haley," Evelyn said softly. "It's nice to see you."

"What are you doing here?" I asked.

She twisted her fingers together and said, "I mentioned to you that I was going back to work."

"Yes, you did," I realized. "But I didn't know you meant here. At the *store*."

This is where the *incident* caused by *that certain some-*

one had occurred, the one that had so traumatized Evelyn that she'd made herself a prisoner in her own home for months. Prior to that, Evelyn had been an assistant department supervisor working in ILA—that's retail-speak for Intimates, Lingerie, and Accessories.

"I'm giving it a try," Evelyn said quietly.

Oh, great. With that attitude, she wouldn't last two days dealing with customers—and employees.

"Remember what we talked about at your house," I said. "If you're going to do this you have to be a little more assertive."

Evelyn drew in a breath, straightened her shoulders, and stopped twisting her fingers together.

"You're right, Haley," she said, and pushed her chin up. "And that's exactly what I'm going to do."

"Good for you," I told her.

"I'm glad to hear you say that," Evelyn said. She pointed down the hallway behind her. "Could I see you in my office?"

Evelyn had an office?

"You're on the schedule for later, but we may as well do it now," Evelyn said.

Schedule? We were supposed to *do* something?

"Aren't you working in ILA?" I asked.

"Didn't I tell you?" Evelyn asked. "I'm the corporate training supervisor. It's my job to make sure every employee has completed all of their training, as required by the corporate office."

Oh, crap.

Evelyn went inside her office and I reluctantly followed. She sat down at the desk and pulled up something on her computer.

"Let's see. According to the corporate log, you—oh dear, this can't be right." Evelyn looked up at me, stunned. "There's no record of you attending five of the last six sessions, Haley."

"You're kidding," I said, and managed to sound surprised.

It was an outright lie, but what else could I do?

Evelyn turned back to the computer, hit some keys, and looked at me again. "That's exactly what it says."

I leaned across the desk and studied the spreadsheet on the screen. Bright red filled five of the blocks next to my name.

"Obviously, there's an error in record keeping," I said.

Evelyn frowned. "This presents quite a problem."

"Not really," I said, using my what-could-be-simpler voice as I gestured to the spreadsheet. "Just plug in the info that says I attended the classes. Problem solved."

Yeah, okay, I knew I was taking advantage of Evelyn's demure nature, our friendship, and her first day on a new job. And, yeah, I knew it was awful of me. But, come on, this was five incomprehensively boring training sessions. No way could I sit through them—which was why I'd ditched them in the first place.

Evelyn sat there for a couple of minutes studying the spreadsheet and I knew she was thinking it over, weighing everything I'd done for her over these past months against five training sessions. My spirits lifted a little.

"There's only one thing to do," Evelyn finally said. "You're going to have to make up the sessions, Haley."

"What?" I might have said that louder than I meant to.

"It's the right thing to do," Evelyn insisted.

"What?" I'm sure I yelled that.

She looked up at me. "You told me that if I went back to work I would have to be firm in my decisions. Remember?"

Heck, yeah, I remembered. But I didn't think she'd use her powers for evil—against *me*.

Evelyn rose from her chair and straightened her shoulders. "I'm sorry, Haley, but you're going to have to make up those training classes. All five of them will have to be completed within the next two weeks."

"*Two weeks?*" I think I was still yelling.

"And because the classes weren't completed as scheduled," Evelyn went on, "you'll have to take a test at the end."

"A *test?*" I'm positive I was still yelling.

"If the sessions aren't completed within the designated time period, or if you don't pass all the tests, you won't be eligible for a pay raise, a promotion, or any of the corporate contests or events."

Oh my God, I don't *believe* this.

Not that I wanted a promotion, and the corporate contests and events were usually pretty lame, but I sure as heck wanted a pay raise.

"That's corporate policy," Evelyn said softly.

I just stared at her. No way could I sit through five training sessions in two weeks. Some of those sessions were three hours long—some were even longer. I couldn't do it. I absolutely couldn't.

Evelyn burst out crying.

Yikes! What happened?

"I'm so sorry, Haley, to give you this bad news," she said, tears rolling down her face. "You've been such a wonderful friend to me and now I'm forced to put you through *this*. I should never have tried to come back to work."

Oh, jeez, no.

"I should have known it would be too much for me," Evelyn insisted between sobs.

"Don't say that, Evelyn, you're doing great," I told her.

"No." She shook her head. "No."

I dashed around the desk, plucked tissues from a box sitting on the file cabinet, and pressed them into her hand.

"You're handling everything just fine," I told her as I

gently patted her shoulder. "And you're right about the training. I need to do it. Really."

Evelyn dabbed at her cheeks and continued to shake her head.

"You're doing a super job," I told her.

She sniffed, getting her tears under control. "Do you . . . do you really think so?"

"Absolutely," I said, giving her my cheerleader wanna-be smile.

"And you're really okay with making up those training sessions?" she asked.

"Of course," I told her, and waved the idea away as if it were a clearance purse at an outlet mall.

She gulped down the last of her sobs. "Thank you, Haley. You . . . you always make me feel better about things."

"I'll be in the shoe department tonight," I said. "If you get upset again, or if you need me for anything, just call."

Evelyn blinked back a fresh wave of tears. "Thank you, Haley."

I gave her one last encouraging smile and left the office.

Heading down the hallway, my heart ached a little for Evelyn. I didn't know what it was about her, but she always got to me. I was glad that I talked her into not quitting her job tonight. And I was proud of her for sticking up for the corporate policy she'd been charged with upholding.

I was still going to have to figure a way to get out of doing those training sessions, of course.

As I passed the customer service booth, I saw that the line was long, lots of customers with returns and complaints, or wanting a price adjustment on sale merchandise. Right now, the shoe department looked pretty good.

"Haley?" someone called.

Thinking it was a customer wanting actual service, or perhaps a supervisor with a problem, I kept walking.

"Haley?" the voice called again. It sounded familiar—in a good way.

I stopped and saw that it was Detective Shuman.

My heart did its usual little flip-flop—which was really bad of me, I know—as he walked over.

But his expression didn't look all that flip-flop-worthy. A knot the size of a Chanel tote jerked in my stomach.

Shuman leaned close. "We've got a problem. A big problem."

Oh, crap.

CHAPTER 17

Immediately I knew that Detective Shuman hadn't come to the store tonight to invite me to a dinner party he and his girlfriend were giving. He had on his cop face—which was kind of hot—so I figured I wouldn't be eating German food at their place anytime soon.

"Let's go somewhere," Shuman said, keeping his voice low.

I led the way past the customer service booth, through the door into the stock room. The place was quiet, as usual at this time of the night. It was chilly back here and the Hub's music track—no way you'll hear any of this stuff at the Grammy's—played softly.

"I got a phone call from Dempsey Rowland today," Detective Shuman said. "They hired a consultant to do the background investigations on the new hires."

I recalled that Max Corwin had given me that choice bit of info this morning. I hadn't thought much about it at the time, but seeing the look on Shuman's face now—yikes!—I figured this couldn't be good.

Jeez, had they already found out that my UM graduation was really the University of Mixology? How could they have learned that so quickly? Was my file the very first one they'd worked on?

Maybe so, if Detective Madison had said something to them.

Not a great feeling.

I shifted into I'm-guilty-but-I'm-going-to-look-innocent mode. Luckily, I've had lots of practice at this.

"Did they find something about Max?" I asked, thinking a little misdirection at this point couldn't hurt.

"It's not what they *found*," Shuman said. "It's what they *didn't* find."

I had no idea what he meant, but I got the feeling this would be bad for me.

I have a sixth sense about things like that.

"Your personnel file is missing," Shuman said.

Wow, was this a break for me or what? If my file wasn't there, it meant they couldn't—

Hang on a minute.

"You think I stole my own personnel file out of H.R.?" I asked. "So they couldn't do my background investigation?"

"Detective Madison is convinced you're involved in Violet Hamilton's murder," Shuman said. "He thinks you have something to hide. Is that true, Haley?"

I didn't want to lie to Shuman, so what could I do but avoid his question?

"If my file was missing, why would Madison think I took it?" I asked. "It was in the H.R. office, along with all the other new hires'."

"The others were there. Yours wasn't," Shuman said.

"It's not my fault if Adela lost it," I pointed out.

Shuman hesitated a moment, as if he needed a beat or two before delivering the next punch.

"You were seen in Adela's office. Alone. Near the personnel folders," Shuman said. "We have witnesses."

Oh my God. The day I'd been formulating my Plan B and needed contact info for Max, Tina, and Ray. I'd gone into Adela's office. But my oh-so-brilliant plan had been thwarted when Adela and Mr. Dempsey walked in.

"I didn't take my personnel folder," I told Shuman.

I saw no need to mention that I'd intended to lift info from the other new hires' folders.

"Besides," I added. "I'd e-mailed my résumé to Adela. Even if my personnel folder wasn't available, all my info would be in her inbox."

"It's not," Shuman said.

Oh, jeez. Now they thought I'd stolen my file *and* deleted my résumé from Adela's computer?

"There are a lot of older women who work there. Some of them probably aren't so great with computers—I'm sure they're still trying to figure out how to program their VCRs," I said. "Any of them could have deleted it accidentally."

"Maybe," Shuman said. "But you know how this looks."

Yeah, I knew how it looked—like I was guilty of Violet's murder and attempting to hide evidence.

This seemed like an excellent time to throw someone else under the bus, so I said, "Have you checked out Tina Sheldon?"

"Do you know something?" he asked.

"I happened to see her leaving her house on Sunday morning in a white van," I said. "She took the Five south—"

"You *happened* to see her leave? And *happened* to follow her down the Five?" he asked, giving me a don't-expect-me-to-believe-that cop look—it was way hot.

I ignored his expression—except for the way-hot part—and said, "Anyway, this morning when I saw her in the breakroom, she claimed she hadn't been out of her house all weekend."

Shuman frowned his cop frown, and I could see his mind was processing the info.

"Why would she have lied?" I asked. "Unless she was hiding something."

He nodded and I knew he'd check it out.

"Any progress in the case?" I asked. "Did you find the murder weapon, maybe? Or a suspect that's not—me?"

Shuman gave me the closest thing to a grin he could manage during a murder investigation discussion.

"A few suspects that aren't you," he said, then shifted into cop mode again. "According to the coroner, the murder weapon was a flat, blunt instrument. And, the victim's laptop is unaccounted for."

So somebody smashed Violet over the head with her own laptop. I didn't like that picture in my brain, so I pushed it aside.

A minute or so passed but Shuman didn't leave. We just stood there together in the quiet stock room. I didn't want to talk about Violet's murder investigation anymore, and I got the feeling he felt the same.

"How's the German food?" I asked.

Shuman grinned that special grin I'd seen him wear when he'd been in the store with his girlfriend while she shopped for a stand mixer. My belly got a little gooey recalling how he'd looked at Amanda that night.

Ty flashed into my head. He'd sent me flowers today—twice. That was the same as Shuman's awesome grin, wasn't it?

"German food's not so great," Shuman said, his grin getting bigger. "But the cook . . . now, she's something."

I couldn't help but smile along with Shuman, and for a few seconds—okay, more than a few—I envied Amanda.

"I'd better go," Shuman said quietly.

"Yes, you'd better," I replied.

Still, neither of us moved. We just looked at each other for a little longer, then we both bolted for the door.

"See you," Shuman called over his shoulder.

"Yeah," I answered, and headed for the shoe department.

"Surprise!" Ty shouted as I opened the door of my apartment.

I was surprised, all right. He must have been watching for me to return from my shift at Holt's—which was unusual—plus, he was smiling from ear to ear and that was *way* unusual. Ty almost never smiled.

My spirits lifted, seeing him in such a good mood. I'd had a really long day and figured a quiet evening snuggling with Ty was the perfect way to end it.

"I bought you something," he declared, his smile growing even wider.

Visions of emeralds, sapphires, and rubies flashed in my mind. Or maybe a—oh my God, the Temptress tote I'd been dying for!

"Close your eyes," Ty said.

He took my hand and led me inside my apartment. My heart raced. I couldn't remember whether I'd told him about wanting the sizzling hot Temptress, but even if he didn't get me that, jewelry would be fantastic. Or maybe cruise tickets. Oh, wow, that would be awesome. I'd need new bathing suits, of course, along with sun block and sandals. Sundresses. Oh my God, I'd need so many sundresses. And shorts, of course, with—

"Okay, open your eyes," Ty announced.

My eyes sprang open.

"Ta-da!" Ty gestured grandly to a—oh my God, it was a television.

What the hell?

A huge television, and I mean super huge, was bolted to a wall. It looked like one of those old drive-in movie screens.

The artwork I'd had there was stacked in a corner next

to my TV and stand, which he'd moved out of the way. A ripped-up brown box and packing materials were scattered all over the room, and my chairs were pushed back.

"After being here so much, I realized you needed an updated TV," Ty said proudly. "This one's got everything. All the bells and whistles. The latest technology."

I opened my mouth to speak, but nothing came out.

"Look, it's got six speakers for the highest quality sound," Ty said, pointing.

Wires and cables snaked out from behind the television, up the wall, and around the room to speakers that he'd mounted high in the corners. Everything was held in place with—oh my God, that was duct tape.

"And look at this remote," he announced as he pulled it out of his pocket like a gunslinger in a high-noon walkdown. "Impressive, huh?"

The thing was huge, black with shiny silver buttons.

It looked like a pay phone.

"Do you like it?" Ty asked, with that puppy dog I-already-know-you-love-it expression on his face.

Oh my God. My apartment. My fabulous apartment that I'd worked months—and maxed out an impressive number of credit cards—to decorate. I'd shopped relentlessly—retail stores, vintage shops, outlet malls, catalogs—to select just the right colors, accent pieces, and furniture. And now it looked like the showroom at Honest Bob's Discount TVs For Less or something.

But Ty looked so proud and so happy, and he'd gone to a lot of work—and expense. I couldn't ruin it for him.

"It's—" My throat closed off. I coughed and tried again. "It's great. I love it."

Ty threw his arms around me and pulled me tight against him. He held me like that for a minute, then stepped back.

"Let me show you how this bad-boy works," he said, and dropped onto the couch with the remote.

I stepped over a mound of packing paper and sat down beside him. He flipped channels, pointed, explained things, and I hung in there pretty well. But when he got out the manual and started reading aloud, I had to stop him.

"That's enough for now." I'm pretty sure I shouted that, but Ty didn't notice because the TV volume was turned up so loud.

He muted the sound and nodded. "You've had a long day. How's the new job?"

I'd never gotten around to telling Ty that I was an actual suspect in the murder of Violet Hamilton, and I saw no need to mention that now I was accused of hiding evidence as well. So I went with the safest topic I could think of.

"I talked to someone in the contracting department today," I said.

"That's where you were assigned when you were hired," Ty said.

I guess I shouldn't have been surprised that he remembered that little bit of info. Ty's way smart, and he has an awesome memory.

"I hoped I could get some info on what exactly contracting does," I said. "But Beatrice seemed a little reluctant to divulge much."

"They'll tell you everything after you get your security clearance," Ty said. "But it's pretty straightforward. Dempsey Rowland is a civilian company that bids on government contracts for big construction projects. They build post offices, government buildings, infrastructure. They do lots of jobs overseas in places like Russia, Oman, Kuwait, Iraq, Indonesia—most everywhere, really."

See how smart Ty is? He knows everything.

Jeez, why didn't I think to ask him in the first place?

"The bidding is very competitive," Ty said. "There's lots of oversight by the government. That's why the contract department is so important. Dempsey Rowland, and companies like it, has to be extremely careful that they adhere to the exact terms of the contract. It's the government's money they're fooling around with."

"But there are always those news stories about fraud, waste, and abuse in government spending," I said.

"True," Ty said. "But in the case of these government contractors, if things get screwed up, the government won't let them bid on projects anymore. That means that places like Dempsey Rowland would be done. Out of business."

Yikes! And I was supposed to work in that department and make sure that didn't happen?

Ty shrugged. "It's a good company, and a good place to start your career, but I don't see you working there for long. But with that experience, you'll be able to work most anyplace. Procurement specialists and sub-contract administrators are always in demand."

Yuck. This job was sounding worse and worse.

Maybe I should just confess that my alma mater was really the University of Mixology and get a fun job bartending at a cool club somewhere.

Ty grinned at me. "Knowing how you like to buy things, it's a natural job for you."

My spirits lifted. I'd buy things? That's what the job was all about?

"Every company has to buy things," Ty said. "Hotel chains, cruise lines, movie studios, theme parks. And department stores, of course."

Oh, wow. I could work at one of those cool places? Buying things? With the experience I'd gain working in the Dempsey Rowland contract department?

My thoughts raced ahead. Maybe I could work at someplace really fantastic like Universal Studios or Disneyland—or maybe even Neiman Marcus. I could spend my workdays buying thousands—no millions—of dollars' worth of merchandise. Talk about the ultimate shopping experience.

My brain locked up, and a feeling of horror swept over me—sort of like when you spot the perfect bag in the Nordstrom display case and realize you don't have quite enough credit left on your Visa card.

To get one of those fabulous jobs meant I'd have to keep my job at Dempsey Rowland. And to do that, I'd have to pass my security check and get clear of this murder accusation.

Impossible? Maybe not.

Stranger things had happened.

The person doing my background investigation might not look all that deep, or might not question what the "UM" I'd put on my résumé actually stood for. I'm mean, jeez, you're always hearing those news reports about a guy who'd never been to medical school working for a big hospital as a doctor, or a lawyer who'd faked her credentials after graduating from community college. It could happen to me, right?

"Anything new on the murder investigation?" Ty asked.

"I ran into Shuman at the store tonight," I said.

I saw no need to mention he'd come there specifically to ask me if I was impeding the investigation by hiding evidence.

"Detective Shuman." Ty nodded thoughtfully. "Detective Madison's partner."

Ty had met both of them a few months back when they'd investigated deaths at the Holt's store.

"Shuman said they have some leads," I said. Then, anxious to change the subject, I said, "He was in the store a few days ago with his girlfriend. She was experimenting with German food and mentioned having a dinner party."

"Would you like to go?" he asked.

"Sounds like fun."

Ty was quiet for a couple of minutes, then gave me a big smile.

Oh, jeez, what now?

"I have another surprise," he said.

I considered bolting for the door, but he took my hand and led me into the kitchen.

"Ta-da!" he said, pointing to a huge metal box sitting on the counter.

Okay, so maybe this wouldn't be so bad.

"You bought a tool box?" I asked.

"No," he said. "It's your lunch box."

My—what?

"I know you're working diligently to stick with your new plan to eat healthier, and I know it's hard to find nutritious food when you're in an office all day," Ty explained. "So I'm going to pack your lunch for you."

He was going to—what?

"Every day," he promised. "You'll never have to be tempted by chocolate or chips or any of that junk food in the vending machines again."

Oh, great.

CHAPTER 18

It was fruit and fiber day, apparently.

I gazed into the lunch box Ty had proudly presented to me on my way out of my apartment this morning. Inside was a variety of fruits and nuts, along with packages of things that were purported to be food and that probably tasted like shredded shoe boxes.

Yuck.

Not that I didn't appreciate all the trouble Ty had gone to. He'd been thoughtful and considerate helping with my whole-new-me plan. Just the sort of thing an involved, committed, devoted boyfriend should do.

I guess. Ty had never been an involved, committed, devoted boyfriend before.

I stashed the lunch box under my desk and sat back in my chair. I'd spent most of the morning doing actual work, so I figured I was due a little me-time.

True, in the past Ty hadn't been the kind of boyfriend I wanted, and he'd known that. He'd explained—more times than I wanted to hear—that his position at Holt's made it impossible for him to be the sort of boyfriend I deserved.

So now he was doing that—or at least he was being the kind of boyfriend he thought I wanted. But he'd been so different lately I couldn't help but wonder what the heck was going on.

Was it just that he'd had a scary wake-up call after his car accident? Or was something else happening?

That whole thing about him canceling his appointments, renting a car, changing clothes at a convenience store, then going to Palmdale for no known reason still bothered me.

I didn't know what he had been doing with his days, since he wasn't going to Holt's now. He never gave me any real info when I asked. I figured that he deserved some downtime. He'd been running Holt's twenty-four-seven for years so it was okay to sit around and do nothing—although I did hope that today he'd clean up that mess he'd left in my living room.

I got up from my desk chair and picked up my purse—a stunning Marc Jacobs satchel. I desperately needed to have lunch with Marcie today. Ty's whole world's-best-boyfriend thing was starting to work my nerves ever so slightly, and I needed her advice.

But today I had other lunch plans. I left my office.

I recognized Dale Winslow right away. As I walked up to the outdoor café on Figueroa Street where she'd agreed to meet me after I'd phoned her yesterday, I spotted her at one of the tables, the only woman there alone.

Even seated, I could see she was tall and willowy with long legs and arms. I figured her for about my age. She had light brown hair and blue eyes, and she wore denim capris, a white shirt, and a gauzy coverup teamed with chunky jewelry that gave her casual look an air of sophistication. Hanging on the back of her chair was a—oh my God, she had a Temptress tote. Immediately, I knew we'd be BFFs.

"Dale?" I asked, as I approached the table.

She smiled up at me. "Haley?"

"I love your bag," I said. I might have moaned when I said that.

Dale threw a quick glance at my satchel—jeez, was I ever glad I'd armed myself with a Marc Jacobs today—and touched her Temptress tote.

"I picked it up just this morning," she said. "You wouldn't believe what I went through to get it."

"Tell me," I said, and dropped into the chair facing her. "And don't leave out *anything.*"

"I was on a waiting list for weeks," Dale said. "When the sales clerk called this morning, I rushed to the store only to be told there had been a mix-up and they'd given my bag to someone else."

"Oh, no!" I imagined the devastating pain she must have experienced at that moment, and my own heart ached.

"I told the clerk that I'd come there to get a Temptress, and I wasn't leaving without one," Dale told me. "So I went to the stock room myself and took one off the shelf."

Oh, yeah. Dale and I would be BFs *forever.*

She smiled. "By that time the clerk had called her supervisor and we were all in the stock room together. They said I could buy it—"

"Like you'd leave without it," I said.

"Exactly," Dale agreed. She patted the tote again and smiled. "So I have a Temptress."

"Which store was it?" I asked.

"Nordstrom at The Grove," she said.

I made a mental note to go there immediately after work. If they had them in stock, I'd get one—no matter what.

The waiter appeared and I was relieved when Dale ordered a tuna sandwich. That meant I could order something decent to eat, instead of a crappy salad I always felt forced to eat when dining with other females.

"Sorry about your grandmother," I said, figuring it was time to get down to business.

Grief tightened Dale's expression. "It's been awful. Just awful."

The waiter brought the ice teas we'd ordered. I stirred in two sugars, rather than the substitutes—just to keep my brain functioning at peak level, of course.

"Grandma devoted her life to Dempsey Rowland," Dale said. "I never thought she'd actually be murdered there."

"Everybody I've talked to said Violet was the backbone of the company," I said. "Any idea who'd want to hurt her?"

Dale shrugged. "Let's face it, when you work anywhere, you're going to make enemies as well as friends. But I don't know of anyone who'd push it this far."

Our sandwiches came. The waiter fussed over us for another minute or so, then left

"You two were close?" I asked, even though I already knew the answer, and bit into my sandwich.

"Very," Dale said, and managed a little smile. "Grandma was the best. She stepped up like you wouldn't believe after my mom died. She pushed me, which I didn't like at the time, of course, but I'm glad she did. She paid for my private school, college, everything."

"I heard that Violet wanted you to work for Dempsey Rowland with her," I said.

I'd been told there was a big blowup between Violet and Dale over the whole thing. Office gossip has a way of getting stretched out of shape sometimes—not that I would ever do that, of course—so I wanted Dale's take on it.

"Oh, that." Dale rolled her eyes and put her sandwich down. "I thought the job was a lock—and so did Grandma. She was livid when it fell through."

"You mean Dempsey Rowland refused to hire you?" I asked.

Dale started in on her sandwich again. "I'd just graduated from Harvard with my MBA, but I had no work experience. Maybe that was it."

Okay, this was weird. I'd been hired just a few months after Dale had been rejected. She had an MBA from Harvard. I had a BA—supposedly—from University of Michigan. Dale had a recommendation from a founder of the company. I'd been referred by a friend of a friend.

"Grandma wanted me to sue," Dale said.

"Sue Dempsey Rowland?" I asked. "Her own company?"

"It wouldn't have been the first time they'd been sued," she said.

"Couldn't Violet get Mr. Dempsey to step in on your behalf when H.R. turned you down?" I asked.

"I guess not," Dale said.

Okay, that was even weirder.

"Grandma was adamant that I bring suit, but I didn't want to. It hardly seemed the best way to start my career. You know how these company bigwigs talk at their lunches and golf games," Dale said. "I didn't want to get a bad reputation before I even got a job—not that I've had any offers yet."

"You're still not working?" I asked, a little surprised. "You seem like just the kind of person any company would want."

"I'm sending out résumés every day," Dale said. "I wanted to stay here in L.A. to be close to Grandma, but now, well, I guess it doesn't matter."

We were quiet for a few minutes, neither of us interested in finishing our lunches.

"It's good that you're doing the memorial service for Grandma. I'm surprised, frankly, that the company is allowing it," Dale said. "But I don't want to attend. Getting through the funeral was hard enough."

"I understand," I said. Then, for some odd reason, Ty popped into my head. "Listen, my boyfriend runs Holt's Department Stores—yeah, I know the clothes are awful— but he's a Harvard grad, too, so if you'd like, I'll mention you to him."

Her eyes widened. "That would be great."

"E-mail me your résumé," I said, and we both whipped out our cell phones and entered each other's info. Dale sent me her résumé.

"Thank you so much, Haley. I really appreciate this," she said. "Oh, listen. Have you contacted any of the Dempsey Rowland retirees about the memorial service?"

"Not yet," I said.

"A number of Grandma's longtime friends retired in the past year or so. She stayed in touch with almost all of them," Dale said. "You should call Erma Pomeroy. She was one of the first people hired after the company was founded. She and Grandma were really close. Erma worked in payroll so she knew everybody who worked at the company. She can give you a list of names to invite."

Dale scrolled through her phone and e-mailed Erma Pomeroy's number to me.

"Thanks for meeting me," I said. "Lunch is on me."

I passed the waiter my Dempsey Rowland corporate card. I figured the company would want to pay for Dale's lunch—and mine, of course—since her grandmother had been killed there. Right? Well, okay, maybe not. But I was doing it anyway.

We said good-bye and, as I headed back to work, I sent Ty an e-mail about Dale and attached her résumé.

I was feeling really great about doing a good deed and was considering treating myself to a Starbucks as I stepped off the elevator on the fifth floor.

The reception area was crowded with about a dozen men in suits, typical for early afternoon when so many employees were headed out for lunch, or just returning. A

FedEx guy stood at the reception desk zapping a stack of packages with his handheld computer.

"Haley?" Camille called from behind her reception desk.

I kept walking but the lobby was packed, slowing my escape.

"Haley?" Camille called, louder this time. "There's someone here to see you."

Just then, a really hot-looking guy in a tuxedo rose from one of the lobby chairs. He was a little younger than me, maybe, with jet black hair, a strong chin, and killer blue eyes. He must have been one of those men who spend their every waking moment in the gym because he had a smoking hot body—not that I really noticed or anything, since I have an official boyfriend who was devoting himself to me completely.

"Haley Randolph?" the guy asked, looking at me.

A few of the men standing in the lobby gave him the eye also.

"Yes," I said.

"This is from Ty," he announced. He picked up a guitar from a case lying on the floor, and started singing "Close to You."

What the heck?

He sang—loud.

He played his guitar—loud.

All the men in the lobby stopped and stared. The FedEx guy turned to look. Camille leaned across the reception desk to get a better view.

Oh my God, what was this guy doing?

Heat swept up my back—and not because he looked so hot.

From the corner of my eye, I saw three more men venture out of their offices down the hallway and stare.

Tuxedo guy kept singing.

I felt my cheeks turn red and—and, oh, jeez, what if I perspired in my new suit?

The song dragged on with tuxedo guy belting out lyrics about birds showing up, stars crashing down, moon dust and starlight—or something. I don't know, it was all too humiliating to comprehend.

Finally—thank God—the song ended. The singer whipped a single red rose from inside his guitar case and presented it to me with a flourish.

"Ty wants you to know he's thinking of you," he said.

"Great," I mumbled, then snatched the rose from his hand and hurried back to my office.

When I got there, I dashed inside and slammed the door, ready to—oh, jeez, not again.

A large arrangement of red roses sat on my desk, wedged between the white and yellow bouquets Ty had already sent. Good grief, my office was starting to look like a mortuary.

I shoved the single red rose into the bouquet and plopped down at my desk. The whole incident had been more embarrassing than anything. I knew Ty meant well, but, jeez, couldn't he do something more private?

I knew I should call and thank him for the flowers and the singer, but I couldn't quite bring myself to do it yet. Then my office door burst open and I wished I had.

Darth Vader—I mean Ruth—stomped over to my desk.

"I received your memo on the memorial service," she said, and pursed her lips as if she'd just tasted something bad. "It is adequate—barely."

Before I'd left for lunch, I'd taken a copy to her office. She was gone so I had left it on her desk. I'd thought about e-mailing it to her, but even though I'd heard she had a laptop, I wasn't sure she used it all that often. When I saw her desk I figured I'd done the right thing. No sign of the laptop, but I did see Mr. Dempsey, who gave me triple-stink-eye, like he thought I might steal something.

Now, with Ruth being such a snot, I wished I'd held onto it a little longer.

"Since getting this information was so difficult," Ruth said, "I'm going to have to follow up more closely with you on Mr. Dempsey's event."

Mr. Dempsey was having an event?

"Absolutely nothing can be left to chance," Ruth declared. "Every aspect of the event must be carefully orchestrated. It is the premier moment in Mr. Dempsey's entire career and must be treated as such."

Oh, crap. His retirement party. I'd forgotten all about it.

No way was I telling Ruth that, though.

Instantly I channeled my mom—thank goodness she's occasionally useful for something—and shifted to you-can't-out-bitch-me mode.

"First of all, Ruth," I said, "you aren't my supervisor, so you have no business insinuating yourself into anything corporate events does."

Her eyes bulged and her face turned red.

"Second of all," I went on, "everything involving Mr. Dempsey's retirement party is being handled with the care and attention it deserves. When—and if—I require anything from you, I will let you know."

Ruth narrowed her eyes at me and squeezed her lips so tight I thought her face might implode—which, by the way, would have improved her looks considerably.

"See that you do," she hissed, then stomped out of my office.

I collapsed in my chair.

Oh my God. That stupid retirement party. How was I going to pull it off? I had no idea what Constance had or hadn't done because everything was still locked in her office, sealed shut by the LAPD crime scene tape.

Oh, crap.

CHAPTER 19

"Haley? Haley Randolph?"

I looked up from my desk and saw a guy in a sharp looking suit standing in my doorway. I put him at late twenties, maybe thirty already, tall, with dark hair spiked up above a Homer Simpson forehead.

My Holt's training kicked in and I wanted to bolt for the door, but he was blocking the way, trapping me in my own office.

I hate it when that happens.

"Yes," I mumbled.

"Haley! Oh, good gracious! I heard the singer mention your name. It's so great to meet you—finally!" He rushed toward me, his hand outstretched. "I'm Jerry Spicer. Sarah's friend."

Thank goodness. Somebody who was genuinely friendly. I rose from my chair and shook his hand.

"You're Sarah Covington's friend," I realized. "You got me the job here."

He modestly waved away my words. "Oh, shoot. All I did was recommend you to H.R. after Sarah contacted me. Your qualifications got you the job!"

"Well, thank you," I said.

"I can't believe they brought you on board so quickly," Jerry said. He chuckled. "You're leading the force, my dear. Forging ahead, changing the face of Dempsey Row-land—which it desperately needs, of course."

"Wow, I didn't know I was doing all of that," I said.

"You sure are. Out with the old, in with the new—or the young, I should say," he declared. "And, listen, don't you give a thought to all those lawsuits. All that's coming to an end now. Everybody says so."

"Lawsuits?" I asked.

Jerry waved away my words. "Hey, listen. The company is finally moving into the twenty-first century. With all these old folks heading for retirement, we will actually have a staff that can send an e-mail—with an attachment!"

Jerry laughed at his joke and I laughed, too. Not a lot of funny moments here at Dempsey Rowland.

But I doubted the staff here at Dempsey Rowland was quite that bad with computers. Sure, many of the women I'd seen here were older. While I doubted many of them were downloading iTunes or checking out YouTube, I was sure they were all comfortable enough with the technology it took to do their jobs.

"I've got to run," Jerry said. "We'll have lunch some-time. Promise."

Thanks to Jerry, I skated through the afternoon in a pretty good mood. I ordered cakes and balloons for next week's birthday club recipients, and made reservations for three upcoming luncheons. Since I was in such a generous frame of mind, I decided the contracting department ought to have lunch on Dempsey Rowland tomorrow, and since I hoped to one day work over there, I figured it wouldn't do any harm to ingratiate myself to them. I sent out an e-mail announcing the luncheon, then phoned the deli down on 8th Street and ordered sandwich trays, sal-ads, drinks, and three kinds of desserts.

Yeah, okay, all of that was good for office morale, team spirit, and the other b.s. management was always yammering on about. But the real reason I did all that was because I didn't want to come out of my office.

What if somebody saw me and asked about the singing tuxedo guy Ty had sent? I just didn't want to get into it with anyone. Honestly, it wasn't the type of incident I wanted to have define my role here at Dempsey Rowland.

Not that I didn't appreciate Ty's efforts, of course. But still.

I sat at my desk breathing in the scent of three dozen roses, the refrain from "Close to You" still stuck in my head.

Ty claimed he would devote himself to being the kind of boyfriend I wanted, the kind I deserved. Did he really think flowers and a singer were *me*?

Something else kept rattling around in my head. Lawsuits.

Jerry had mentioned them earlier, so had Dale. So what was going on that the company kept getting sued?

A lot of big companies were the target of frivolous lawsuits. It kept law firms in business. But from what I'd heard, this seemed like more than your usual petty grievances.

There was one way to find out what was going on. From my days at Pike Warner, I knew attorneys had access to every lawsuit that had ever been filed. Just why such a database existed, I didn't know. Maybe it was a we're-already-suing-so-back-off warning, or it could have been a hey-the-more-the-merrier-let's-all-pile-on sort of thing.

Jack Bishop could find out for me. Jeez, I owed him so many favors now. I wondered when he'd expect me to repay him.

I mean that in the most platonic way, of course.

I pulled out my cell phone and called him. He answered on the first ring.

"You need a favor," Jack said.

I heard soft music and highway noise in the background

and figured he was in his Land Rover somewhere, doing
something way cooler than planning luncheons and buying birthday club balloons.

"So you're a mind reader now?" I asked.

"Good thing you're not," he said, using his Barry White
voice.

A little tremor went through me. My toes curled.

"I'll catch up with you later," Jack said, using his business voice once again.

"Okay, I'll be at the—"

"I'll find you," Jack said, and hung up.

I sat there for another minute holding my phone—
which seemed to have heated up a few thousand degrees
or something—then glanced at my watch. It was 4:45.

Close enough.

I got my purse and left.

Visions of the Temptress bag danced in my head as I got
off the elevator in the parking garage and headed for my
car.

Thanks to my disregard for the established hours of operation at Dempsey Rowland—which I'm sure were flexible; well, kind of flexible—I could get to Nordstrom at
The Grove ahead of everyone else ending their workday
and get the jump on those Temptress totes waiting in their
stock room to be claimed.

Yes, I knew they were intended for other women higher
up on the waiting list than me. Yes, I knew I should wait
my turn. And, yes, I knew that would be the decent thing
to do.

But it wasn't going to happen.

If Dale could get a Temptress bag, so could I.

As I got in my car, I noticed that I wasn't the only one
slipping away a little early today. About a dozen parking
spaces down, I saw Max Corwin get into his minivan. Not

a flashy ride, but I figured he needed the seats for all those kids of his.

I backed out of the space and followed Max out of the garage.

Of course, the sales clerks at Nordstrom were highly trained and excellent at their jobs. For me to waltz into their handbag department and lay claim to a Temptress would take some finesse on my part.

I'm not great at finesse.

But I'm great at confrontation and, really, most of the time that worked better than finesse.

As I approached the freeway entrance, I noticed that Max's blue minivan was a couple of cars ahead of me. I intended to pull up alongside of him, give him a little toot and a wave, and be gone.

But Max took the northbound entrance ramp, which was odd. He should have headed south to get to his home in El Segundo. Maybe he had a doctor's appointment or something equally dull.

Tina flashed in my mind. I'd thought she was seeing family or shopping when I'd followed her down the 5, then turned back. Maybe that's exactly what she'd been doing, but since she'd lied to me about spending her weekend at home with sick kids, it had made me suspicious.

Immediately I shifted into private detective mode, swung onto the northbound freeway entrance, and followed Max.

Traffic was bumper-to-bumper, creeping along at the usual L.A. afternoon slow crawl. I kept thinking Max would exit the freeway at any moment, but he kept going, putting The Grove, Nordstrom, and the soon-to-be-mine Temptress bag farther behind me. Following him was really boring—maybe I should limit tailing a suspect to twisting mountain roads in a vintage Mustang Shelby, somehow—but I didn't want to give up, as I had with Tina.

Yet this hardly needed my full concentration. I plugged in my Bluetooth and called Marcie.

"You're not going to believe what Ty did," I blurted out as soon as she answered.

Marcie didn't even respond. She knew there was no reason to, as a best friend would.

"He sent a guy in a tuxedo to the office today who played the guitar and sang 'Close to You' to me," I said.

"He did—what?"

"In the lobby. In front of dozens of people," I said.

"That sappy old Carpenters' song?" she asked. "Not good."

"And Ty's already sent me three huge bouquets of roses," I said. "My office looks like the *American Idol* green room."

"Sounds like he's trying to be a good boyfriend," Marcie said, sounding reasonable.

I hate it when other people are reasonable.

"Yes, I know," I agreed. "But what on earth made Ty think I'd want my boyfriend to do this kind of thing?"

"Did you tell him?" she asked.

Okay, now she'd completely lost me.

"Tell him what?" I asked.

"Did you tell Ty what kind of boyfriend you want?"

"Well—" I stopped, realizing she was right.

I hate it when other people are right.

"Ty never asked," I told her. "He just assumed he already knew."

"You still should have told him, Haley, a long time ago," Marcie said.

Okay, now she was starting to get on my nerves.

"You have to admit," Marcie said, "that you seldom really talk to Ty. You never tell him what's going on with you."

Yeah, now I was really irritated.

"You should ask yourself why that is," Marcie said. "I mean, if you and Ty are meant to be together, like you think you are, why wouldn't you tell him everything that's going on with you? He should be the first one you tell. The one you run to when things go bad."

Marcie was making way too much sense at the moment.

"Your call is breaking up," I said to Marcie. I killed the connection and yanked the Bluetooth out of my ear.

I know that was a crappy thing to do, but, jeez, you call a friend for a little sympathy and she ends up telling you the truth—which was the very last thing I was prepared for.

I changed lanes, just to distract myself from my own thoughts, and saw that Max's minivan was about four cars ahead of me. No way would he get out of my sight, with traffic chugging along at jogging speed.

I switched on the radio and tried to sing along with Madonna's "Material Girl," but even that couldn't keep me distracted from my own thoughts.

My chest felt heavy—kind of like when someone dies—and tears threatened. As much as I didn't want to admit it, Marcie was right—Marcie was almost always right. Ty and I seldom talked—*really* talked. I kept things from him. I didn't share much of anything more than my desire for the latest handbag. I never *ran* to him when I was upset. Most of the time I even forgot to tell him when something good happened.

This definitely said something about our relationship. But what?

Well, really I knew what.

Ahead of me, Max started working his way over to the right-hand lane so I did the same. I figured his exit was coming up. I followed as we transitioned to the westbound 118. Traffic lightened up a bit as we headed toward Simi Valley.

My spirits lifted a little when I followed Max onto the Tampa Avenue off ramp and turned left, because I knew the Northridge mall was nearby.

Maybe Max was going shopping. Maybe he intended to

do nothing more incriminating than hit a couple of stores, then go home. That meant I could do a little shopping my- self—plus check out Macy's for a Temptress.

But Max turned right into a residential neighborhood before we got to the mall.

Darn. I hate it when that happens.

At this point, I figured Max was just visiting a friend or relative and the chances of me pulling up to the place and seeing evidence of Violet's murder lying on the lawn were pretty slim. Still, I'd come this far so I stuck with it.

A couple of blocks later, Max hung a left, then swung into the driveway of a house halfway down the block. The minivan paused, then the garage door rolled up. Max pulled inside. The door came down.

Okay, that was weird.

My wanna-be private detective instincts kicked into high gear. I drove slowly past the house. At the corner, I hung a U and drove back, then pulled against the curb on the opposite side of the street.

The house Max had entered looked just like all the other homes here. The neighborhood was well established, the houses probably thirty years old, the kind of place where couples hunkered for the long haul of raising their kids. SUVs and minivans lined the street and filled drive- ways. Bikes, tricycles, and toys were scattered across the front lawns.

I watched the windows, thinking maybe I could spot Max or someone else and figure out what was going on there. But the blinds were closed so I figured he'd gone into the kitchen on the back of the—

Wait a minute.

Hanging by the front door was one of those wooden signs with the names of the family members carved into it. I'd seen one of those before, just recently, I realized. It was hanging by the front door of Max's house in El Segundo.

This one looked just like it except that the names were different.

I locked my gaze onto the sign. The names read Max, Melanie, Misty, Mace, Miles.

I fell back in my seat, trying desperately to come up with some reasonable explanation. But I couldn't. All I could figure was that—oh my God—Max had *two* families.

That sure as heck was a good reason to change jobs every year or so, as Detective Shuman had told me Max had done. It was one whale of a reason to be concerned about a background investigation.

And an excellent motive for murder.

CHAPTER 20

"You want me to—"
I couldn't get the words out.
I tried again.
"You're suggesting that I—"
The words hung in my throat. They wouldn't come out.
I gave it another try.
"You think that I should—"
Forget it.

I stared down at Evelyn seated behind her desk in the Holt's office. I couldn't—*could not*—believe what she had just said to me. If it had been anybody but Evelyn, I might have gone across the desk after her like a spider monkey.

I mean, jeez, I'd worked all day at Dempsey Rowland, given up my chance to claim—yeah, okay, some other woman's—Temptress tote at Nordstrom, to follow Max Corwin out to Northridge.

And now *this?*

"Remember? At your training review, we talked about how you'd missed several of the training sessions," Evelyn said, sounding completely reasonable, "and your need to make them up on a timely basis."

Yeah, I knew Evelyn had mentioned it, but I didn't think she really *meant* it.

I am, after all, *me.*

"So, as I said, I worked out a schedule that will allow you to complete your missed sessions quickly," Evelyn explained.

She pointed to the computer printout she'd placed on the desk a few minutes ago, the one that had rendered me momentarily speechless.

"Since you missed the facilitator-led, in-store sessions, you can use the CBT version," Evelyn said, then added, "That's computer based training."

Which was code for clear-the-room-of-sharp-objects-because-a-suicide-attempt-was-likely.

Evelyn gestured to yet another printout. "I've set everything up so you can do the CBT training this weekend. That means you'll work a full eight hours on Saturday and on Sunday."

Eight hours—for two straight days—isolated alone in a room, reading the Holt's policies and procedures. Nobody to talk to. No way to slip away for candy—just to keep my energy level up, of course.

"And don't forget, you'll have a test at the end of each segment," Evelyn said.

A test? Yikes! That meant I'd have to actually pay attention to what I was reading—and remember it. How was I supposed to text my friends and update my Facebook page under those conditions?

Evelyn gave me a kind smile. "I know this is a taxing schedule. So don't worry if you don't pass some of the tests. You can continue the training sessions into next week, if need be."

More of this? Into next week? Was this nightmare ever going to end?

No way—*no way*—could I sit through this.

"Actually, Evelyn," I said, and managed to sound calm and self-assured, "the other clerks who went through the training told me everything about it. Absolutely everything. I feel completely confident that I'm up to speed on all the new policies and procedures."

"I'm so glad all the employees are sharing information," Evelyn said with a broad smile. The corners of her mouth turned down. "But everyone must go through the training and learn the material firsthand. That way, there is no misunderstanding or misinterpretation."

I didn't want to get rough with Evelyn, but I couldn't just sit here and let this happen.

I tried another tactic.

"As much as I appreciate Holt's desire to keep every employee well trained—"

I almost gagged when I said that.

"I just don't feel right not being on the sales floor. Rita is such a conscientious cashiers' supervisor. I can't leave her shorthanded," I said.

My temples started to throb.

"And I certainly don't want to diminish the high standards of service Holt's is known for, by not being available to help customers," I said.

My right eye began twitching.

"I understand completely," Evelyn said. "But you must go through the training, Haley. I've already had your schedule approved by the corporate office."

No. No, no, no. There *had* to be a way out of this.

Maybe I could get some sort of special dispensation. Or a waiver. Maybe I could bribe someone. Yeah, that might work.

Under normal circumstances, I wouldn't even consider doing something like that, but these weren't normal circumstances. We were talking about training. That elevated the situation to a whole other level. Desperate measures were called for.

Maybe I could have sex with someone at Corporate.

Hang on a minute.

I was already having sex with someone at Corporate.

Oh my God. Ty. I could just have him sign a waiver and—poof!—this whole training thing would go away.

Whew!

"Thanks so much for working out the training schedule for me," I said, rising from my chair. "I really appreciate everything."

Evelyn smiled. "You're very welcome, Haley."

I left the office.

I love being me.

I left Holt's feeling pretty darn good about myself. Yeah, okay, maybe it was kind of crappy for me to get out of the training when all the other employees had to endure it, but I didn't see anything wrong with special treatment—as long as it benefited me, of course.

I walked into the near-empty parking lot with the other employees. Only a few cars were left. The security lights had been cut back—Holt's claimed it was to reduce their carbon footprint, but I'm pretty sure they were more concerned about their electric bill.

My spirits lifted a little when I saw a man standing beside my car. His back was to me, but I knew it was Jack Bishop. I'd called him earlier and he'd said he would find me. It was way cool—but I wished he could have found me in some hot club looking hot, instead of here at Holt's.

"Hey, you found me," I called, as I walked up.

He turned around. I froze.

Oh my God. It wasn't Jack. It was Mike Ivan.

How had he found me here? How did he know I worked at this Holt's store? Did he know absolutely everything about me?

Mike gave me a hint of a grin.

"I didn't want to scare you this time," he said.

Like having a maybe-connected-to-the-Russian-mob guy even knowing who I was *wouldn't* be scary?

I forced myself to calm down.

"I got you the information you asked about," Mike said.

It took me a minute to recall that I'd asked Mike about checking for a Russian or Romanian connection to Juanita's disappearance. My concern for Juanita zapped me.

"What did you find out?" I asked. "Is Juanita okay?"

He shook his head. "I got nothing. Whatever happened to your friend, it has nothing to do with any of my distant—and I emphasize *distant*—associates."

I felt a little let down. Of course, I was glad Juanita hadn't been kidnapped by some crazy Romanian band of gypsies or the Russian mob, but if something like that hadn't befallen her, where was she? What had happened to her?

"Listen, Mike," I said. "I really appreciate this. Sincerely I do."

"You want me to look somewhere else?" he asked.

I shook my head. "I can't think where else to check. I've called all the usual places—hospitals, police, morgues—and gotten nothing."

We were quiet again while I ran the list of places to look for Juanita through my head. I didn't come up with anything new. In fact, I was stumped.

"Sorry I couldn't help," Mike said.

"Thanks, Mike," I said.

We just looked at each other for a few more seconds.

"We're even now," I said. "Favors swapped. We're square."

He hesitated a minute, then nodded. "Sounds right to me."

Mike walked away through the darkened parking lot, and disappeared into the shadows.

Twin high-beam headlights hit me and I spotted a big car barreling through the parking lot toward me. *Mob hit* flashed in my mind. Was somebody about to run down Mike? Would I be the only witness? Forced to testify, then whisked away into the federal Witness Protection Program?

A black Land Rover slid to a stop near me and Jack Bishop jumped out.

Mob hit with Jack and me forced into WITSEC together bloomed in my head—which was really bad of me, I know.

Jack didn't look anxious to be forced into anything that included me at the moment. In fact, he looked downright angry—always a hot look.

"What the hell are you doing?" he demanded, and stabbed his finger at the parking lot where Mike had disappeared. "That was Mike Ivan, wasn't it? I told you to stay away from him."

What was it with men sometimes? They actually expected you to do something just because they told you to.

I decided not to get into it with Jack.

"Mike and I are even now," I said. "I did him a favor, he did me a favor. That's the end of it."

Jack wouldn't let it go.

"That man is dangerous, Haley," Jack said. "Steer clear of him. If you need something, come to me—not him."

Jack stared hard at me for a few seconds. I stared right back. He looked away first.

"So what do you need?" he asked.

Now, I was the one who didn't want to let it go.

"Are you sure you're finished being all worked up?" I asked.

"I'm not likely to be finished getting worked up over you anytime soon," he said, and gave me a wicked little grin.

I'm completely helpless against Jack's grin.

"Okay, so here's the deal," I said, thinking it better to stick to business. "I'm hearing a lot about Dempsey Rowland and lawsuits. I need to find out who's suing who, and why."

"You think this is connected to the murder?" Jack asked.

He was all business now—which was kind of disappointing, but for the best.

"Maybe," I said. "I'm not sure, but it's worth checking out."

Jack gave it a few seconds' thought, then nodded. "I'll get back to you."

He walked around to the driver's side of my car. I punched the remote and he opened the door for me. I moved to climb in, but he blocked me with his body.

"I knew you'd contact Mike Ivan," he said, gazing down at me.

It hit me then that Jack Bishop knew me better than Ty—my official boyfriend.

Jack edged a little closer. "Maybe I need to hang a little tighter with you."

My heart started to beat faster. Jeez, Jack smelled great, and some kind of crazy heat rolled away from him—the kind of heat that could make me do crazy things.

But not crazy enough to make me forget I had an official boyfriend.

"I'd hate to see you embarrass yourself, when you can't keep up," I told him, with a wicked little grin of my own.

I put my hand against his chest—oh my God, did he have great muscles—and gave him a little nudge. Jack stood fast for about two seconds, then stepped off.

I got in my car and drove away.

"Surprise!"

Oh, no. What now?

Ty had that you're-going-to-love-this smile on his face when he met me at the door of my apartment. Immediately, I braced myself.

"Remember when you mentioned Detective Shuman

and his girlfriend cooking German food and planning a dinner party?" Ty asked, blocking my entrance.

My mind raced. Oh my God. What did that mean? How had Ty interpreted my statement? Was I about to be serenaded by an oompah band of musicians dressed in lederhosen? Did my entire apartment smell like sauerkraut, because he'd been cooking all evening?

Of course, maybe a good strong German beer wouldn't be so bad right now.

"Ta-da!" Ty stepped back. He waved his arm and gestured grandly into my apartment.

I walked inside. The first thing I noticed was that all the packing paper from yesterday's TV was piled up on my couch. The television was tuned to a baseball game with the sound cranked up to only-dogs-can-hear-this level. A beer bottle sat on my coffee table—no coaster.

The next thing I saw was what appeared to be a light armored army vehicle partially assembled in the middle of my living room. It was surrounded by nuts, bolts, and other metal parts I didn't recognize. Thrown into the mix were several power tools, a thick orange extension cord, bubble wrap, more packing paper, and a huge red, white, and blue shipping box with GRILLIN' AMERICA printed on the side.

"Is that a . . . a—"

"A grill," Ty announced. "It's the Turbo 2000 Mega Grill. This thing is all stainless steel, with ten burners, twelve hundred inches of grilling space, side burners, a warming oven with two settings, and the most BTUs of any grill on the market today."

"It's a beast," I said, and looked through my patio door. "Is that going to fit on my balcony?"

"I'll make it fit," he told me, and waved away my concern.

I cringed. Oh my God, what was *that* supposed to mean?

"When you told me about Shuman and his girlfriend having a dinner party," Ty went on, "I got the feeling you'd like to do the same. So I bought this grill today. What's better than a thick, juicy steak cooked to perfection over an open flame, shared by friends? So I figured we could have friends over and cook dinner for them."

Visions of my mom flashed in my head—I hate it when that happens—but, oh my God, did Ty expect me to *cook*—at my *own* dinner party?

I gestured toward the Turbo 2000 Mega Grill and what looked like a couple billion parts surrounding it.

"Are you going to be able to get that thing put together?" I asked, and left *before the next decade* unspoken.

"Well, I don't do this kind of thing often," Ty admitted. "But I'll get it figured out. Hey, guess what else I bought today?"

Before I could hazard a guess—or even emotionally prepare myself—Ty took my hand and pulled me into the kitchen.

The cute little drop-leaf dining table I'd found at a vintage furniture store, haggled over the price and maxed out my Visa for, had been shoved into a corner. Next to it was a—oh, jeez, what was that thing?

"It's a freezer," Ty announced. He opened the lid. "I filled it with steak—three different cuts."

I peered into the freezer at what looked like—yikes!—approximately five hundred pounds of meat inside.

"And that's not all," Ty said. "I bought lots of chops and roasts. And hot dogs—twelve packs. They were on sale."

Twelve packs of hot dogs? *Frozen?* I mean, jeez, how bad could you need a hot dog?

"So we're ready to have friends over for dinner at a moment's notice," Ty said, with a little nod of satisfaction.

"That's really . . . something," I managed to say.

Ty wrapped me in his arms and gave me a long hug. It felt nice, really nice. Then he leaned back and said, "You must be hungry. I'll fix you something to eat."

Visions of something warm, oozing with cheese and mayo, drifted into my thoughts.

"While I was at the grocery store today buying the meat, I found a soup I know you'll like," Ty said. "It will fit right in with your new eating plan. It's got barley, veggies, lots of whole grains."

Eek!

"No, really, it's fine," I said. "I'm not all that hungry."

"It won't take a minute," Ty insisted, pulling out a couple of cans from the cabinet.

"Are you planning to go back to work anytime soon?" I asked.

I said that in the nicest way imaginable—*considering*.

"I hadn't even given it a thought," Ty said. "By the way, I looked at that résumé you sent me. Dale appears to have a lot of potential. I'm going to meet with her, see if there's a place for her at Holt's."

My distress over my apartment and the soup Ty was fixing for me vanished in a heartbeat. He really was trying hard to be a great boyfriend. He'd put a lot of time, money, and effort into doing things he thought would make me happy.

Marcie was right. If Ty had missed the mark on some of the things he'd done, it was my fault—well, partially my fault. Even if Ty had never asked what I wanted, the truth was that I had never told him.

Of course, Marcie—being really annoying, as only a BFF can be at times—had gone on to remind me that I seldom talked to Ty about some of the big things that were happening in my life.

Marcie was almost always right, so I decided to tell him something—something that didn't make me look bad, that is.

"Did I mention that Mom's housekeeper has disappeared?" I asked.

Ty grabbed a pot from the cabinet by the stove and looked back at me. "Juanita disappeared? What happened?"

I shrugged. "I don't know. She just didn't show up for work one day. I called her several times, I went by her house, I checked with the hospitals, the police, and the morgue. Nothing."

"She didn't have vacation scheduled and your mom forgot?" Ty asked.

Ty had met my mom. He knew how she was, so this was a reasonable question.

"Mom had a dinner party scheduled," I said. "No way would she let Juanita have vacation if she was expecting guests."

"So what happened before?" Ty asked, popping the top of the soup can and pouring the soup into the pot.

"Before what?" I asked.

Jeez, what was that smell?

"Before Juanita left," Ty said. "Things like this don't happen for no reason. People get hurt, they get angry, they get scared. Something triggered her disappearance."

My mind shifted gears to the day the nurse in the emergency room called and told me Ty had been in an accident near Palmdale. What had triggered *that* event? He'd never really told me—because I'd never really asked—why he was headed there in the first place.

"That reminds me," I said. "Did you ever make it to Palmdale?"

Ty stopped stirring the soup. He didn't turn to face me. "No," he said.

"What were you doing up there?" I asked, and managed to make it sound light.

"Business." Ty stole a quick glance at me, then turned

back to the soup. "Just business. Thinking about opening a store up there."

Okay, so maybe I didn't tell Ty everything that was on my mind. Maybe I didn't mention my deepest, darkest secrets, all my screw-ups or problems. Maybe that was one of the aspects of our relationship I needed to work on.

But I knew Ty well enough to know when he was holding back, not telling the complete truth.

And that could only mean that he'd just lied to me.

CHAPTER 21

Wwhat were friends for if not to use for your own personal gain? I mean, really, wasn't that what relation-
ships were all about?

I figured they were, as I settled into my office the next
morning. With practiced ease, I ignored the work I was actually being paid to do, pulled out my cell, and called Marcie. She answered right away.

"Are you up for booking a couple of purse parties next
month?" Marcie asked, after we'd exchanged morning
pleasantries.

Marcie and I had been giving purse parties for months
now, selling knockoff bags to deserving women who
couldn't afford the real thing. We'd made tons of money,
which had really helped me through my financial lean
times. Plus, the parties were super fun and we both really
loved hosting them.

Since that whole background-investigation thing was
still hanging over me, along with the possibility of losing
my job—unless a miracle happened, of course—I figured
that keeping the purse parties going was definitely the way
to go.

"Sure," I said. "Set up as many as you can. I'm in."

Marcie was employed at a huge bank just a couple of

blocks from here. She'd worked there for years, moving through many different departments, so she knew almost everybody in the building. This, of course, benefited our business because she knew tons of women who liked attending purse parties—and today it benefited me personally because I had a favor to ask.

"Are you still working in the mortgage department?" I asked.

"That was two months ago," Marcie said, then paused, and gasped, "Are you and Ty buying a house?"

She sounded really excited and I hated to burst her bubble, but I couldn't help it.

"No, nothing like that," I said.

I had a feeling Marcie was about to ask me how things were going with Ty and me—we're BFFs so we just know these things about each other, even when our conversation was bouncing off a couple of satellites orbiting the planet—but I wanted to avoid the topic of my so-called relationship.

I knew I should tell her about my conversation with Ty last night, and how I got the icky feeling he'd lied to me about his reasons for going to Palmdale, but I just couldn't do it. Not now, anyway.

A conversation of that magnitude demanded lots of time, beer, and chocolate.

"Do you still know someone in the mortgage department who could do you a favor?" I asked.

"What do you need?" she asked.

"I need one of those reports," I said. "You know, the one from the title company that tells who owns a piece of property, who's on the deed, who has liens or judgments or mortgages"

"You mean a title search?" she asked.

"Yeah," I said. "Remember? You told me about it that night at that place when you had on that teal dress, and you were telling me about that jerk-face guy who worked at the title company that asked you out and he was really married."

"Oh, yeah. *Him,*" Marcie grumbled. She was quiet for a moment, then said. "Do I want to know why you're doing this?"

"Not really," I said.

At this point, my suspicion that Max Corwin had two families—and, thus, an excellent motive to murder Violet Hamilton—was just that, suspicion. I didn't see where telling Marcie about it would do any good. But I couldn't take it to Detective Shuman without some sort of evidence.

"Yeah, I can get that for you," Marcie said. "Just send me the property info you want checked."

For a minute, I thought she might ask me to have lunch with her, but I didn't want to think about it. Today was antioxidant and ancient grain day, according to Ty when he'd presented me with the lunch he'd packed for me this morning. I'd smiled and thanked him, and I really did appreciate his thoughtfulness and the effort he'd put into it, but *yuck*.

Marcie and I hung up and I texted her the two addresses I'd found for Max. Of course, if the info from the title company showed that he was on the deeds of both homes, it could just mean that he owned two houses. Maybe he lived in one and the other was a rental unit or something.

But I'd been to both places. I'd seen those wooden signs hanging by the front doors listing the names of the family members, with Max's name featured prominently at the tops of both, above what I assumed was a wife's name and a bunch of children's names.

Detective Shuman had told me that Max had fallen under suspicion because he'd changed jobs often in the past few years. If it were true that Max had two families, switching employment made sense. Sooner or later, something would happen at the office that would require the wife and kids to show up—a company picnic, an award ceremony, the annual Christmas party. It probably would require an impressive juggling act on Max's part to remember the right names and show up with the correct wife and children. Much easier to just change jobs.

So that put Max at the top of my personal he-probably-did-it suspect list.

I mean, jeez, if Max really was married to two women and had two sets of children, and everybody found out about it, he could lose a whole heck of a lot more than his job.

I glanced at my watch and saw that I'd managed to get through a big chunk of the morning without doing any actual work, but I saw no reason to launch myself into a frenzy to get something accomplished. I'd already booked the upcoming luncheons and ordered items for this week's birthday club—I'd upgraded the celebrations by adding an iTunes gift card, courtesy of the Dempsey Rowland corporate credit card—and I still had Violet's memorial service to finish up. But nothing pressing needed my immediate attention, which meant that I could—

Hang on a second.

Yikes! Mr. Dempsey's retirement party.

I slumped down in my chair. Good grief. I had to find out what was going on with that thing.

I stared at the common wall between my office and Constance's office next door. Adela had told me that Constance had been working on the retirement party for months, so she probably had everything done.

But what if Constance was one of those employees who claimed they did their work but actually put it off to the last minute—can you imagine? What if she really hadn't done much of anything yet? I'd be the one looking like a total idiot—not her.

There was only one way to find out for sure.

I had to get my hands on the info in Constance's office. But it was still sealed off by the LAPD, and since Detective Madison knew I wanted to get inside, I knew he would keep it sealed just to make my life harder.

Maybe I could ask Detective Shuman. Maybe he would let me inside just so I could get the retirement party info.

I mean, what harm could it do? It wouldn't take long and, really, how could there be any actual evidence of Violet's murder left in there? Both of the detectives and the crime scene investigators had been all over it. Surely they'd found everything of importance.

Shuman floated through my mind, along with the image of that special smile I'd seen him use when he looked at his girlfriend, or talked about her, or thought about her.

Nice.

Then Ty popped into my head. I was sure I'd seen him give me that special kind of smile at some point in our relationship, but I wasn't quite up to searching my brain to pinpoint the exact time, location, and occasion at the moment. Instead, I thought about what he'd said about Juanita and how *something* must have happened that caused her disappearance.

Ty's really smart like that.

Then my brain hopped to another topic—that just happens sometimes—and I thought about Violet's murder.

Something had happened before her death, something that caused her killer to take action. So far, I'd discovered nothing that would indicate what that might be.

I needed to find out.

I made it through the gauntlet of sneers, frowns, and dirty looks from the gals in the Support Unit and found Iris at her desk in the payroll department. She'd been really helpful when I'd spoken with her before, so I hoped she didn't regret her loose lips and wouldn't clam up on me this time.

"Hi, Iris," I said, giving her my I'm-a-nice-person smile. I don't find a need to use that one very often.

She looked up from her desk, glanced around—checking to see if her supervisor was watching, probably, a standard move for anyone employed in an office setting—then gave me her I'm-a-nice-person smile in return.

I think she uses hers more often.

And really means it.

"Got a minute?" I asked, then stepped into her cubicle and sat down before she could answer.

Iris held up a stack of papers. "Well, actually, I have to get this report finished."

"This won't take long," I told her.

I leaned toward her a little, assuming the classic here-comes-the-gossip stance, and lowered my voice. "I heard something and I wanted you to be the first to know."

Iris leaned in a little, responding with the time honored let's-talk-smack position.

"I got in touch with Violet's granddaughter, Dale," I said, then paused a few seconds to let the drama build. "She says there was absolutely no problem between the two of them."

Iris looked confused. "Not even after Dale didn't come to work here, as Violet had wanted?"

I leaned in a little closer. "Turns out Dale wanted to work here, but the company wouldn't hire her."

Iris's eyes narrowed and she rocked back in her chair.

"I guess I should have expected that," she murmured. Then her mood lightened again. "Well, I'm relieved there were no hard feelings between Violet and Dale. She loved that girl so much."

My let's-talk expression morphed into my I'm-confused expression with practiced ease.

"When I spoke with you before, you mentioned that Violet had been very upset in the months leading up to her murder," I said. "So if everything was fine between her and Dale, what was she so troubled about? Do you have any idea?"

Iris frowned. Obviously, I'd stumped her with my question.

I didn't have time to wait around for her to come up with an answer, so what could I do but suggest one of my own?

"Did it have something to do with Ruth?" I asked.

Yeah, okay, I knew Iris had said absolutely nothing about Ruth in our previous conversation, and I'd found no evidence whatsoever of a problem between the two of them. Still, Ruth had been so dreadful to me I just thought it would be nice if I could somehow incriminate her in the whole murder thing.

It was worth a try.

Iris lurched toward me and whispered, "Violet and Ruth never got along. Ruth was—and still is—very possessive of Mr. Dempsey. Always making excuses for him and covering for him. But Violet had known him from the very inception of the company. She resented Ruth sticking her nose in where it didn't belong, and running interference for him."

Oh, wow. This was good stuff, really good stuff. Maybe Ruth actually had murdered Violet.

This was working out better than I'd hoped.

I ran with it.

"Did something happen between Violet and Ruth just before Violet's death?" I asked. "An argument, or a confrontation, maybe?"

Iris gasped and her eyes flew open. Her body went stiff. For a couple of seconds—eek!—I thought maybe she was having a stroke.

"Oh, my goodness," Iris exclaimed. She gulped in a couple of deep breaths and said, "I—I didn't even think about it, but the day before Violet's body was discovered, I saw her in the hallway."

"Did she tell you something?" I asked.

I had to keep her talking in case she really did have a stroke.

I mean that in the nicest way, of course.

Iris shook her head and her eyes got a glazed look, like she was remembering something—or maybe she really was having a stroke.

"I saw Violet in the hallway that day. I was headed over to H.R. Violet looked furious. Absolutely furious," Iris said. "In fact, she looked so mad I was afraid to approach her. You know how it is when you're friends with somebody for a long time. You just know when they need to talk and when they need to be left alone."

I understood completely. That's the way it was with Marcie and me.

"So did you talk to her later?" I asked.

"No, I didn't. I was planning to ask her out for lunch the next day and find out what was going on," Iris said. "But, of course . . . she was found dead that morning."

Iris fell silent, and I couldn't think of anything to say.

I'm really not good in these situations.

"And you know what?" Iris said quietly. "That day when I saw Violet and she was so upset? She was coming out of the Executive Unit."

I gasped. Oh my God, this was a major clue.

The whole thing bloomed in my mind.

Maybe Violet had a confrontation with Ruth. Maybe their argument had continued until the next day, somehow, and they'd ended up in Constance's office, for some reason. Maybe Ruth had gotten so angry she'd attacked Violet and killed her.

Admittedly, there were still a lot of holes in this argument-turned-to-murder scenario, but the important thing was that I had a new murder suspect.

And it was Ruth.

Cool.

Chapter 22

I left the office a little before noon—it's never too early to leave, really—to have lunch with Erma Pomeroy. Dale had told me that Erma and Violet had been BFFs since back in the day, and that Erma could give me a list of Dempsey Rowland retirees who would want to attend Violet's memorial service.

I had another motive for talking to Erma when I called her and asked if she could meet me.

That's how we super-stealthy-wanna-be-private-detectives do things.

I headed up Figueroa Street toward Wilshire Boulevard, enjoying the gorgeous Southern California weather and feeling great about the brown business suit I'd worn today, and went inside the restaurant Erma had suggested.

The place was small, with booths along one wall, a full bar on the other, and table-chair combos filling the space in between. There were lots of dark wood, green plants, and numerous shades of brown.

The lunch crowd had already started to filter in, but I had no trouble spotting Erma—the only gray-haired woman dining alone. She had on white capris, red sandals—neon-pink toenail polish—a red print blouse with a matching scarf tied around her head, and she was drinking a beer from the bottle.

My kind of gal.

"Erma?" I asked, as I approached her table.

"That's me," she declared as she pushed the facing chair back with her foot. "You must be Haley. Sit it down, honey."

"Thanks for meeting me," I said as I took a seat.

"I'm retired now. Not that many people want to have lunch with me these days. At least, not many people who can remember where we're meeting, get themselves there, and not wet their pants on the way." Erma drained her beer, then called to the bartender, "Bring another one of these, George. And one for my young friend."

The guy behind the bar nodded. He was young and kind of hot looking—not that I really noticed, or anything.

"You'd better eat something," Erma said, and passed me a menu. "We girls from Dempsey Rowland used to eat here all the time. This place has changed hands more times than I want to count. Like everything else, change, change, change."

I glanced over the menu as George approached the table with two beers balanced on a tray.

"I'll have a cheeseburger all the way," I said, as he put the beers on our table. "Thanks, George."

"My name's not George," he said quietly, giving me a smile. "It's Jeremy."

"I can still hear," Erma announced. "You look like a fellow who worked here a few years ago. His name was George. Heck of a guy. Died of cancer. Sad. But, hell, it's better than wasting away in some nursing home, waiting for kids that are never going to show up and visit."

Jeremy gave me a good-luck-getting-through-lunch-with-her smile and went back to the bar.

"So," Erma said, tipping up her beer, "you're planning a memorial service for Violet, are you? Does Arthur know about it?"

It took me a minute to realize that Arthur was Mr. Dempsey's first name.

"The service is his idea," I said.

"I doubt that," Erma told me.

I'd wanted to talk with Erma to find out what she knew about Violet during her days at Dempsey Rowland, and had used the memorial service for cover. I figured I'd have to use my aren't-I-sly-and-clever-at-manipulating-a-conversation skills to get the info I wanted. But it seemed Erma was ready to dive right in.

I think the beer helped.

"Actually, that's what Ruth told me," I said.

Erma made a grunting noise. "Ruth. That bitch."

"I don't like Ruth," I said.

"Smart girl," Erma declared, and took another pull on her beer. "Violet never got along with Ruth. She was all over Arthur, screening his calls, his visitors, putting herself between him and most everybody else, especially Violet."

"Isn't that what most executive secretaries do?" I asked.

"Not like Ruth," Erma said. "She protected him, cleaned up after him, saw to his every need."

My eyebrows bobbed as the vision of—ugh, gross!—Ruth and Mr. Dempsey doing the wild thing sprang into my mind.

Erma must have read my horrified expression because she said, "Nothing like that. Ruth was more like Arthur's mother, fussing over him the way she did. Hell, she probably thought—and still might think—she'll be the next Mrs. Arthur Dempsey. But even the current Mrs. Dempsey won't be Mrs. Dempsey much longer."

"They're divorcing?" I asked, and did a quick calculation in my head. "They must have been married—forever."

"Forty-some years," Erma said. "So after putting up with that bastard all this time, she's being pushed aside for a younger version."

"Oh my God. How do you know that?" I asked.

Erma shrugged. "I worked in payroll. I interacted with everyone in the company. I got the dirt on everybody."

Wow, cool. Maybe I should get a job in payroll.

"Arthur is just waiting for his retirement," Erma said. "He has to keep up appearances, make sure the company's reputation is unblemished. Any hint of impropriety and the government contracts that are the foundation of Dempsey Rowland would vanish in a heartbeat."

"Does Ruth know about the new Mrs. Dempsey waiting in the wings?" I asked.

"If she suspected it, she wouldn't believe it," Erma said. She took another swig of beer. "*That's* how obsessed she is with Arthur."

Jeremy brought my cheeseburger and another beer for Erma, even though she hadn't asked for one, then retreated behind the bar again. More customers were in the restaurant now. The noise level amped up a bit.

"Violet started with the company alongside Arthur— but not as a partner, mind you. She had a big stake in it, emotionally, anyway. She resented Ruth always trying to keep her away from Arthur." Erma shook her head. "Ah, hell, I told Violet she should leave that place years ago. I begged her to go. But she wouldn't."

I bit into my cheeseburger. Delicious—especially since I doubted it had antioxidants or ancient grains like in the lunch Ty had packed for me today.

"Violet was loyal—too loyal," Erma declared. "She thought the place needed her—and she was right about that. Arthur . . . he's a real piece of work. Who knows what would have happened to the company if Violet hadn't been there."

I ate a couple of fries while Erma worked on her beer. I could almost see the wheels turning in her mind, remembering everything that had happened at Dempsey Rowland before her retirement, probably thinking about what had gone on since she left.

"Violet was a good person, a good friend. She deserved better than to die the way she did," Erma said, her voice softer. "Hell, after what I did, I should take responsibility for what happened to her."

I gulped down a bite of cheeseburger, my senses shifting to high alert. Was Erma about to confess to something? Killing Violet, maybe?

Damn. I'd really hoped it would be Ruth.

I leaned in a little and shifted into I'm-your-friend-you-can-tell-me-anything mode, which was totally fake, but still.

"So what happened?" I asked.

Erma drained half her beer, then shook her head. "You talked to Dale, right? She told you about Violet trying to get her a job at Dempsey Rowland, right?"

"She said the company wouldn't hire her," I said.

"That's a load, if I ever heard one," Erma declared. "It was Arthur. He wouldn't sign off on hiring her."

"Mr. Dempsey himself refused to hire Violet's granddaughter?" I asked, just to be sure I understood. "She was superqualified. Violet had worked there since the beginning. You couldn't ask for a better recommendation than that. Why wouldn't he hire her?"

"Because Arthur liked throwing his power around," Erma said. "And because—"

Erma clamped her mouth closed.

I hate it when people do that.

"Because?" I asked, hoping to draw her out again.

Erma stewed for a minute or so, then said, "Because Arthur knew Violet and Dale would discuss her starting salary, and Arthur didn't want that happening."

Okay, I was completely lost now.

"Why not?" I asked.

Erma puffed up a bit, as if she were mad—at what, I didn't know.

"I told Violet to quit the company," she grumbled. "I told her years ago that she should leave, go someplace else. But she wouldn't. No matter how many times I said it, she refused. She had some ridiculous misplaced sense of loyalty, and she wouldn't leave."

Something clicked into place—and I hadn't even had any chocolate with my lunch.

"You worked in payroll," I said. "You knew how much everybody at the company was paid."

Erma nodded. "Yes. And I knew that bastard Arthur Dempsey consistently paid Violet thirty percent less than her peers."

"*Thirty* percent?"

Oh, yeah, that was crappy, all right.

"Just because she was a woman," Erma said.

That was double crappy.

"Did Violet know?" I asked.

"Of course not. She thought Arthur paid her fairly because she started the company with him and worked like a dog to keep the place going," Erma said.

Something else clicked into place.

"You told Violet that she was being underpaid?" I said.

"Hell, yes, I told her," Erma declared.

She was fired up now—and I don't think it was from all the beer she'd been drinking.

"Violet knocked herself out for that company, year after year, decade after decade. There wouldn't have even been a company if that power-hungry, egotistical, self-centered, underhanded Arthur Dempsey had run it by himself," Erma said. "Then, when he refused to hire Dale and Violet was so devastated, I told her about her salary. I thought it would make her—finally—see the truth and leave. Just take her retirement and go, enjoy her life and have some fun, for a change. But instead . . ."

Neither of us said anything for a few minutes while the weight of Erma's words hung over us like a bad haircut.

"You want to hear something else?" Erma asked softly.

I wasn't sure if I did or not—which wasn't like me, but there it was.

"Arthur is retiring with a four million dollar bonus," she said.

Okay, now I started to fume.

"He cut Violet's pay for years, and now he's getting a huge bonus?" I asked.

"You got it," Erma said.

"Did Violet know about his retirement bonus?" I asked.

"I told her everything," Erma said. She shrugged. "At that point, I figured what the hell, why not?"

Jeremy brought our check over and I presented the Dempsey Rowland corporate credit card. I figured if the company could give Arthur Dempsey a megabonus, it could pay for our lunches—along with a huge tip for Jeremy, of course.

"Here. I brought this for you," Erma said. She dug into her tote bag and handed me a folded piece of paper. "It's the names you asked for. People who retired who'd want to come to Violet's memorial service. I added the names and contact information of people who worked for companies we did business with. Some government people, too. Violet knew everybody. They'd all like to be there for her."

I put the list in my handbag.

"Thanks," I said, and rose from my chair. "I'd better get back to the office."

Erma nodded. "Sure thing, honey. I'll see you at the memorial service."

As I turned to leave, I was surprised to see that the restaurant was full now, and that people were lined up for tables. I'd been so caught up in what Erma was saying, I hadn't noticed.

A face in the crowd caught my attention. One of the Volturi—I mean, Ruth—stared straight at me. She shifted her gaze to Erma, then back to me, giving me serious stink-eye. I glared right back and walked out of the restaurant without speaking to her.

I hit the street desperate for a breath of fresh air, some time to think about everything Erma had told me—and a mocha frappuccino, of course.

By the time I walked down the block to Starbucks, I decided the whole office could use a treat. Sipping my frappie, I went a few doors down to the bakery and ordered two hundred cupcakes to be delivered to Dempsey Rowland tomorrow. That should sure as heck give the employees a boost and improve office morale.

And maybe it would cut into Arthur Dempsey's bonus a little.

I took my time getting back to the office. Everything Erma had told me kept running around in my head and I needed some time to process it all.

Violet's beloved granddaughter had been denied a job at Dempsey Rowland, then Violet learned from Erma that she'd been significantly underpaid for decades. Iris claimed she saw Violet coming from the Executive Unit the day before her murder, looking absolutely furious.

Had she had a confrontation with Arthur Dempsey? Or maybe with Ruth, since she kept everyone away from Dempsey at her own whim, it seemed.

And, regardless, was it a motive to murder Violet?

I took the elevator up to five. Camille waved to me as I stepped off. Thankfully, she only had some messages for me. No sign of another guy waiting to sing a love song in the lobby.

"I'm having cupcakes delivered tomorrow at noon for the entire staff," I said. "Let me know when they arrive, will you?"

"Of course," Camille said. She smiled—I think. "That's

so sweet of you, Haley. Constance never did anything like that for the staff. And the birthday club is so much nicer now that you're running it."

I decided to take this opportunity to use Camille's compliment for my own benefit.

"Do you remember when I told you about the memorial service for Violet?" I asked. "You were surprised when I said Mr. Dempsey knew about it. Why was that?"

"Mr. Dempsey and Violet didn't always get along. I often heard them disagreeing," Camille said. "It was Violet's fault, really. She just wouldn't let things go."

"I guess she felt like she should have a say in things, since she helped start the company," I said.

"But she wasn't a partner, or anything," Camille pointed out. "Ruth told me many times that Violet could be quite pushy and overstep herself, especially where Mr. Dempsey was concerned. Ruth and Violet never really got along either."

"I see," I said.

I didn't really, but it was easier to just walk away.

I headed for my office, the effects of my mocha frappuccino zapping my brain cells like price scanners at a clearance sale.

If neither Ruth nor Mr. Dempsey liked Violet, why give her a memorial service? Was it just to keep up appearances?

Or maybe to throw suspicion off of her killer?

Despite my lack of real evidence, I still hoped that Ruth was the murderer. Violet, according to Iris, was furious with somebody in the Executive Unit the day before she died. It could have been Ruth.

What about Mr. Dempsey? He wasn't exactly the nicest man on the planet, but that wasn't motive for murder. In fact, it seemed like Violet had a heck of a good reason to kill *him*.

And why would either of them kill Violet here in the office? A murder and a police investigation sure as heck weren't good for the company image that everyone was so concerned about.

Either somebody else had killed Violet—like Max or Tina, my other two suspects—or Ruth or Mr. Dempsey had a megahuge reason to murder her on the spot.

But what was it?

I turned the corner and spotted Adela walking toward me. Her pace picked up when she saw me, and I could see that she was in there's-a-problem mode, big time. She stopped in front of me.

"I need to speak to you immediately," Adela said.

Her jaw was clinched so tight, her lips barely moved.

Not a good sign.

Adela whipped around and headed back down the hallway, leaving me to follow her into my office. Inside, I saw that yet another arrangement of roses had been delivered. I knew without looking at the card that they were from Ty.

It was really sweet of him, of course, but, come on, enough already. My office was starting to resemble a wedding chapel.

Adela wasn't the least bit touched by the lovely ambience or sweet floral scent in my office. She turned on me like a soccer mom on double-coupon day.

"I just spoke with Mildred in accounting," Adela declared. "*What* is going on with your corporate credit card?"

I didn't think she really wanted an answer, because she didn't wait for one—which was good, since I didn't know what the heck she was talking about.

"According to Mildred, you're not using approved vendors," Adela said.

Vendors had to be approved?

"You've purchased balloons for the birthday club. Balloons aren't authorized," she said.

Birthday club items had to be authorized?

"And you're dangerously close to going over budget," Adela told me.

There was a budget?

"What is going on?" Adela demanded.

It sounded to me as if Adela already knew perfectly well what was going on, thanks to Mildred in accounting—whoever that was—ratting me out. But, luckily, I'd worked in a corporate environment before and was very familiar with the time-honored tradition of passing blame along to someone else.

Immediately I shifted into I'm-right-and-you're-wrong mode.

"First of all, I'd suspected there were some irregularities on accounting's end regarding the corporate card," I told her. "In fact, I planned to speak with Mildred this afternoon."

Lying was another time-honored corporate tradition—which was really bad of me, but what else could I do?

"If you'll recall, Adela," I went on, "I accepted this position in corporate events planning under extremely difficult circumstances. I'm working with directions, lists, and models put together by Patty and Constance, which concerned me from the start. Now, after hearing of these questions from accounting, I can see that my concerns were well-founded."

Yeah, I know, it was all b.s., plus it was super stinky of me to throw both Patty and Constance onto the sacrificial I'm-desperate-to-keep-this-job corporate altar. But if they didn't want people talking smack about them behind their backs, they should have come to work.

Adela didn't say anything for a couple of minutes, then went into back-down mode.

"Fine," she said. "I'll leave this situation to you. But I expect it to be handled promptly."

"It's been my experience that *promptly* is the only way to handle an incident of this nature," I told her.

"Fine," Adela said again, then whipped around and left my office.

I pushed my door closed and launched into full-on, all-out, big-time total panic mode.

Oh my God, oh my God, *oh my God.*

I could get fired for scheduling lunches at restaurants where the food actually tasted good? And for buying balloons? *Balloons?*

If Mildred in accounting was blabbing to Adela now, what would happen when the charges for today's lunch with Erma and the zillion cupcakes I'd bought rolled in?

I couldn't—*could not*—lose this job. Sarah Covington would find out. Ty would find out. *Everybody* would find out.

The pay here was beyond fabulous, and there was no end to all the things I wanted to buy.

There was no time clock here—something crucial to my employment success. Nobody paid any attention to when I got to work, when I left, or even if I stayed all day, making this my all-time perfect job situation.

And, besides, I'd bought eight—*eight*—business suits. Where would I wear them if I didn't work here?

I forced myself to calm down. I had to think.

There was still an outside possibility that whoever was doing the background investigations now might not bother to verify that the UM I'd listed on my résumé was really the University of Mixology and not the University of Michigan. I mean, really, who would question that? I might actually pass the background check and get my security clearance.

I paced back and forth through my office, my brain pounding, searching feverishly for a solution.

Wow, could I ever use a Snickers bar or two right now.

Nobody had asked for my résumé—I still didn't know why mine was the only one that had been lost—so that meant my background investigation hadn't actually begun yet. I still had time to redeem myself for my unapproved restaurant and birthday club faux pas.

I hate the birthday club.

Now I hate balloons, too.

Then an idea blasted through my brain. I knew just how to salvage this situation.

I'd have to do a stellar job on Mr. Dempsey's retirement party. Yeah, that was it. Any minor screw-up I'd made with the corporate credit card on a few cupcakes, lunches, and unauthorized balloons would be forgiven in a heartbeat once everyone saw what a fabulous job I did on that party.

My entire future came down to one party.

Was that crappy, or what?

Anyway, I heaved a sigh of relief that I'd figured everything out. I had a plan—a great plan—to put into action.

But first I had to rearrange my office, call a friend—and go shopping, of course.

I grabbed my purse and left.

Chapter 23

Five o'clock was the official quitting time at Dempsey Rowland and the place emptied out pretty much on time—I knew this because I was usually among the first wave of employees to hit the elevator.

Of course, there were always a few kiss-asses who lingered, hoping to be seen by senior management and score some points toward their next promotion and pay raise. Today, I was one of those people who stayed late—but for an entirely different reason.

I sat at my desk, staring at my watch, willing my phone to ring. Right on cue, at three minutes before the hour, Camille called.

"You have a visitor," she said. "I told him the offices were closing, but he insisted."

"Thank you, Camille, I'll be right there," I said.

It took everything I had not to run through the halls to the reception area, but I forced myself to walk slowly. In the lobby—looking way hot in jeans, a dress shirt, and sport coat—stood Jack Bishop.

Wow, what a sight at the end of a long day.

"Miss Randolph, thank you for seeing me so late in the day," Jack said as he came forward extending his hand.

I'd asked Jack to come to my office and pretend he was a visitor during a phone conversation we'd had this afternoon. He'd agreed to do it—but he didn't know what else I had in mind for him.

Yeah, okay, it was crappy of me not to explain everything to Jack before he got here, but some things were better when presented in person.

"Thank you for coming by," I said as I took his hand.

My knees wobbled. Talk about a warm, firm handshake.

"Let's go to my office," I said. That might have come out in a breathy little sigh.

Jack threw a quick, questioning glance at Camille. She looked particularly skeletal this afternoon, her face more drawn and waxy than usual.

"I'm pretty sure she came back through time to kill John Connor," I whispered.

He nodded and followed me down the hall.

"Nice," he commented as we walked past the LAPD crime scene tape still covering the door to Constance's office.

"The cops won't take it down," I told him as we walked into my office. "That's why I called you."

Jack eyed the massive floral arrangements filling my office.

"Did someone else die?" he asked.

"The day's not over," I said.

I pushed my office door closed and turned to face Jack. Fading sunlight filtered in through the window. The room seemed smaller. Jack seemed—

Never mind. I had to stick to business.

"I need a favor," I said. "It's nothing big. Really. And it's not illegal—technically. I don't think. Well, probably not. But you have to be quick."

"I'm never quick."

I wish he hadn't said that in his Barry White voice.

My stomach got kind of gooey, but I fought it off.

"Come over here," I said, moving past him to the tall

file cabinet in the corner. "All you have to do is help me get up there, then wait while I climb through the ceiling into the office next door, and pull me back up when I'm finished over there."

Jack just looked at me. He didn't say anything. He didn't have to. Jack had a way about him that affected me in lots of ways, and forcing me to blab on with his silence was one of my least favorite.

I'd come up with this plan after Adela's oh-so-pleasant visit to my office this afternoon. If I had any hope of keeping my job, I absolutely had to pull off a fabulous retirement party for Mr. Dempsey. Everything I needed to do was locked up in Constance's office, sealed behind LAPD crime scene tape. I had no idea where the key was kept, and even if I managed to find it, I didn't want anyone to see me going inside. If word got back to Detective Madison—and it would because that's just the way offices work—he would be down here in a superhero flash, slapping on the cuffs.

"Look, I need information that's in that office," I told Jack.

I saw no need to mention my renegade balloon purchases or my flagrant disregard of the corporate list of authorized restaurants.

"There's no way to get what I need except to climb in through the ceiling," I said.

"What kind of information?" Jack asked.

"It's nothing illegal or top secret," I said in my let's-move-on voice.

"What kind of information?" Jack asked again.

Good grief. Why can't he just roll with this?

"It's information about a party," I said.

His left eyebrow crept up a half-inch. "A *party?*"

What was it with men? Why did they have so much trouble understanding the most basic concepts?

"The less you know, the better," I told him. "Nothing illegal is happening here. We're not breaking and entering because nothing is being broken, and *entering* doesn't count if you're already in the building. Probably. And if it does, it shouldn't."

Jack just stared at me.

Okay, now I was getting annoyed. I couldn't hang around inside the building after office hours forever. Someone would notice my leaving later than usual and it might arouse suspicion. Plus, I had to work at Holt's tonight and I didn't want the hassle if I was late.

"Your total involvement is to help me get over the wall, then pull me back again," I said.

I remembered from being inside Constance's office that she had no furniture in the back corner of the room, the spot that corresponded to the tall file cabinet in my office, leaving me no way to get back into my office.

Of course, once I was inside I could move something over to stand on while I climbed back up, but what if Detectives Madison or Shuman came back to check something? They'd probably made a diagram of the office—that's what they do on all the TV crime shows—and they'd know the furniture had been moved, and I'd be their one and only suspect.

"It's no big deal," I insisted. "I go to the gym and work out, but I concentrate on my thighs and legs, not my arms."

Jack's gaze dipped a bit. "Time well spent," he said.

"Are you going to help me, or not?" I asked.

He hesitated a few seconds, then said, "I'm in."

"Good. Now turn around while I get undressed," I said.

Both eyebrows shot up.

"A covert op in lingerie?" he asked. "Why didn't you say that in the first place?"

"Just turn around," I told him.

When I'd decided to climb into Constance's office this

afternoon, I knew I couldn't execute the necessary moves in my business suit and heels. No way could I go home to get something op-worthy to wear, with Ty there. So I'd found a store a couple of blocks from here and bought sweatpants and a T-shirt—in black, of course.

I grabbed my shopping bag from under my desk and retreated to the far corner of my office near the door, but away from the glass panel that allowed anyone in the hallway to see inside. Jack turned his back and stared out the window.

"Hey, did you find out about the Dempsey Rowland lawsuits I asked you about?" I said, and kicked off my pumps.

"You mean the last favor you asked?" Jack said.

"Yeah, okay, I've asked a lot of favors lately," I said as I took off my suit. "I owe you dinner, or something."

"I'll take or something," he said.

Jeez, I wish he'd stop talking that way when I'm half-dressed.

"Dempsey Rowland has been the target of a number of lawsuits," Jack said.

"Nuisance suits?" I asked, pulling on sweatpants. "That's pretty standard stuff for any big company."

"More than that," Jack said. "Sex discrimination suits filed by women who worked here. Executive-level women complaining about low salaries, slow promotions, things like that."

"Maybe that explains why so few younger women work here, except in the Support Unit, and why so many women in support never get promoted," I said. "Word got out that Dempsey Rowland wasn't a good working environment for females."

"Try hostile environment," Jack said. "Arthur Dempsey has been sued personally for sexual harassment."

Okay, that really explained why so few young women

worked in the Executive Unit. Human Resources must have figured that with Dempsey retiring, it was finally safe to hire women—thus, my new job.

Wow, did I have great timing, or what?

"The suits that were settled all had a confidentiality clause," Jack said.

"That figures," I said, as I pulled on my T-shirt. "Dempsey Rowland is crazy concerned about their public image."

I pulled the tote I'd bought this afternoon from the shopping bag. It was a no-name canvas bag—the Temptress would have been perfect for the occasion—and I felt a familiar wave of nausea at carrying a nondesigner bag, but I powered through.

I can do that sometimes.

"Okay, let's do this," I said.

Jack looked me up and down, from my head to my bare feet—thank goodness I had a fresh pedi—and said, "It's going to be dirty up there."

"No problem," I said.

"It's a small space," he told me.

"Doesn't scare me."

"With bugs," he added.

"Bugs?"

"And spiders."

"*Spiders?*"

Oh my God, I'd never thought about bugs and spiders. I didn't want to crawl around with bugs and spiders—not in this outfit. I needed a hazmat suit with goggles, gloves, and boots.

I drew in a breath, forcing myself to calm down. Icky as it would be, I had to go through with this. I absolutely had to get that retirement info from Constance's office. My entire life depended on it. Sort of.

"That's okay. I'm doing this," I said. I might not have said that with as much conviction as I should have.

"Let's go," Jack said.

I pushed my desk chair over to the file cabinet, then removed Ty's roses and put them on my credenza. When I looked again, Jack had his jacket and shirt off revealing a snug, sparkling white wifebeater and drool-worthy muscles. In a flash, he stepped onto the desk chair, climbed onto the file cabinet, lifted out the panel in the drop ceiling, and disappeared.

My knees gave out and I dropped into the chair. Oh my God, was that hot or what?

Then I came to my senses and scrambled up the chair and onto the file cabinet.

The crawl space was creepy, all right, dark and dusty, with all kinds of cables and wires running alongside duct work. It didn't smell so great. The ceiling panel in the adjoining office was gone. I raised onto my tiptoes and peered over the common wall.

Jack stood below looking up at me.

"What do you need?" he asked, in a low voice.

"I'll be right there," I said.

Oh my God, who cared about dirt, bugs, and spiders? I was desperate to get into that office with Jack—just to make sure nothing was missed, of course.

He glanced at the glass panel in the office door. At any second, somebody could walk down the hall and see him inside. Or peek into my office and see me on the file cabinet.

"The clock's ticking, Haley," he said.

Jack was right.

I hate it when other people are right.

"Look in the desk for files labeled 'retirement party' or anything to do with the Roosevelt Hotel," I said.

Jack blasted through the cabinets, the credenza, the desk drawers, pulling out file after file. He handed them up to me.

"I'll check the computer," he said quietly, and went back to the desk.

From the number and weight of the files he'd given me, I figured this had to be everything. Plus, Constance probably wasn't any better with her computer than most of the other women in the building, which was why she'd had Patty—her second brain, as Adela had called her—to help.

Jack perched on the edge of the desk chair and started pecking away at the keyboard. I climbed down from the cabinet, dumped the files on my desk, then shimmied up again.

From the angle of the computer, I could see Jack paging through screen after screen—obviously, Constance didn't believe in password protecting anything—then he stopped. I knew he'd found something.

I squirmed higher on the wall and leaned into Constance's office as far as I dared. Jack went through the drawers again, then stopped and pulled out a box of CDs. He flipped through the jewel cases, then selected a disk, which must have been blank, and popped it into the tray on the tower.

Wow, he was superfast.

If I was going to be a private detective, I was definitely going to have to up my game.

Seconds ticked by while the disk copied. Jack sat perfectly still, watching the screen. I glanced at the glass panel in the door to the hallway. Nobody outside. I scanned the drawers to make sure Jack hadn't left anything open. He hadn't.

Somebody walked past the door. Yikes!

"Hide," I whispered.

I ducked down behind the common wall. A couple of seconds passed. I straightened up and peered into Constance's office. Jack had the CD out of the tower. He snapped it into a jewel case, logged off of the computer, then gathered up all the cases.

Something caught my eye. One of the cases had a cover that looked familiar.

"Bring that one," I whispered.

Jack looked up at me and shuffled through them one by one until I nodded. He put the rest back in the drawer, did a quick sweep of the room, then headed toward me.

I scrambled down from the file cabinet. A second later, Jack's face appeared over the wall. He must have pulled himself straight up—how hot was that?

He climbed over the wall, put both panels back in place, then jumped down from the file cabinet.

"Wow. That was awesome," I said.

"Damn right it was," he told me, then presented me with the CDs he pulled from his back pocket.

I recognized one of the covers right away. It was a pink and black Burberry.

"You owe me," Jack said.

I'd seen this pattern several years ago when they'd come out with a limited edition line of handbags and accessories.

"I'll tell you what I want," Jack said.

Only, I'd seen it recently. But where?

"When I want it," he said.

Jack's hand splayed across my cheek. His palm was hot. He tilted my face up until I met his gaze. His eyes were hotter.

He leaned down until his mouth hovered above mine. His breath was smoking hot.

Jack angled closer and his lips moved closer.

I put my finger across his mouth, stopping him.

I've got an official boyfriend. And that's that.

Jack just hung there for a minute, then backed away.

"You still owe me," he said.

He picked up his shirt and sport coat, and left.

"My boyfriend and his new girlfriend broke up," Sandy said.

Bella and I sat across from her at a table in the Holt's

breakroom as the minutes remaining on our break ticked away and we all waited for the store to close so we could get on with something interesting.

For a change, my evening shift had flown by—probably because I couldn't stop thinking about what had almost happened between Jack and me in my office a few hours ago.

I desperately needed to talk to Marcie about this. Only a BFF could help me process this whole thing.

Sandy's comment blew me out of my own problems and landed me squarely into hers.

"You mean your *ex*-boyfriend?" Bella asked.

She still had the tropical thing going on with her hair. Tonight she'd sculpted it to resemble an erupting volcano. Or maybe it was a whale with a waterspout. I couldn't be sure.

"You two broke up," I said. "He and the new girlfriend were going to Hawaii, weren't they? You went shopping with him for clothes."

Sandy nodded. "They broke up. Things weren't as serious between them as I thought."

"You mean he didn't buy her an engagement ring when he went into the jewelry store?" Bella asked. "While you sat outside holding all the bags?"

"No," Sandy said. "He bought her earrings. See?"

She pulled back her hair and pointed to gold loops swinging from her earlobes.

Bella and I looked at the earrings, then at each other. If somebody had held a match to us, we'd have launched straight through the roof.

"Those are the earrings he bought for *her?*" Bella demanded.

"And he gave them to *you?*" I asked.

"They're really quite lovely," Sandy said.

"And you *took them?*" Bella asked.

"And *kept them?*" I asked.

"He said he really had me in mind when he bought them," Sandy said. "He said I truly deserved them."

"Lord help me," Bella murmured, as she rose from the table. "Get me out of here before I say something that ought to be said."

She left the breakroom.

I, however, couldn't hold back.

"Dump that loser," I told her. "He treats you like dirt."

"He's an artist, Haley," Sandy said.

"He does tattoos."

"That's how all artists are," she said. "That's the price they pay for being so creative."

Sandy and I had been friends for a long time, but for a moment I thought I might bitch-slap her—just to knock some sense into her.

The breakroom door swung open and Jeanette, the store manager, walked in. Tonight she had on an I-paid-big-bucks-for-this-six-years-ago-and-I'm-going-to-wear-it-until-the-buttons-pop-off suit which, from the look of things, could happen at any moment. She'd gone urban, for some unknown reason, with a gray skirt and a matching jacket that had wide shoulders covered with crystals.

She looked like the Chrysler Building.

"Haley, could I see you for a moment?" Jeanette asked.

Immediately, I shifted into no-can-do mode. I've found that when a supervisor seeks you out, it's only because they want you to do something—like a special project, or additional duties. No way was I saying yes to anything.

That's how I roll.

"I just sat down for my break," I said, which was a total lie but absolutely necessary under the circumstances.

"You can come back," Jeanette said. "There are some people in my office who need to speak to you."

Somehow, I doubted this was anything that would benefit *me*.

"Immediately," Jeanette added, using her I'm-the-boss voice.

I hate that voice.

I followed her out of the breakroom and down the hall to her office. Jeanette paused outside the closed door.

"You can ask for a lawyer," she said, then pushed the door open and walked away.

I looked inside. Detective Madison sat behind Jeanette's desk and Detective Shuman stood behind him.

Oh, jeez, this couldn't be good.

"And so we meet again," Detective Madison called. He reared back in his chair and gave me a wide I've-got-you-now smile. "Come in, come in. We have lots to talk about."

"I doubt that," I said.

"Oh, but we do," Madison said. He was still grinning, still thoroughly enjoying himself—at my expense, of course.

I glanced at Shuman. He looked tense. I'd seen that expression before—but not in a good way. I was sure his girlfriend had never seen it.

"Let's start off with Erma Pomeroy," Detective Madison announced.

I got a weird feeling.

"You saw her today, didn't you," Madison said.

It wasn't a question. He already knew.

My weird feeling turned sickly.

"What happened?" I asked. "Is Erma okay?"

"She's dead," Madison told me. "Murdered in her own home. And you were the last person to see her alive."

Oh, crap.

CHAPTER 24

Erma was dead. I could hardly believe it.
I sat in my office the next morning ignoring my official Dempsey Rowland duties, lost in the recollection of my confrontation with Detectives Madison and Shuman in Holt's last night.

Well, actually, it wasn't really a confrontation. When Madison had claimed I was the last person to see Erma alive and suggested that I was responsible for her death, I just walked out. I was surprised—and relieved—that neither detective came after me. At first I thought it was kind of odd, since they'd come all the way to the store to talk to me, then I figured Madison was just trying to scare me by showing up, and he had no real evidence against me.

Jeez, I really hope he has no evidence against me.

My cell phone made a familiar pinging noise. I glanced at it on the corner of my desk and saw that I had a text message from Marcie, but I wasn't ready to read it. Erma was still in my head, big time.

I'd just seen her at lunch yesterday, and now she was gone—not just gone, but murdered. She seemed like a nice lady who'd worked hard most of her life and deserved to enjoy her retirement. Now that wouldn't happen.

I was grateful she'd given me the list of retirees and people Dempsey Rowland had done business with over the years who knew Violet. I'd contacted them all yesterday afternoon, and most everyone wanted to attend tomorrow's memorial service.

I wondered if anyone would have that kind of service for Erma.

I gave myself a mental shake. Enough with the depressing thoughts. I had to move on.

The files Jack had retrieved for me from Constance's office last night were stacked on my credenza. I had to go through them and figure out just what the heck was going on with Mr. Dempsey's retirement party.

Jack looking way hot in that white wifebeater sprang into my mind.

I forced the image away.

Jack, trying to kiss me.

Jeez, maybe I should stick with the depressing thoughts of Erma dying.

I decided to call Marcie. I had a lot to talk to her about and she always made me feel better about things.

I called and she answered right away.

"Were the reports what you expected?" Marcie asked.

What the heck was she talking about?

"The reports," she said again, like she could read my mind, or something—which, I guess, she kind of could. "The title searches you asked for. I sent them to you a few minutes ago."

Jeez, that must have been the text message she'd sent. I'd forgotten all about it.

"They're great," I said. "Thanks. I owe you."

"Want to go shopping on Saturday?" Marcie asked. "I'm itching to go to the factory outlet mall in Camarillo. We can leave early and spend the whole day."

My spirits lifted.

"You bet," I said. "We can stop at that—oh, crap."

I was supposed to be at Holt's all day on Saturday making up those stupid training sessions.

I hate training.

"What's wrong?" Marcie asked. "You can't make it?"

No way was I missing out on a trip to the outlet mall.

This morning when Ty handed me my lunch—it was omega-3 and magnesium day, apparently—he mentioned that he had a meeting at the Golden State Bank & Trust at one o'clock today.

He explained why, but I drifted off.

I'd just go to the B&T—if I interrupted an important meeting, oh well—and have him sign a statement excusing me from making up those training sessions, and I'd be free to shop all weekend long if I wanted.

"No problem," I said to Marcie. "I'm in."

We hung up. I got on my computer and generated a statement for Ty to sign—on fake Holt's letterhead—and tucked it inside my purse, a totally fabulous Dior clutch. This put me in the mood to work, but I fought that off by reading the text message Marcie had sent me.

Just as she'd said on the phone, the two title reports I'd asked her to do on Max Corwin were complete. She'd e-mailed them to me.

My heart rate picked up a little as I logged onto my e-mail account. If the title reports contained the info I hoped for—that Max Corwin owned two houses and had two families—that meant he had a humongous motive for murdering Violet.

Of course, that might also mean that he'd killed Erma. I figured the two murders had to be related. I didn't know how, exactly. I'd worry about that later.

I opened the files with the title reports. They contained all kinds of information about the property—the legal description, taxes, mortgages. Most of it I didn't understand—or care about.

The property on Tampa Avenue in Northridge showed the legal owners were Maxwell Corwin and Melanie Corwin, husband and wife.

The El Segundo property was vested to Maxwell Corwin and Mandy Corwin, husband and wife.

I couldn't help it. My mouth flew open.

Oh my God. I'd been right. Max secretly had two families.

Bastard.

If this wasn't a motive to murder the person doing background investigations, I didn't know what was. I grabbed my cell phone and called Detective Shuman, as I printed out the title reports.

"We need to talk," I said when he answered.

I could hear voices and phones ringing, and figured he was in the squad room. Madison was probably seated nearby.

"About what?" Shuman asked.

"Don't get your hopes up," I said. "I'm not confessing to anything."

I wanted to talk to Shuman alone, and tell him what I'd learned. If the info I had on Max Corwin turned out to break the case, no way did I want Madison to take any of the credit for it.

"Starbucks on Fig at twelve-thirty," I said.

Shuman paused for about ten seconds, then said, "I can do that."

He hung up and so did I.

It was still early and my meeting with Shuman was hours away, so there was nothing to do but perform some actual work.

I hate it when that happens.

Mr. Dempsey's retirement party—and, thus, my opportunity to keep my job—had to be my priority. I picked up the files from my credenza and started looking through them.

Immediately, I was overwhelmed.

Constance—whose handwriting resembled that of a serial killer—had written comments on everything, but in no particular order. Pink sticky notes were plastered over yellow sticky notes. Orange highlighter struck through blue highlighter. There were list after list of names, addresses, places, and times. A huge stack of papers that looked like legal contracts was clipped together.

Jeez, how was anybody supposed to make sense out of this?

I drew in a big cleansing breath and blew it out slowly.

There was nothing to do but buck up, dig in, and hunker down.

But, well, no sense in getting into this thing too deep right now. Somehow, there had to be an easier way.

Maybe Constance had straightened out all this mess when she'd input it into her computer. I hunted through the pile of files for the disk Jack had copied last night and, instead, found the one with the pink and black Burberry case.

Huh. I knew I'd seen this pattern recently, but where?

The new employee orientation session on my first day of work here flashed in my mind. I'd seen this pattern on Violet's laptop case.

A great idea zapped me. If this Burberry pattern was on her laptop, that must mean this CD case belonged to her, too.

Oh my God. What if there was a major clue on the CD?

I popped it open. Inside was a disk labeled DEMPSEY ROWLAND THROUGH THE YEARS.

Damn. Not exactly the smoking hot piece of evidence I was hoping for. More like a stroll down Dempsey Rowland memory lane.

Violet had worked for the company since its inception, so she probably had photos from day one. I figured she'd scanned them onto the disk so Constance could show them at Mr. Dempsey's retirement party.

Or maybe Constance had made the CD herself and just borrowed the case from Violet, or perhaps Constance had her own pink and black Burberry office accessory collection.

Regardless, nothing on the disk was going to help me figure out what was up with Mr. Dempsey's party and get it staged in an I-can't-possibly-be-fired fashion.

My office phone rang.

"Your cupcakes have arrived," Camille said when I answered.

"I'll be right there," I said, and hung up.

Wow, I hadn't realized it was noon already. I'd put several hours into trying to figure out what was going on with the retirement party, but hadn't gotten very far.

I figured I could always go to the Roosevelt Hotel and try to fumble my way through an interview with their event coordinator and not look like a complete idiot, but I wasn't confident I could pull that off.

Amber, Ty's personal assistant, popped into my head. She was a whiz at absolutely everything. I was sure she could make sense of Constance's notes in no time.

I shoved all the files into the no-name tote I'd purchased yesterday—oh my God, I desperately needed that Temptress—along with the title reports I'd printed out and planned to show Shuman. I'd call Amber after I finished with him, and ask her to meet me somewhere.

Wow, am I good at this, or what?

I went to the reception area, relieved to see that the guy from the bakery hadn't taken one look at Camille and bolted. She made him sign in—good grief—then he helped me deliver the cupcakes to all the breakrooms.

They looked really yummy. I ate one—okay, two—but only to be certain they were the top quality cupcakes Dempsey Rowland employees deserved.

By the time I got back to my office and sent out an e-mail to all the employees announcing that cupcakes were available, it was nearly 12:30. I grabbed my handbag—a gorgeous Dior—along with the tote, and left.

As promised, Detective Shuman sat at a table by the window in Starbucks. He had on his usual dress-shirt-tie-sport-coat combo that didn't look all that great together. I figured that meant he and Amanda weren't living together—no way would she have let him out of the house looking like that—and for some reason I was kind of glad. Just *kind of* glad. Not *really* glad. Okay, well maybe a little more than kind of glad.

Anyway, Shuman was working on a coffee. A mocha frappuccino waited at the spot across from him.

"My favorite," I said, sitting down. "How did you know?"

"I am a detective," Shuman reminded me.

It was nice—really nice—that he had paid attention to what my favorite drink was and had bought it for me. So I certainly couldn't refuse it. How rude would that be? Besides, one exception to my whole-new-me plan wouldn't hurt anything, and I did have Ty's barley and bean broth soup waiting for me back at the office. It was low sodium day, apparently.

"Thanks," I said, taking a long sip. "Oh, and by the way, I didn't kill Erma Pomeroy."

Shuman gave me a half grin, then shifted into detective mode.

"Madison thinks her death is connected to Violet Hamilton's murder," he said.

"Because Violet worked for Dempsey Rowland, and Erma had recently retired from there?" I asked.

"Cause of death, too," Shuman said. "Blunt force trauma to the skull."

I flashed on Erma getting hit on the head with something big and heavy. Not good. I forced the image out of my thoughts.

"Any other connection?" I asked.

"You."

Oh, crap.

"Look, I saw Erma at lunch to get the names of Dempsey Rowland retirees who might want to come to Violet's memorial service. That's the first time I'd met or talked to her. And I only knew Violet because of the new-hire orientation class I was forced to attend," I said. "That's not much of a connection."

"It's more than we've got anywhere else," Shuman admitted.

Oh, jeez. This wasn't good.

"So, what? You think I had some problem with Erma, invited her to lunch, then followed her home and bashed her over the head with something?" I asked.

Shuman sipped his coffee. "If not you, then who?"

"How would I possibly know?" I asked.

Okay, I was getting a little fired up right now. I didn't come here to get grilled over Erma's murder. I was here to pass along my newly discovered, sizzling hot evidence against Max Corwin. Apparently, Shuman didn't realize I was about to do his career a huge favor.

"You might have been on to something with Tina Sheldon," Shuman said.

What the heck was he talking about?

I mentally changed gears and remembered that I'd told Shuman about the mysterious trip Tina had taken down the 5 the morning I'd followed her, and that she'd lied to me about it the next day.

"Seems Ms. Sheldon makes numerous trips to Mexico in her van, according to her GPS," Shuman said. "She drives down, crosses the border, stays for a few minutes, then comes back."

I gasped. "Oh my God. Do you think she's smuggling people into the country?"

"Could be," Shuman said. "A middle-aged white woman in a nice van wouldn't attract much attention from the border guards. They wouldn't be likely to search her vehicle."

"Yeah, but if she got caught she'd be in major hot water," I said.

"And if she didn't, she'd make major bucks," Shuman said. "We alerted the border patrol. They'll target her vehicle and search it next time she crosses back into the U.S."

Oh, wow. I'd actually solved a crime—but it was the wrong one.

I hate it when that happens.

"Tina wouldn't have known Dempsey Rowland required a background investigation," I said. "Sounds like a motive for murder, if you ask me."

"Madison is working that angle, but I don't like it," Shuman said. "Doesn't make sense. Sure, killing Violet Hamilton would delay the new-hire investigations, but sooner or later they would be completed. Anybody with something to hide would be exposed. The best anyone could hope for would be to work there awhile, pick up a few paychecks, maybe network a little in the hope of finding another job somewhere."

I'd thought those same things myself. But so far, the only lead I'd had that wasn't connected to the background investigations had turned out to be nothing.

I guess Shuman was having the same problem.

"Maybe that's exactly what Tina is doing," I said.

He frowned his cop frown—it's way hot—and I knew he was considering the possibility.

"I'm not crazy about it, but it's our strongest lead." Shuman shrugged. "People have murdered for less."

Now I wasn't sure if I should tell him about Max Corwin's secret double life. Shuman was convinced Violet's murder had nothing to do with the background investigations so my telling him about Max would only distract him, maybe slow him down and delay his discovery of the actual murderer. Besides, for all I knew, Shuman had already uncovered Max's duplicity, and I didn't want to look like an idiot by telling him something he already knew.

"So if you didn't kill Erma," Shuman said, "do you know who did?"

I huffed, just to be sure he knew this question didn't suit me.

"Look, it's like I already told you," I said. "I had lunch with Erma. We talked about the olden days at Dempsey Rowland. She told me about Violet and how she didn't get along with—"

Hang on a second. Something did happen at lunch—or after lunch, when I was leaving. Why hadn't I put this together sooner?

Shuman leaned toward me. His cop sensors were on high alert.

"Erma told me that Violet never got along with Ruth Baker, Mr. Dempsey's executive secretary," I said. "As I was leaving the restaurant, I saw Ruth waiting for a table. She was giving both of us triple-stink-eye in a really creepy way."

Shuman didn't say anything.

"Ruth might have followed Erma home and murdered her," I said.

Cool.

CHAPTER 25

I was mega stoked thinking that Voldemort—I mean, Ruth—had actually murdered both Violet and Erma.

The evidence spun through my mind as I walked up Figueroa Street toward the Golden State Bank & Trust on Wilshire Boulevard.

From everything I'd heard, Ruth was protective of Mr. Dempsey and Violet had resented it, understandably so, given her history with the company. Ruth hadn't liked Violet for the same reason. The two of them had probably battled it out for years over Mr. Dempsey's attention.

Iris had told me that she'd seen Violet the day before her murder coming back from the Executive Unit absolutely furious about something. Had Ruth not let Violet see him? Had that been the last straw between them? Had the two of them had one final confrontation in Constance's office the next morning, and Ruth killed her?

And what about the memorial service? Ruth must have been the one who insisted I plan a memorial service for Violet, as a way to throw suspicion off of herself. She'd told me it was Mr. Dempsey's idea, but everyone I'd talked to doubted his involvement.

Oh, yeah. Ruth was suspect numero uno—to my way of thinking, anyway. Shuman wasn't quite as thrilled when I laid it all out for him in Starbucks, but he at least listened.

I hoisted my tote higher on my arm—jeez, I really hope nobody important sees me with this thing—and reached into my handbag for my cell phone.

I had to call Amber and see if she could meet me somewhere this afternoon and sort out the details of the retirement party. Her voicemail picked up so I left a message.

Next, I had to find Ty at the Golden State Bank & Trust and have him sign my letter about those stupid Holt's training classes. Hopefully, Amber would call back by then.

My afternoon would be perfect—if I could just get people to put aside their own plans and problems and help me with mine.

I didn't see why that shouldn't happen.

The day was beautiful, of course, as it most always is in Southern California. Lots of well-dressed people were on the street, headed somewhere important, or having lunch with someone who mattered.

I drew in a breath, taking in the sweet smells of the plants blooming at the open-air dining plaza as I walked by, thinking about how I'd like to—

Wait a second.

I froze, too stunned to move.

Ty sat at one of the tables. He had on a suit.

Seated across from him was a woman.

I glanced at my watch and saw that it was a few minutes after one. Ty should have been at his appointment at the GSB&T that he'd told me about this morning.

Of course, his appointment could have been canceled or rescheduled. Or maybe he'd gotten there early, handled whatever he'd gone there to handle, and left.

But none of that explained why he was having lunch—with a woman.

I got an icky feeling in my stomach.

Maybe Ty hadn't had an appointment at all. Maybe

he'd told me that as cover in case I spotted him downtown today. Maybe he'd lied to me.

I intended to find out.

My feet felt really heavy, like I was walking in slow motion. The two of them were talking. The remains of their lunch were on the table between them. They'd been there for a while.

I looped around to the right to get a better look at her. From what I could see, she was young, maybe my age, with light brown hair, which she'd pulled back in a low ponytail. She had on a business suit, but she'd amped it up with some incredible accessories that really—

I stopped again. Oh my God. She was Dale Winslow. I'd sent Ty her résumé and he'd told me he wanted to talk to her about a position at Holt's. That's what was going on.

Whew!

Wow, what a relief. And how silly of me. Jeez, why would I think—even for a minute—that Ty had gone behind my back to see someone else?

Maybe because he'd lied about his trip to Palmdale. And because he hadn't gone to work for over a week and he'd never told me what he did all day, where he went, or who he saw.

I pushed those thoughts—reasonable though they were—out of my mind. I didn't want to think about them now. Besides, I was sure there was a logical explanation for everything Ty did.

Even if he never told me what it was.

As I walked closer, I saw Dale lean forward just a bit and say something. Ty laughed. He really laughed. He threw back his head and laughed.

I don't think I'd ever seen him do that.

Then Ty leaned forward and said something to Dale. She giggled, and Ty started laughing again. They bantered back and forth, oblivious to everyone and everything around them.

Including me.

Ty finally composed himself and smiled across the table at Dale.

My heart thumped hard and seemed to sink into my belly.

I'd seen that smile before. But not on Ty's face. Never. Not once.

I'd seen that smile on Shuman's face when he looked at his girlfriend.

I just stood there, unable to move. A minute or so later, Ty must have caught a glimpse of me from the corner of his eye because he did a double take and rose from his chair.

"Haley, this is a surprise." He held out his arm and I walked over, then he brushed a kiss against my cheek.

He didn't smile.

"It's so good to see you again, Haley," Dale said.

She sounded as if she truly meant it. She wasn't uncomfortable with me finding her having lunch with Ty.

Whatever was going on between them was one-way.

"We were just discussing my coming to work for Holt's," Dale said. "Sit down. Join us."

"Yes," Ty said, pulling out an extra chair. "Join us."

My stomach felt queasy. My head hurt. I wanted to cry.

"I've got to get back to the office," I said. It came out sounding kind of strained.

"Oh, well, if you're sure," Dale said.

"I'm sure," I said.

I left the table. At the sidewalk, I glanced back. Ty just stood there watching me.

Still no smile.

I walked away.

I spent most of the afternoon staring out my office window at the pedestrians and traffic on Figueroa Street.

Ty didn't call.

He didn't send flowers.

I couldn't bring myself to call Marcie and talk to her about the whole Dale and Ty thing because I wasn't sure exactly what had happened.

I just knew that something had changed.

My cell phone pinged. It was a text from Amber saying she was more than willing to help me sort out the retirement party info, and that we could hook up later tonight.

Movement in the hallway outside my office caught my attention and I realized employees were leaving. Jeez, it was five already? How had that happened?

I didn't really want to go home and see Ty. I wasn't sure if he'd be there or not, but, either way, I wasn't up to talking to him yet.

I almost wished I was scheduled to work at Holt's tonight.

Good grief. What has my life become?

I got my purse and tote, and left my office.

There was nothing to do but go see my mom.

In the whole maybe-dead-maybe-kidnapped situation with Juanita, I figured I'd done all I could do. I'd looked everywhere I knew to look. I'd checked with the police, hospitals, and morgue. I'd been to her house. I'd phoned her. I'd talked to her neighbor. I'd even called in a major favor with the maybe–Russian mob.

I only knew one more thing to try.

When I pulled into the driveway at Mom's house and went inside, the place was deadly silent. My dad wasn't home yet. He usually worked late—not that I blamed him, of course.

From the look of things, Juanita had either come back to work or Mom had hired another housekeeper.

"Mom?" I called as I walked through the house.

"In here, sweetie," she answered.

I followed her voice and found her in the family room.

She was stretched out on the chaise, and looked like she had just stepped from the pages of the magazine that was on her lap.

A Prada ad, specifically. Slacks and sweater in browns and golds, three-inch heels, accessories that equaled the median income of most Midwesterners. Hair perfectly coiffed, makeup expertly applied.

Just another L.A. housewife. That was my mom.

"I'm so glad you're here, Haley," Mom said. "I just had the most wonderful idea."

Oh, dear God, no.

"You're going to love this," she declared.

My left cheek started to twitch.

"I'm going to start my own clothing line," Mom said.

I began to blink uncontrollably.

"And now that you have your college degree," she said, "we can be partners."

I'm pretty sure a big chunk of my hair fell out.

"Won't that be fabulous?" Mom asked.

"You know, Mom, I just stopped by to ask you about Juanita," I said. "Has she come back to work?"

Mom frowned slightly, careful as always not to cause undue premature wrinkling.

"She most certainly has not," she told me.

"Have you heard from her?"

"Not a word," Mom reported.

When I'd mentioned Juanita's disappearance to Ty, he'd asked what had happened just before she left Mom's house the last time. Maybe I should have thought of that myself when this whole thing started and saved myself some time and effort.

Because, really, I should have known from the beginning who was responsible for Juanita's disappearance: Mom.

"So what happened before she left?" I asked.

Mom looked totally lost now.

"Something must have happened," I said. "Did you two have a disagreement of some kind?"

"No, of course not," Mom insisted.

"Did Juanita have some sort of problem? Did she need something?" I asked. "Anything at all?"

Mom was quiet while she pondered my question—either that or she'd forgotten what I'd asked.

"Well, she did mention her daughter," Mom said finally. "But it was only in passing."

"Which daughter?" I asked.

I knew Juanita had two grown daughters. One lived near her in Eagle Rock and the other had recently moved to Arizona.

"Her oldest, the one who's living in Scottsdale now," Mom said. "Juanita mentioned she wanted to go visit her because she was pregnant and was having some problems."

"You *did* tell her to go, didn't you?" I asked.

Mom paused, thinking back—I hope.

"She didn't *ask* to go," Mom said. "Why would she? Juanita was well aware of my dinner party scheduled for Saturday evening."

Oh, jeez.

"You didn't tell her to go right away?" I asked. "You didn't tell her that her daughter was more important than your dinner party?"

Mom looked completely baffled. "She didn't *ask* to go."

I wanted to tell Mom that she should have insisted that Juanita leave immediately, that her daughter and unborn grandchild were far more important than a dinner party. That's what Juanita wanted to hear. That's what she deserved to hear.

And that, even as hurt as she must have been—that's most likely why she was crying when her neighbor saw her leave her house with what must have been her husband and another male relative—Juanita had probably sent that young woman to Mom's place to help with the dinner party. The woman spoke so little English that Mom interpreted her comments to be a ransom demand.

But, somehow, I didn't think Mom would get it, and I sure as heck didn't want to hang around and try to explain it to her.

"I have to go," I said, and headed for the door.

I drove around for a long time, got a burger and fries from the Jack-in-the-Box drive-thru, stopped for a mocha frappuccino at Starbucks, and pretty much chucked my whole-new-me policy. I still wasn't ready to go home yet so I brought my totally embarrassing nondesigner tote into Starbucks and set to work trying to figure out Mr. Dempsey's retirement party plans.

Luckily, Amber called and promised to come right over. One more mocha frappuccino later, she showed up.

"Okay, what have we got here?" she asked, flipping through the files. "Wow, this is a real mess."

"I'll get you a coffee," I said, figuring she'd need the caffeine jolt.

When I brought it back to the table, she had a tablet out, making notes. I didn't want to just sit there and watch her work—nor did I want to do any actual work myself—so I asked if I could borrow her laptop.

"Sure," she said, and pulled it from the bag she'd brought in with her.

I was all set to surf the Net, visit my favorite fashion sites, and check the availability of the Temptress at all the major department stores, when I remembered the CD that Jack had copied from Constance's computer during our covet op.

I pulled the disk out of my tote.

"This might have some info on it," I said, placing it on the table.

Amber nodded as she flipped papers, made notes in the corners, and clipped them together in separate batches.

"I'll check it out in a sec," she said.

Not that I was feeling guilty, or anything, that Amber was working so hard and I wasn't, but I decided I should at least try to look like I was doing something constructive. I opened the Burberry jewel case and popped the CD with the history of Dempsey Rowland into the laptop, thinking maybe I could use some of the photos at Violet's memorial service tomorrow. A lot of old-timers would be there and would probably get a kick out of seeing themselves looking younger and, no doubt, thinner.

I grabbed my frappie and settled in, ready to be bored to tears by the upcoming retrospective of Dempsey Rowland company picnics, Christmas parties, and corporate facts and figures.

Instead, I saw photos of Arthur Dempsey as a young man, in middle age, and then as I knew him from the office now. He was in luxury yachts, private airplanes, limousines; going in and out of hotel rooms with young, sexy, big-boobed girls, and huddled with other men in informal meetings.

Arthur Dempsey—nor anyone else in the pictures—had not posed for these shots.

Interspersed with the photos were black and white pics of bank statements and what appeared to be legal documents.

"What the hell?" Amber asked.

I realized then that she was watching the CD with me.

"I'm not sure," I said.

Amber turned up the volume. I hit the PLAY button and the CD started over.

I'd only heard Violet's voice for a few grueling hours during orientation, but it had left an impression on me. I recognized it right away.

While the CD played, Violet's voice-over described Arthur Dempsey's forty-year history of corruption—photos thoughtfully included: Divulging bids to competitors for kickbacks; using overruns in government contracts for his personal use; accepting—and giving—bribes to anyone and everyone whom he could benefit from.

"Damn," Amber mumbled.

"Yeah," I agreed.

I realized that Violet had probably made this CD in retaliation for Arthur Dempsey's refusal to hire her granddaughter, compounded by her discovery that he'd grossly underpaid her for years. She'd probably put up with a lot from him. She'd worked tirelessly behind the scenes to insure the company's sterling reputation despite Dempsey's actions. That whole thing with her granddaughter and her salary had probably been the last straw—along with Dempsey's multimillion dollar retirement bonus.

Violet had gone into Constance's office that morning, no doubt, and put the incriminating CD with the retirement plans. Maybe she'd thought it was a good place to hide it, or maybe she wanted Constance to show it at Arthur Dempsey's retirement party—his greatest moment of triumph—so everyone would know exactly what kind of man he really was.

That's what I would have done.

But someone must have found out about the CD, confronted her, and then smashed her in the head with something big and heavy.

I thought I knew who that was.

But I also thought I knew who else it might be.

Arthur himself had the most to hide. When all this information came to light, not only would his reputation be ruined, but so would his company.

I wasn't sure Ruth would stand by and let that happen.

Maybe on that last day when Violet had gone to the Executive Unit, she'd threatened Arthur with exposing his underhanded dealings. Ruth might have overheard and decided to stop Violet herself.

Another thought popped into my head. Somebody had told me they'd seen Ruth with a laptop. Shuman said Violet's was missing.

Was that the murder weapon?

Had Ruth murdered Violet? Or had it been Arthur Dempsey himself?

I had to find out. And I knew just how to do that.

I started by calling Detective Shuman.

CHAPTER 26

It was a Louis Vuitton day. Definitely a Louis Vuitton day.

I stood with the fabulous LVT organizer Ty had given me last fall—long story—checking off items on the list I'd made for Violet's memorial service. So far, everything was going great.

The main conference center was the perfect venue for today's service. The large stage at the front of the room was fully equipped for a theatrical production, with curtains, lights, microphones, the works. I didn't need any of that today, though, just the giant TV screen that hung over the stage; I'd had help from the tech people this morning to get it working like I needed.

Along one wall I'd placed the refreshment table, and the caterer I'd hired had stocked it with six kinds of coffees, three flavored teas, water—sparkling and mineral—pink and sugar-free lemonade, every soda on the market, and three kinds of fruit juices. In the adjoining full kitchen, the staff was preparing to serve the bountiful array of meats, cheeses, salads, and desserts I'd ordered, courtesy of my Dempsey Rowland corporate credit card.

In keeping with my own personal policy of spending as much of Dempsey Rowland's money on Violet's behalf as possible, I'd hired a florist to decorate the entire room with floral bouquets. Flowers and greenery abounded. On the stage, the podium was draped in garland and a giant funeral spray stood beside a large photo of Violet.

Yeah, I know, I could get into real trouble for blowing my budget big time. But if everything went as I expected, in another few minutes nobody would care.

I'd scheduled the memorial service for three o'clock on Friday afternoon. That way everybody could attend the half-hour service, have refreshments, pretend to talk about Violet as an excuse not to go back to their desks, then leave early.

Do I know how to play an event, or what?

Employees, retirees, and guests were starting to arrive. Arthur Dempsey stood at the entrance to the room greeting everyone. Ruth had positioned herself a half step behind him, as expected.

It looked like a good turnout. I'd invited about fifty people, in addition to the Dempsey Rowland employees, and it seemed they were all here. I didn't recognize many of them, but I knew city and federal government officials and corporate executives with whom Dempsey Rowland had done business for years were in attendance.

Two guests no one knew about were positioned offstage in the wings.

I glanced at my wristwatch and saw that the service was scheduled to start in ten minutes. Time to make my move.

After viewing the CD last night in Starbucks with Amber, I'd figured that either Ruth or Arthur Dempsey had murdered both Violet and Erma. All I had to do was prove it.

I didn't have any hard evidence, but that was no reason not to pursue the theory.

That's how we private eye–event planners do things.

So I'd come up with a plan to expose the real killer, and as long as that person didn't go nuts and try to murder someone else—like me, maybe—everything should be fine.

I waited until there was a gap between arriving guests, then crossed the room and stepped in front of Mr. Dempsey.

"I need to speak with you right away," I said in my low it's-important voice.

Dempsey glared at me, as if thoroughly annoyed that I'd dared interrupt him.

"I know who murdered Violet," I said.

That got his attention.

"I have proof," I said. "I want you to see it before I call the police."

I walked away and crossed the room, weaving my way between employees and guests who were milling around, talking, and helping themselves to beverages. When I climbed the stairs at the edge of the stage and walked into the wings, Arthur was behind me.

The big TV screen illuminated the stage with the Dempsey Rowland corporate logo, but it was dark back here. A gooseneck lamp turned to face the wall offered minimal light.

"I found a CD," I said. "Violet made it."

I'd set up my laptop earlier—with the help of the tech people—on a small table near the heavy, dark stage curtain. Mr. Dempsey glared at it.

"What the hell is going on?" he demanded.

"Just watch," I said, and turned the laptop toward him. "Come a little closer so you can see better."

He did. I stepped behind the table and I hit the PLAY button.

The scenes I'd witnessed last night in Starbucks rolled, and Violet's voice once again gave a vivid, detailed description of Arthur Dempsey's years of excess, abuse, fraud, and corruption.

When the CD ended, I hit a couple more buttons, hoping Dempsey wouldn't know what I was doing. He didn't seem to. He stood frozen in place, but his eyes swept back and forth, and I figured his brain was frantically searching for the best way to spin what I'd just showed him.

"Lies. Facts twisted to make them look like something they're not," Dempsey said, pointing at the screen. "Put together by a disgruntled employee who was barely hanging onto her job. I should have fired that bitch years ago."

"Violet threatened to expose you," I said.

His gaze came up sharply and pinned me with a look of sheer hatred.

"That's why Ruth murdered her," I said.

Dempsey's expression shifted. He was a crafty old bastard who'd had decades of experience at seeing an opportunity and going for it.

"Violet was seen returning from the Executive Unit the day before she was murdered," I said. "She was furious over something. I believe she came to your office, threatened to expose you, and Ruth decided to stop her."

He didn't say anything so I kept going.

"Violet was struck over the head with a blunt object," I said. "It was probably her laptop. Violet's is missing, and Ruth was seen carrying one through the office shortly after her murder."

Dempsey began to nod slowly.

"I had lunch with Erma Pomeroy to discuss the memorial service," I said. "Ruth saw us together. She must have thought Erma knew something that would incriminate her. After all, Erma worked in payroll. She knew how you'd underpaid Violet all those years. She had friends in accounting and contracting who could back up Violet's claims that you'd made and accepted bribes for government contracts."

"Damn," Dempsey swore. "I should have gotten rid of Ruth a long time ago, too. Stupid bitch. Just another idiot woman I had to put up with. Now she's murdered two people and brought scandal to my company."

"Arthur!"

From the edge of the stage curtain, Ruth rushed over. She'd followed Arthur and me back here, as I knew she would, then stood aside as a good assistant should, and listened to everything that was said.

"Arthur, how can you say those things?" Ruth exclaimed.

She was frantic, on the verge of tears, totally confounded by what Dempsey had said about her.

"You don't mean that. I know you don't," Ruth insisted. "How can you say I murdered Violet and Erma when you know very well that I didn't?"

"I don't know anything of the sort," Dempsey told her.

"But Arthur, I've devoted my entire adult life to you. I took care of you. I protected you." Ruth touched his arm. "I didn't tell you this because I wanted to surprise you, but I'm retiring, too, when you do. We can go places. Finally, we can truly be together."

Dempsey jerked away. "What the hell are you talking about?"

"I know you never loved your wife," Ruth said.

"You're right about that. He's divorcing his wife," I said. "But he's already picked out the next Mrs. Dempsey, and she's young enough to be—well, me. With bigger boobs."

Ruth looked at me, then back at Dempsey again. She was totally lost now.

"You're . . . you're marrying someone else?" she asked.

"Hell, yes," Dempsey told her. "What the devil made you ever think I'd want you?"

A full minute passed while Ruth just stared at Dempsey, then I guess the truth finally sank in.

"I didn't kill those women! You know I didn't!" she shouted at Dempsey. "I heard Violet in your office that day, threatening to expose everything you've done."

"Enough!" Dempsey told her.

"You're the one who gave me that laptop," Ruth said. "You're the one who told me to get rid of it."

"Shut up," he demanded.

"I told you I saw Erma and Haley at lunch together, then you left for the afternoon." Ruth gasped. "Oh, Arthur, you killed them. You really killed both of them!"

"Damn right I did!" Dempsey shouted. "I wasn't about to let those two bitches bring me down!"

"Oh, Arthur, no!" Ruth shook her head frantically. "I was afraid you'd done it, but I didn't want to believe it. That's why I had Haley plan this memorial service and said it was your idea, so you wouldn't look guilty."

"Be quiet," Dempsey insisted.

I hadn't known which of them had done the killings, but I figured one of them would rat out the other when it all went down.

Ruth turned on me. "This is all *your* fault! None of this would have happened if you hadn't found that CD. You've been nothing but trouble since you came here. I found your personnel folder hidden in Arthur's briefcase, and I'm glad he took it from Adela's office so the police would think you murdered Violet!"

I flashed on the day I'd been nosing around in H.R. looking for the folders of the other new hires. Adela had shown up and interrupted me. Mr. Dempsey had been with her. He must have figured incriminating me was a way to keep suspicion off of himself and lead the detectives down a dead end.

"For God's sake, will you shut up!" Dempsey roared. He pointed at my laptop. "That CD is company property. Give it to me."

"Sure," I said. "How much are you willing to give me for it?"

His eyes narrowed to two beady pinpoints of hatred.

"You're known for taking bribes, and offering them, of course. It's all documented. How much is it worth to you?" I asked. "Or do you plan to kill me like you did Violet and Erma?"

"Listen to me, you little twit," Dempsey said. "I'll do anything I have to do—including murder—to keep my company in business. You're expendable—and so were those two."

He glanced around, as if suddenly remembering where we were and who was in the conference room just steps away. "This isn't the time or place for this discussion."

"Don't worry. Everyone here already knows." I pointed to my laptop. "The CD played on the big screen over the stage while you saw it here."

Fury rolled across his face as he looked from the laptop to me.

"And everyone saw your confession," I added.

I pointed to the webcam affixed to my laptop, which I'd switched on after the CD played. I'd figured Arthur wouldn't know enough about computer equipment to realize I'd mounted a webcam on my laptop, and even if he had, I'd doubted he'd notice it, either because it was dark backstage or because he was so caught up in the CD Violet had made.

"Wave to the audience," I said.

But Dempsey didn't wave. He let out a growl and swiped my laptop off the table, then lunged at me. Ruth screamed. I dodged left. Dempsey overturned the table and grabbed for me.

"Stop! Police!"

Detective Shuman ran from behind the stage curtain and wrestled Arthur Dempsey to the floor. Detective Madison trailed along behind, holding a gun.

Dempsey fought and cursed as Shuman put the cuffs on. Ruth began to cry. Noise from the employees and guests in the conference room grew.

"You, too," Madison said. He holstered his weapon and grabbed Ruth's arm.

"What? What are you doing?" she wailed.

"Accessory after the fact," Madison said, as he snapped handcuffs on her wrists.

"Good work," Shuman said to me, as he got to his feet.

My heart was pounding pretty good and—yikes!—I'd started to sweat, but I forced myself to calm down.

"Thanks," I said.

"Not so fast," Detective Madison said, over Ruth's cater-wauling. "You still have a lot of questions to answer."

All the other Dempsey Rowland employees left early, but not me. Detective Madison insisted I wait around the conference room, tell, and retell the facts leading up to Dempsey's confession until even he was sick of hearing about it.

I fudged a little—okay, I outright lied—about how I'd come into possession of Violet's CD. I claimed I found it in my office.

No sense in getting into the whole thing too deep.

It helped that I'd called Detective Shuman last night when I'd made the discovery and he'd come to Starbucks and looked at it. He'd agreed to setting up Dempsey and Ruth today.

Madison had called in other investigators who were doing whatever it was investigators do in these situations, but they were closing up their cases, putting away equipment, and heading for the door. I guessed there was a lot more action in Arthur Dempsey's and Ruth's private offices.

Detective Shuman walked over.

"You're free to go," he said.

"Yeah, but am I really free?" I asked.

If Madison still thought I was involved in these murders somehow, I wanted to know.

"You're cleared," Shuman said. He gave me a totally non-cop grin. "You do good work."

My stomach felt a little gooey.

"We make a good team," I said.

A few seconds passed while we just stood there looking at each other, then we both seemed to come to our senses.

Shuman backed away. "See you around."

"Whenever," I said.

I left the conference room. The reception desk was empty. I saw only a few employees in their offices as I headed down the hallway.

When I turned the corner, I spotted Max Corwin coming out of the breakroom. He spotted me and hurried over.

"Good news for us, Haley," he said. "With all the problems Dempsey Rowland will have now that this bribery and fraud has come to light, our background investigations will be pushed way back."

At one point I'd thought Max might have murdered Violet. Now I knew he hadn't. But, somehow, the crimes he did commit seemed worse.

"Tampa Avenue in Northridge," I said. "Melanie, Misty, Mace, and Miles."

Max just stared at me.

"El Segundo," I said. "Mandy, Maddie, Micha, and Minnie."

He turned white. His eyes got big.

"Make it right," I told him.

Max's face flushed bright red.

"Well, Haley . . . well, now, I think you've got the wrong idea—"

I was in no mood.

"Make it right," I told him again. "Or I will."

I walked away. Maybe Max's personal life was none of my business. Maybe I should have left it alone. But what he was doing wasn't right, and sooner or later it would blow up in his face. If Max was the only one who would suffer, well, okay. But he wasn't. And that's what bugged me about the whole thing.

Tina and her mysterious trips to Mexico flew into my

mind. I'd suspected her in Violet's death also. I now knew she wasn't guilty of murder, and maybe she was innocent of other crimes. I figured the border patrol would catch Tina if she was really doing something illegal.

As I turned the corner and headed toward my office, I saw Adela walking toward me. She looked frazzled, weary, and super stressed out.

I wished she'd retire before she died on the job.

"Haley, I'm glad I caught you," Adela said.

She spoke in her this-will-be-bad-for-*you* voice.

Great.

"I've just come from a meeting with senior management. In view of these new developments and allegations, the future of Dempsey Rowland is in question," Adela said. "Police officials are hauling away all sorts of documents from Mr. Dempsey's office. It's a given that a team of government auditors will be dispatched from Washington, probably by Monday. This will be a far-reaching, in-depth probe, going back decades."

A little ray of hope fluttered in my belly. Maybe that meant I wouldn't have to work corporate events anymore. Maybe they'd want me to work with the government auditors.

Wow, that would make a great addition to my résumé.

"We can expect congressional hearings, eventually," Adela said.

Cool. Maybe I'd get a free trip to Washington.

"At the least, there will be substantial fines and penalties," she said.

Did that mean my pay would be cut?

"It's doubtful the company will survive this," Adela said.

I got a weird feeling.

Adela drew herself up and straightened her shoulders. "I'm sorry to have to tell you this, Haley, but we're letting you go."

They're letting me—what?

"We're laying off almost the entire staff," Adela said. "Effective immediately."

A couple of seconds passed before her words sank in.

"But—but I'm the one who solved Violet's murder," I said. "I'm the one who exposed Mr. Dempsey's corruption."

"Yes, and thank you so much for that," Adela said.

I don't think she really meant it.

"Clear out your office tonight," she said. "Any further dealings with what's left of the company will be handled by mail."

Adela walked away.

I trudged down the hall and into my office, feeling kind of numb.

Jack flew into my mind as I glanced at the ceiling panel.

I forced my gaze onto Ty's flowers—not that I had a guilty conscience about the time I'd spent here with Jack, or how great I'd thought he looked, or that he'd tried to kiss me. Really. Well, okay, maybe a little.

But how could I help having those thoughts when he'd looked so hot in that white wifebeater? He'd said that he expected to be paid for his help. He'd said he'd tell me what he wanted, when he wanted it. He'd told me that before, lots of times. Only this time—

I decided not to think about it anymore. I had bigger things to deal with.

I took one last look out the window at the Starbucks, gathered my things, and left.

CHAPTER 27

O h my God, what was I going to do now?
The question had been raging in my head all the way
home and still I hadn't come up with an answer. I'd lost
my job—my really cool, mega-salaried, no-time-clock,
corporate-credit-card job. How was I going to pay my rent,
my bills, my car payment? And, more important, what the
heck was I going to do with eight fully accessorized business suits?

I got out of my Honda and headed up the stairs to my
apartment, desperately searching for a silver lining in this
pitch-black cloud that hung over me. I still had my job at
Holt's, of course, but that didn't make me feel all that
much better. I had my certificate of completion from the
University of Mixology. Maybe I could get a bartending
job.

I pulled my keys from my purse and opened my front
door. At least I was home now. I'd had a totally crappy
day. Things couldn't get any worse.

I walked inside.

Things got worse.

The place was still a wreck. The half-assembled grill
stood in the middle of the floor surrounded by power
cords, tools, and metal parts. Packing boxes, paper, and
bubble wrap from the grill and the new TV were strewn

everywhere. Some of the television cables that had been affixed to my walls with duct tape had come lose and hung
in long loops. My furniture was still out of place, and two
beer bottles—no coasters—sat on my coffee table.

But none of that was the worst part.

Ty stood in my living room. His duffle and garment
bags were packed and lying on the couch.

A few minutes passed while we just looked at each
other. I couldn't bring myself to say anything. My chest
felt heavy, my stomach rolled, my head ached, and my
heart hurt so bad I could hardly stand upright.

Ty didn't look like he was doing so great either, but he
spoke first.

"I'm sorry, Haley, but I can't be the kind of boyfriend
you deserve," he said.

I just stood there.

"I miss my work," Ty said. "I can't spend my days
shopping, or sending flowers and thinking up thoughtful
things to do."

I didn't need all the things he'd done for me, but I did
need more than he'd been able to give when he worked at
Holt's.

Yet I knew that wasn't everything.

I'd seen that smile he gave Dale when they were at
lunch, the look on his face when he'd spoken to her, when
she spoke to him, when they laughed together over something. It was the same look Shuman gave his girlfriend.
The look Ty had never given me.

And all the flowers, packed lunches, frozen steaks, TVs,
tuxedoed singers, and grills couldn't make our relationship something it wasn't.

"I . . . I understand," I said, because, really, I did.

"This is killing me," Ty said. "But I think it's for the
best."

"So we're . . . done?" I said.

"I'm sorry," he said.

"Me too."

We came together and hugged. Then Ty stepped back, picked up his duffle and garment bags, and left.

I just stood there staring at the door for a long time, then pushed aside a mound of bubble wrap and collapsed onto the couch. I knew I should call Marcie, or at least go get myself a beer, but I couldn't get up.

From the looks of my apartment and the number of floral arrangements I'd left in my office, Ty didn't really know what kind of boyfriend I wanted. But if he didn't know, it was because I never told him.

He thought I wanted one thing, when I really wanted something different. We'd come together but, somehow, we'd totally missed each other.

Maybe if I'd talked to him more—really talked to him. Maybe if he'd done the same. But we hadn't, and that meant something.

I wished I could cry. That way, at least I'd get my emotions out. But they just kept banging around inside of me, along with all kinds of thoughts.

Ty had never told me why he was headed to Palmdale the day of his car accident. I hadn't exactly been up-front with him about a lot of things in my life.

We never really talked. I doubted we were alone in that. A lot of people probably had the same problem.

I thought about Juanita. She hadn't specifically asked Mom for time off to go see her daughter, but she'd been hurt when Mom hadn't offered it.

Ruth had mistakenly thought Arthur Dempsey cared for her, to the point where now she was involved in a murder. A few well-placed words would have cleared that up a long time ago.

Maybe if Erma had told Violet about the despicable discrepancy in her salary years ago, both of them would be alive today.

I slumped down on the couch, my thoughts spinning.

I'd gotten a whole-new-me, all right. But it wasn't the *me* I'd wanted.

My apartment was a total disaster. I had a freezer I didn't want, filled with food I didn't need. I still hadn't gotten that Temptress bag. I'd lost my great job, and tomorrow when I went in for my shift at Holt's, I'd have to spend eight long, miserable hours doing make-up training because I'd forgotten to have Ty sign my waiver. I never found out for sure what happened to Juanita, or exactly what Ty had been doing in Palmdale. There wasn't an ounce of sugar in my apartment, and my cabinets and fridge were filled with totally gross healthy food.

How the heck had absolutely everything gone so wrong?

A loud knock sounded on my front door. My heart jumped and I sprang off the couch.

Ty? Was Ty coming back?

I leaped over a packing box and raced across the room.

No, wait.

I stopped. Ty wouldn't have knocked.

I approached the door and looked through the peephole.

Jack Bishop stood outside my door.

He banged his fist again, harder this time.

"I know you're in there, Haley," he called. "You owe me. I decided what I want, and I want it *now*."

Oh, crap.